Elaine Faber

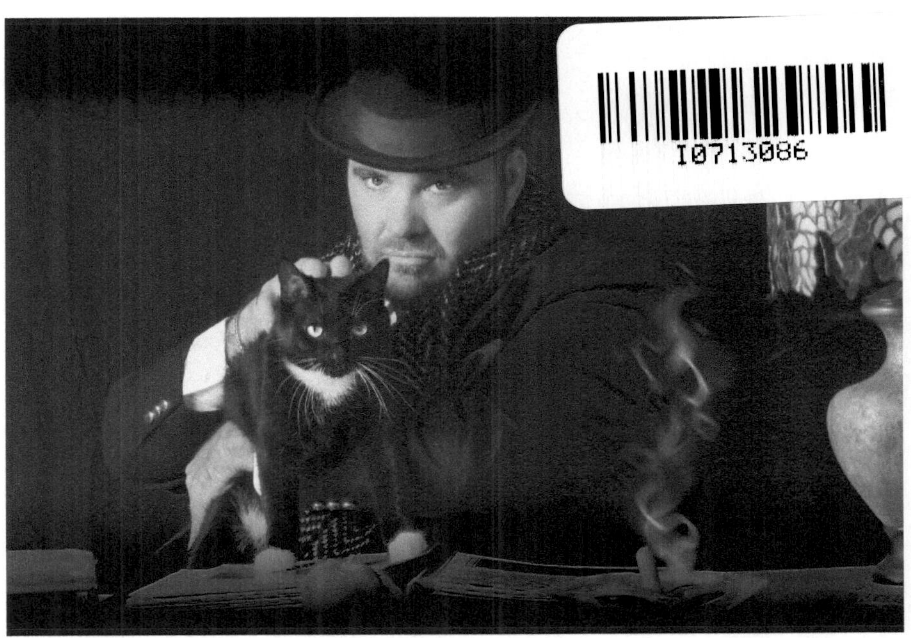

Black Cat
and the
Lethal Lawyer

Elk Grove Publications

Black Cat and the Lethal Lawyer

Published by Elk Grove Publications

ISBN-13: 978-1-940781-06-8

A portion of the proceeds from the sale of this book are donated to support feline rescue projects.

This novel is a work of fiction. Names, characters, places, and incidents either are the product of the author's imagination or are used fictitiously. Any resemblance to actual events, locales, organizations, or persons, living or dead, is entirely coincidental and beyond the intent of either the author or publisher.

Cover photo *lawyer with cat* © CURAphotography, shutterstock.com image 19277278
Cover layout and book formatting: Julie Williams, juliewilliams.us
Printed in the United States of America

Always humorous, always charming (if murder can be charming!), Elaine Faber's sleuth-stalking/truth-seeking feline, Thumper, finds himself on another cozy caper riddled with calamity of inheritance as Brett and Kimberlee struggle to solve a mystery. If you enjoyed BLACK CAT'S LEGACY, you won't be disappointed in her excellent second book in this Fern Lake series.

Sherry Joyce, Author of *The Dordogne Deception*

Elaine Faber has done it again with another delightful Black Cat adventure. In the second Black Cat Mystery, Thumper and his new family visit Kimberlee's grandmother in Texas along with Kimberlee's recently discovered cousin, Dorian. Mysteries abound as Thumper and his new girlfriend, Noe-Noe, attempt to push their humans in the right direction.

Patricia Canterbury, Author, *Every Thursday*

Elaine Faber blends romance and suspense in her Black Cat Mystery Series. Thumper, the cat with his ancestor's memories, adds an intriguing fantasy element to an already compelling plot.

Cynthia Chow, Reviewer for *Kings River Life Magazine*, http://www.kingsriverlife.com

Thumper, the crime-solving wonder cat is back. And boy does he have his paws full. Not only must he help his humans unravel the mysteries set before them—easy enough if they pay attention—but he has to protect one undeserving character to keep his whole family safe from the Lethal Lawyer.

Elaine Faber is a master storyteller, who knows how to weave a light-hearted tale that keeps the reader guessing until the very end.

Julie Williams, Art Director for Inspire Press

Special Acknowledgements

This book is dedicated to the following special people.

1. To my husband, Lee, and my children, Londa Lee and Michael—for their patience, encouragement and inspiration.

2. To my readers, who have come to love Thumper as I do and never stopped asking, 'When is the sequel coming out?' Your dedication and enthusiasm empower me.

3. To my beta readers, Lois Parrish, Sandy Trezise, Sandy Lassa, Sharon Prewitt and Vidya Shergill—for helping edit and fine tune the manuscript.

And lastly, a special thank you to Julie Williams, my editor, mentor and friend—
    a. for your invaluable advice, for making me dig deeper into the soul of Thumper and his family and bringing them to life
    b. for your extraordinary technical support and design talents
    c. for all you do for me…you are a saint.

Thank you.

Chapter One

Thumper sniffed the wind and shivered, but not from cold. Something was about to change. It wasn't the weather. This perfect day looked as if it had jumped off a picture postcard. A breeze from the lake touched the porch swing and sent it swaying. He turned toward an itch just behind his left shoulder and gave it a quick lick. Sunlight streaming through the vines overhead dappled his fur with wavering spots. He sniffed again. The scent of wisteria blossoms filled the yard surrounding Kimberlee's newly restored house.

He turned in a circle, lay down and began to bathe. First, down his white bib and across his broad black body and then around all four white paws. To finish, he licked his front paw and drew it across his white mustache and then groomed his flowing black tail. His toilette complete, he curled into the swing as his ancestors' memories flashed through his mind like scenes in a drive-in movie.

Ah yes. Thanks to the memories, his life was more exciting than most cats. Why, just last year, Kimberlee returned to Fern Lake to solve her father's murder. Thumper's great-grandfather's memories had guided him, and he in turn guided Kimberlee to clues that helped solve many of the Fern Lake mysteries. She married Brett and they restored this old house with its tragic history of infidelity and murder.

Before Kimberlee returned and he first became aware of his ability to call up his ancestors' memories, Thumper had no particular loyalty to any human. Now he was dedicated to the care and nurturing of Kimberlee, her daughter, Amanda, and to Brett.

Thumper half closed his eyes. His gaze drifted over the yard of the once tumble-down house, now restored to its original Victorian beauty, boasting trimmed shrubs and flowerbeds bursting with color—pink roses, yellow marigolds and blue hollyhocks.

A sudden gust of wind ruffled his long black fur. Change was in the air.

He knew it as surely as when he saw into the past through his ancestors' eyes. More of a sense of *knowing* rather than seeing, but for sure, things would never be the same in the little house.

Kimberlee raised her hand to block out the bright sunlight streaming through the window. Just an inkling of a headache teased between her eyes. Maybe if she closed the sheer drapes, the headache wouldn't blossom into a full-blown migraine. She reached for the curtain and peeked outside.

The mailman opened the gate on the white picket fence and started down the path. Pink petals tumbled onto the cobblestone sidewalk as he brushed against the rose bushes. "Hi, Thumper. How's tricks?"

Thumper lifted his head. He jumped off the swing, stretched, then *ponied* up into the mailman's hand and dropped back down.

The mailman ducked under the wisteria vines crawling around the post. He pushed back the stems reaching their flowered tentacles toward his face.

Kimberlee rubbed her thumb between her eyes, momentarily pushed away the pain, plastered a smile on her face and had the door open before his hand reached the doorbell. "Morning, Fred. What have you got for us today?"

"Special Delivery, Mrs. Clarke. You need to sign for it, right here on the bottom line." He handed her the clipboard and brushed at a strand of wisteria vine, threatening to circle his neck. "They sure smell nice, don't they?"

"They're lovely, but I can't keep up with them. They grow so fast." She signed the form and handed him the clipboard and pen. "Thanks."

She took the letter and shoved it into her pocket. It was probably from Brett's publisher. She'd give it to him later. Didn't want to interrupt his work on his novel.

Fred waved as he ambled back down the sidewalk.

"Thumper, we've got to do something about this wisteria vine before it takes over the house." Collecting her clippers from the garage, she returned to the porch and leaned toward the open window. Inside, Brett pounded on his keyboard. "Will it bother you if I work here on the porch for a while? This wisteria almost strangled the mailman."

Brett didn't look up. "Don't bother with that. I've had that on my *to-do* list for several days. I'll get to it in a few minutes." He glanced toward his notes and then back to the computer screen.

Kimberlee smiled and clipped the vines hanging over the steps. Snippets of purple flowers tumbled to the porch around her feet.

Thumper pawed at the vines, jumped at a branch that wiggled under his foot and nibbled one of the leaves.

"Leave it, Thumper. Leaves aren't good for you."

The hum of a motorboat on the lake sputtered and then stopped. A dog barked. Down by the lodge, Jack, the manager of Herman's Motor Lodge next door, tossed a Frisbee across the lawn. Chance, his golden Labrador retriever, leaped, caught it and dropped it at her master's feet.

Kimberlee waved, moving down the steps as she clipped.

Amanda came around the house and sat on the steps beside Thumper. She dragged a vine in front of his nose. "Fumper and me wants to help—"

"That's it. It's done," Brett shouted through the open window.

Kimberlee laid her clippers on the top of the porch rail and headed for the door. She hurried into the living room.

Amanda followed close behind with Thumper dangling across her shoulder and bumping against her back with each step.

"You're finished? Can I read it?" Kimberlee reached for the top page on the printer. "How did you end the story? Did you decide who the killer was?"

"I'm not going to tell you." Brett pulled her into his arms. "You'll just have to read the book like everybody else. Since it was loosely based on our experiences last year when we investigated your father's murder, who do you think was the killer?"

She put her arms around his neck and leaned against his chest. "I think it was—" Brett's lips came down on her mouth, stifling her response.

"*Oooh.* Mushy stuff." Amanda twirled Thumper in a circle. "Ring a pound of posy. Ashes, ashes, all fall down." She plopped on the floor, the cat sprawled beside her.

Thumper rolled on his back and kneaded his big white feet. "*Yowww.*" He pulled his whiskers back, as if in a contented smile.

After dinner, Kimberlee cleaned the kitchen and fed Thumper while Brett bathed Amanda, read her a story and put her to bed. Kimberlee went to her room, tucked her in and heard her prayers.

She closed Amanda's bedroom door and returned to the living room. The stereo vibrated with the thrum of soft guitars.

Brett sat in his lounge chair with Thumper curled in his lap. Blond curls tumbled over his forehead as he studied the newspaper.

Kimberlee's heart swelled with love every time she looked at him. What a miracle, that she had found such a perfect love last year, so soon after her tumultuous divorce from Amanda's father.

The heat from the crackling fire warmed her cheeks as she approached Brett's chair next to the fireplace. He lowered his newspaper and shoved Thumper off his lap. "Hi there, Mrs. Clarke."

Thumper switched his tail, gave his long fur a shake and huffed out of the room.

"Hello to you, Mr. Clarke… Can we talk?"

"Of course, honey, what's up?" He reached out his hand.

Kimberlee twisted her hands. "My migraines are starting again, worse than before we were married. I had another one this afternoon. I'm scared."

Brett frowned and pulled her onto his lap. "I'm here, honey. It's okay. Why don't we make another appointment with Dr. Johnson? You were doing so well right after we were married. No headaches, no nightmares. Now, what brought this on? Are you worried about the bookstore?"

She shook her head. "Sales have jumped every month since we opened the store last year."

"Is it the memories of your father's murder here in this house? I was afraid this might happen." He kissed her forehead.

"It has nothing to do with moving into the house. You know how much I love it. We've both worked so hard to make everything just right." She gazed around the living room, delighting in the comfort of her new home. "I'm very happy living here."

Brett stroked Kimberlee's hair and kissed her hand. "Whatever's going on, everything is going to be fine. Let's call Dr. Johnson tomorrow. He'll get to the bottom of this."

Kimberlee nodded. If only it was true. She wanted to believe Brett's assurance. She laid her head on his shoulder. "It's probably nothing to worry about. Maybe the doctor can give me another prescription." *If that's all it is. And nothing worse.*

"Why don't you take up painting again?" Brett nodded toward the painting of their house as it had looked when she returned to Fern Lake last year. "You always enjoyed that. And you do such great work."

"That's a possibility." Kimberlee stared at the picture over the mantle. A faded picket fence covered with roses surrounded the two-story Victorian house. Crooked shutters hung from the broken windows. Purple wisteria poked through the broken rafters over the porch. "Maybe I just need a vacation."

He patted her cheek. "Good idea. Let's think about it."

Something in her pocket crinkled as she leaned forward to give him a hug. She pulled out the envelope and handed it to him. "I almost forgot. Here's a letter from your publisher."

He glanced at the envelope. "It's addressed to you, not me. It's from Texas. Didn't you even look at it?"

She shrugged. "I guess I just assumed it was yours." She ripped open the envelope. Three airline tickets fell into her lap. "Well, of all things. Listen to this…

> *My Dearest Kimberlee:*
>
> *It was so good to hear from you last summer when you returned to Fern Lake. Congratulations on your marriage. Though I have not been present throughout your life, I have always held you most dear in my heart and in my prayers.*
>
> *I am planning a wonderful family reunion for you and your cousin. Enclosed are three airline tickets for you, your daughter and husband. Why, you can even bring your pets, if that will make your visit more pleasant.*
>
> *We will have barbecues, a barn dance, romantic moonlight hay rides and a pony for your little girl.*
>
> *While you and your families are here, I will choose a beneficiary of my estate. I will decide which of you girls would best manage my ranch, the horse-breeding program and my overseas holdings in the manner my late husband wished. My attorney, Wilbur Breckenridge, will handle all the legal details. Please say you will come.*
>
> *I look forward to seeing you and your family.*
>
> *Love, Grandmother Lassiter*

Kimberlee caught her breath. The muscles around her mouth tightened. *Me? Running a horse ranch? Not in a million years.* She shook the letter. "It doesn't make sense, does it? She wants us to come to Texas so she can decide who will inherit her ranch? I don't want to live in Texas. I've never been on a horse in my life."

"It does sound a bit…strange, doesn't it? I wonder if she's—"

"I didn't even know I had any other relative. And I'd love for Amanda to meet her extended family." She put her hand to her forehead where the hint of a headache tingled again. Probably from the excitement of Grandmother's ridiculous offer.

Brett stood, cradled her in his arms and walked past the antique spinning wheel in the corner and over to the stereo. "You need to get some rest. Let's talk about this tomorrow." She leaned down and clicked off the music. They laughed as he carried her down the hall, clicking off the switch to the vintage chandelier. She nuzzled his chest.

He stopped in Amanda's doorway and peeked inside. *She's asleep. Good.*

Kimberlee squealed when he dropped her on the bed. "What about Grandmother's letter? We didn't decide what to do. Should I write and tell her we're coming or not?"

"We'll have to give it some serious consideration…tomorrow. Right now I have more important things on my mind."

Chapter Two

hugging and wheezing into the driveway, Kimberlee's Toyota pulled to a stop just as Thumper jumped out from under the wisteria bush with Amanda close behind. She waved a stick over her head and then dragged it in front of his nose. He made several half-hearted swipes at the stick and then abandoned the game.

Kimberlee laughed and crossed the lawn toward the porch. Thumper ran up the steps ahead of her. She opened the door and laid her purse on the table. "I'm home."

Thumper raced across the room and leaped to the back of the sofa.

"Hi, hon." Brett gave her a quick kiss and pulled her down on the sofa beside him.

Thumper grumbled, pulled back his whiskers, leaped to the floor and ambled into the kitchen.

"What did the doctor say, honey?" He stroked her forearm.

"He doesn't think there's anything seriously wrong. He feels the headaches are stress related."

"So, what's the plan?"

"He wants me to try a new prescription. And, he said he thought I needed a vacation." She laughed. "Let's hope it's as simple as that." Kimberlee picked up her grandmother's letter and flapped the envelope toward Brett. "Perhaps we should consider Grandmother's invitation, after all."

"Whatever you say. I'm game for anything that makes you happy."

She laid the envelope on the coffee table. "I've been thinking. We've never been to Texas. I wonder what it's like living on a horse ranch. I haven't seen my grandmother since I was a baby and now it seems I have a cousin I've never met. I think it would be good for Amanda to meet her relatives." She picked up the letter again, tapping it on her hand.

"Since I just mailed my manuscript to the publisher, I'm free for a while." Brett put his arm around her shoulders. "It's probably as good a time to go as any, before he sends it back asking for revisions."

Kimberlee put her hand on her forehead. "Would you get me a glass of water, honey? I think I'll take one of those pills now."

Brett hurried to the kitchen and returned with the water. "Here you go. Where's your new prescription?"

"There on the table, in my purse."

Brett retrieved the purse and the bottle. He read the label and handed her a tablet.

She swallowed the pill and blinked back tears. "Seems like all I ever do is complain about my headaches. It's got to stop. It's not fair to bring all my baggage into our marriage."

Brett touched her cheek. "Don't be ridiculous. I love you, remember? All's fair in love and war. So we have some health stuff… but we'll get through it."

No doubt it was love. He told her often enough how her eyes lit up when she smiled and how he hated the skinny models on TV. Just last night, he'd said, 'If a man can't pinch an inch and feel some meat on a gal's bones, where's the fun in pinching?' Guess that meant the ten to fifteen extra pounds around her middle didn't bother him as much as they bothered her.

Her mouth trembled. "So you don't mind taking care of me when I have a headache?"

He grinned. "I'm not your ex-husband. I love you just the way you are, headaches and all." He stroked her hair and tucked a stray strand behind her ear. "And I love the way your hair curls around your neck." He leaned in and nibbled at her neck. "And your tasty neck, and your—"

"You goofball." She swatted at his straying hand and giggled.

How lucky she was to have such a caring and understanding

husband. She squeezed his hand and planted a peck on his cheek.

Brett stood and walked to the fireplace to examine the painting over the mantle. He turned. "I've been thinking. Are you sure you want to go to Texas for a vacation…or are you thinking about the inheritance?"

"How can you ask that? I hadn't really even considered the inheritance. Grandmother said she wants to leave her estate to someone who will run the ranch the way her husband wanted. We couldn't do that. I sure don't have any intention of giving up our home here in Fern Lake to live in Texas. I just want to get away for a while and meet my family, that's all. Besides, she paid for the airline tickets. What have we got to lose?"

Brett turned to look at the painting again. "I'm not so sure."

"I think it would be fun to take Thumper with us." Kimberlee glanced toward the kitchen where Thumper crouched by his bowl. The *crunch-crunch* of kibbles sounded like mini-firecrackers as he plowed through the tiny morsels. "Grandmother said we could bring our pets. She probably wasn't thinking about a cat, though." She laughed. "But I'll bet he'd love it at the ranch with all those country mice to chase. He's so easy-going, I'm sure he would handle the trip. Amanda would love taking him along."

"Are you trying to convince you or me? It sounds silly taking a cat all the way to a Texas horse ranch, but you're the boss, so whatever you want. You can arrange for Mrs. Wilson to take care of the bookstore. And we can ask Jack to keep an eye on the house. Call Jack and let him know what we're planning. Maybe Dorian will drop by the store a few times, just in case Mrs. Wilson needs anything."

Kimberlee picked up the phone. "Run and check on Amanda while I make the calls." She dialed Dorian's number first. "Hi, Dorian. How's it going? Listen. We've got some exciting news. I got a letter yesterday from my grandmother. She's invited my cousin and us to her ranch in Texas for a family reunion. I guess she's going to rewrite her will and leave her estate to—"

Dorian's shriek pierced through the phone lines.

Kimberlee pulled the receiver away from her ear. "What's the matter? What's wrong? Are you okay?"

"Did you say your grandmother in Texas? What's her name?"

"Whose name? My grandmother? Margaret Lassiter. Why?" Kimberlee's eyebrows squinched together.

"I thought that name sounded familiar when you took title to your house last year. I should have realized then. You aren't going to believe this. Don't go anywhere. I'm coming over. I'll be there in an hour. I need to check on something first."

"What's so important—" The phone clicked in her ear. "…about going to visit my grandmother?" Kimberlee said into dead air.

"What was that all about?" Brett asked.

"Darned if I know. She started screaming and hung up." Kimberlee shook her head. "It's so annoying. She's coming over. I have no idea why she's so excited. She always was a little nuts. I'll call Jack. When should I tell him we're leaving?"

Brett shrugged. "Up to you. The tickets are open-ended. We can call for reservations whenever you decide. Probably the sooner the better before I get revisions back from the publisher."

Within the hour, Dorian rushed into the house with her dog, Sam, at her heels. She flung her sweater onto a chair. "Let me see Kimberlee's letter." She flipped her long beautifully styled blonde hair over her shoulder.

Kimberlee ran her hand over her short curly flyaway hair and sighed. Brett handed Dorian the letter.

"Now, go sit down." Dorian waggled her manicured finger at the sofa. "I want to get a cold drink and catch my breath. I'll be back in a minute." She disappeared through the door.

Sam's gaze followed her into the kitchen, and then he lay down next to the sofa.

Kimberlee sighed and sat on the couch beside Brett. Why did Dorian always look like she just stepped out of a fashion magazine? Even on a spur of the moment visit, her shoes matched her outfit, her eye make-up enhanced her sky-blue eyes, and the color of her lipstick matched her nail polish.

Kimberlee glanced at her nails with the polish chipping off from working in the garden, and felt as though her brown eyes might have just turned a little green. She reached for Brett's hand. *Dorian might have it all; beauty, brains and budget, but I have Brett.*

Dorian sauntered back with a soda in her hand and a cat-that-swallowed-a-canary smirk on her face. She flopped into the recliner.

"Okay, Miss Hoity-Toity," Kimberlee said, "You've got us sitting in a row, waiting with baited breath. Now, what on earth is going on? You about scared me half to death, Dorian, screaming in my ear like that. If this is your idea of a stupid joke, it's not very funny."

"I had to talk to my dad to be sure I had my story straight. I just wanted to see your faces when I told you." She wiggled in the recliner, shifting her bottom from one side to the other, her face beaming. "Look at this." She shoved a letter toward Brett.

He scanned the stationery. "So what? It's Grandmother's letter. We already saw it, remember? We called you…" Brett tossed the letter onto the coffee table, raised an eyebrow and glanced at Kimberlee.

She shrugged. Nothing ever made much sense where Dorian was concerned.

"You're not reading it carefully enough." Dorian giggled. "Look at it again. Read it out loud." She grinned, looked up at the ceiling and began to hum. *It's A Small World.*

Kimberlee picked up the letter and began to read.

"*Dear Dorian; Though I have not been present throughout your life, I have always held you most dear in my heart and in my prayers. Now my life is near an end...* This sounds just like my letter. I don't get it." She glanced at Dorian.

Brett's head jerked toward Kimberlee, his mouth open "What the—"

"Go on, Kimberlee. Keep reading. You'll see." Dorian said with a mischievous smile, picking up her tune again.

Kimberlee read through to the end of the letter. "What does it mean? You're one of the grandchildren? How is that possible?" The letter shook in her hand.

"I got her letter yesterday. I was as surprised as you are. This morning when you called and told me about *your* letter, I called my dad. He told me the whole story. It's kind of complicated, so listen carefully.

"Grandmother was married twice. My mother, Melody, and Kimberlee's father, Mark, were half-brother-sister. They had different fathers so they had different last names. My family moved here after your father died and you and your mom moved away from Fern Lake, Kimberlee. I can hardly believe it myself, but the way I figure it, you and I are first cousins. Well, maybe we're first step-cousins, whatever. Now isn't that a kick?"

Kimberlee's lips moved but nothing came out. She closed her mouth, totally at a loss for words.

Dorian flew out of the recliner and threw her arms around her and squeezed. "Aren't you thrilled? Cousin!"

Thrilled? Was she? Maybe, maybe not. There had been a time when Dorian was a rival for Brett's affections, but when he chose Kimberlee, she and Dorian had become friends. To learn they were related was a surprise at best. "So, all last summer when I was buying my house and talking about Margaret Lassiter, you never realized she was your grandmother, too? I don't get it. How is that possible?"

Dorian shrugged. "I was only four years old when my family moved to Fern Lake. My mother died in an automobile accident a couple of months later. Grandmother Lassiter lived in Texas. I guess she and Dad never got along very well and neither of them tried to pursue a relationship. Eventually, she just drifted out of our lives. Dad never talked about Grandmother. I guess I just didn't connect the dots when you mentioned her name last summer."

"Are you going to accept her invitation and go to Texas," Kimberlee's temples throbbed, "...to visit and find out about the inheritance? Have you thought about what you'd do if she offered you the ranch?"

Dorian laughed. "I guess so... going, I mean, to visit Grandmother. I'm curious to see what this is all about. I don't know. I might consider moving there. I suppose I could learn about horses as easy as the next fellow. She must have ranch hands that perform the actual work."

"Oh, for sure. She probably has a whole staff." Brett waved his hand.

Kimberlee's laugh sounded more like a snort. "I really hadn't given the idea of the inheritance much thought. I just wanted to meet my cousin. Guess I already have, *huh*?" She laughed again and reached for the letter, paused, and folded her hands back in her lap. "Dorian… we won't let this come between us, will we?

"I mean, our friendship got off to a rocky start." Her hands felt cold and clammy.

The color in Dorian's cheeks blossomed pink. "The ranch is supposed to be worth a fortune. We could be talking millions. People have fallen out over a lot less, even killed each other." Goosebumps popped up on Dorian's arms. She shivered. The pink in her cheeks faded to milky white.

"What's the matter? You look like you've seen a ghost." Brett jumped up from the sofa. "Do you want a glass of water?" He started for the kitchen.

"No. No. I'm fine," Dorian said. "I just felt a little light-headed for a minute. Like someone walked over my grave." She rubbed her arms. "Silly of me, wasn't it?" She took a deep breath and sighed. "As far as the inheritance, I agree with you. I don't want anything to change our friendship. Especially now that we've learned we're cousins. I don't have much family. Just my dad. Family means a lot to me." She reached for Sam and stroked his head. "I like my life—living with Sam, and working on the police force. I won't pretend it wouldn't be nice to be rich, but I wouldn't want to risk everything I hold dear. But, who knows, either one of us might change our mind and decide to become ranchers if the right opportunity dropped in our laps."

"We've been talking about taking Thumper. Are you taking Sam?" Kimberlee nodded toward the dog lying at Dorian's feet.

"Of course. I don't go anywhere without him. She specifically said we could bring our pets, so he's going." Dorian reached down and pulled Sam's ears.

"We're going to be quite a motley crew, aren't we?" Kimberlee giggled. A kid, a dog and a cat. Grandmother won't know what hit her."

A square of sunlight shining through the window faded, as though the sun had gone behind a cloud, leaving Dorian's face in shadow.

Chapter Three

 *owww!*

Kimberlee shoved Thumper's carrier into the SUV beside Amanda. He howled again, as the carrier slid across the seat. Did he already know they were going to Texas? If this was a grim hint of what they were to endure throughout the long day before they reached Grandmother's ranch, she might as well pop another migraine tablet now. She gave Amanda's seatbelt a final tug. "It's your job to take care of Thumper, okay?" *Now all we have to do is get through the next six or seven hours.*

Amanda beamed. She shook her finger as she peeked into Thumper's carrier. "You be a good boy and don't cry. We're going to visit our *grandmover.*"

Brett loaded the last suitcase into the back of the SUV and drove to Dorian's apartment. By the time all her paraphernalia was loaded into the back along with Sam's carrier, there wasn't room to wiggle. The boats on the lake cast a bleak outline against the predawn sky as they drove out of town.

After three hours of whining, whimpering and two potty stops, the towers of San Francisco airport loomed through the fog. A five-hour flight took them to San Antonio. From there, they endured forty-five minutes aboard what felt like a single engine crop duster to Eagle Pass, Texas.

Thirty minutes later, they sat in the airport waiting room watching the tiny planes take off and land. Kimberlee checked her watch. Still no sign of the animal carriers from the baggage department. What could possibly be wrong? *Had the animals suffered some ill effect from the flight?*

"Where's Fumper?" Amanda looked up through droopy eyelids.

Kimberlee gripped Brett's arm. "You don't suppose something's happened? Could the carriers have missed the connection between flights? Brett, do something."

"It's likely they had to unload the passengers' luggage before they bring the animals out. Be patient. They probably have limited staff. Look over there, by the front door. 'Spose that's our ride?"

An older man sauntered across the lobby, carrying a sign that read, CLARKE. He might have come straight from a John Wayne movie set, with his red-checkered shirt and tall snakeskin boots. A large belt buckle with a bucking bronco held up faded jeans. Long gray hair slicked back into a ponytail and a neatly trimmed gray beard covered the bottom half of his face. He waved the sign toward Brett and with a toothy grin, raised his bushy eyebrows.

"Must be your grandmother's driver." Brett hurried toward the cowboy.

"We're the Clarke party." Brett extended his hand.

"Howdy. I'm Harold. Are y'all ready? Sorry I made ya wait so long. Got hung up at the ranch. The van's right outside." He nodded toward a battered blue van parked in the passenger loading zone.

"We're still waiting for our animals." Brett gestured to the desk where the clerk sat hunched over her computer. "We've been here for half an hour. I don't know what's taking so long."

"I'll take care of it. Give me a minute." Harold strode to the desk and spoke to the clerk. Within ten minutes, a porter delivered the animal crates. It paid to know the right people. Harold squeezed the family and the luggage into the van and pulled away from the airport.

Amanda wiggled and whined in the back seat, next to Thumper's carrier.

"Won't be long now, folks. It's about ten miles across the prairie to the ranch." Harold's eyes reflected through the rear view mirror.

Kimberlee nodded and pushed her hair off her damp forehead. She rolled down the window an inch and breathed deep. The fresh air was invigorating.

Thumper's cage jiggled. *Rrrowwowwow!*

Sam's intermittent yips from the rear stabbed the air.

Kimberlee put her hand to her aching head. "Thumper. Sam. *Shoosh.* I know you're tired. We're all tired." *If I have to listen to Thumper's howling and Sam's whining much longer, I'll go insane.*

"Amanda, honey. Stop whining and lay your head in Mama's lap. It won't be long now." She turned back toward Dorian. "I swear by all that's holy, if I'd known what we had to go through to get here, I would have thought twice about this trip. And mark my words. Thumper would not have been on the passenger list. I should have given him the tranquilizer the vet suggested. What was I thinking?"

Dorian's laugh came from the third seat in the van. "I told you it was nuts to bring a cat on a trip that involved changing planes twice and two car trips. We're lucky they didn't lose the animals during the flight changes. Hang in there. It won't be long now." She patted Sam's crate. "Quiet, boy."

In the distance, wild horses raced toward the jagged hills, jutting up from the prairie floor. Their coats blurred together in an array of black and gold and brown, creating a collage of color across the prairie.

Kimberlee pointed out across the stone fences. "Amanda, look at the beautiful horses."

Amanda sat up, stared out the window and bounced up and down, straining against the restriction of her seat belt.

Harold glanced back over his shoulder. "They are beautiful, ma'am, but sometimes they sure give us fits. That stallion there, we call him Quantum. He's the undisputed leader of that herd of mares. You'd think with so many wives, he'd be satisfied, but he's alla time trying to get the ranch mares to join his harem."

Beyond the stone fences, the horses moved into the distance across the prairie.

"Has he ever gotten away with one of your mares?" Brett asked.

"We've had a few close calls. He'll bust down a fence once in a while, trying to get at them. He comes every couple 'a months and stirs up the mares. But your grandma, Margaret Lassiter, won't allow none 'a that." A loud guffaw erupted from his barrel chest. "So we keep a close eye on 'em, especially when they're in heat."

"I'll bet you do. You'd lose a big investment if he made off with one of them." Kimberlee leaned forward and touched Harold's shoulder.

"On the other hand, running across them once in a while is one of the pleasures of living here on the prairie. They're gone now. Maybe you'll see them again another day."

Only a cloud of dust remained where moments before wild horses had thundered through the desert.

Kimberlee's stomach quaked when the ranch house and stables came into view. Was she ready for this? *Will she like me?* She had the impression that her grandmother was a rich, sophisticated business woman. Would she think of Kimberlee's family as poor relatives?

Kimberlee glanced into the back seat where Dorian sat gripping Sam's crate. She looked calm on the outside, but her white knuckles suggested otherwise.

Harold pulled the van to a stop in front of the large two-story ranch house. The peaked roof cast a shadow across the twin dormer windows on the second floor. Like a pair of disapproving eyes, they looked down on the new arrivals. Branches on the willow tree in the side yard stirred in the prairie wind. A sudden gust sent the empty rocking chair on the front porch pitching back and forth, as though manipulated by an invisible hand. Kimberlee shivered. Was it an omen of what was to come? For half a second, Kimberlee hesitated.

The screen door squeaked and Grandmother Lassiter stepped onto the porch, her face wreathed in smiles, the wrinkles in her cheeks smoothed out by her grin. She had pulled her gray hair away from her face and arranged it in a bun high on her head. The sleeve on her housedress fell away as she lifted her hand to wave, sending a waddle of skin swaying beneath her upper arm.

Kimberlee stepped out of the car. As she walked down the sidewalk, the prairie wind whipped her hair across her eyes, making Grandmother's image crackled into a fractured caricature. *She looks friendly enough. I'm just being silly.* Her heart beat quickened.

Grandmother bustled toward her. Spots of scrambled egg clung to her checkered dress just above the top button. "Welcome, welcome," she said, throwing her arms around Kimberlee and crushing her against her bosom. "You must be Kimberlee. Welcome to Texas. Come right on in. Harold will bring in the luggage." She smelled of perspiration and talcum powder.

Talcum powder? Scrambled eggs? Not so very sophisticated after all. Kimberlee made an effort not to wrinkle her nose. She patted her grandmother's shoulder. "Grandmother. So nice to see you, at last." She pulled away from her embrace.

Grandmother turned toward Dorian. The clump of scrambled egg tumbled off her housedress and onto the cobbled sidewalk.

"You must have guessed, I'm Dorian, Grandmother. Thanks for inviting us." She reached out her hand. "This is Sam." She smiled down at the dog.

"Why, of course, Dorian." She pulled Dorian into her arms. "I'd know you anywhere. How you favor your mother. My, it's almost like seeing her in front of me again. Almost brings a tear to my eye. So glad you could come. Y'all come on in." She wiggled her finger toward a walkway leading to the side of the house. "You can take the dog around and meet us on the patio, if you like. Save you having to walk the dog through the house."

Dorian glanced toward Kimberlee and raised an eyebrow. "Okay. If you say so..." She started down the cobbled path leading around the house.

Grandmother grinned at Brett. "And you must be Kimberlee's new husband. Welcome to the family. Come in. We're having drinks on the patio. Then, we're planning a barbecue later this evening."

Amanda peeked out from behind Kimberlee's legs.

Grandmother grabbed her arm and pulled her out from behind Kimberlee. "Why, you little darling. Come here to Grandma." She hefted Amanda and swung her around.

Amanda wailed, kicking and pushing against Grandmother's chest.

What on earth was she doing? Kimberlee reached toward Amanda.

"Why, no need to cry. Give Grandma some sugar." Grandmother shoved her face into Amanda's neck and lathered her with wet smooches.

Kimberlee grasped Amanda's arm. "Here, let me take her. She's exhausted from the trip. Give her a little time. Amanda, stop that whining right now." She set her on the ground. "Go help Harold bring Thumper into the house. There's a good girl."

Amanda sniffled and scurried to the back of the van where Harold lifted out the bags. He unloaded Thumper's carrier from the rear seat. His woebegone howling reached a crescendo. *Roww-wow-wow*

"Here you go, little girl, here's your kitty. He's sure raising a ruckus, isn't he? Can you carry him all by yourself? No? He's heavy, isn't he? Well, here, you and I will each take a side and we'll carry him into the house together."

Amanda swiped her sleeve across her wet cheeks and gripped the side of the carrier. She smiled shyly at Harold as they carried the protesting cat into the house. The family followed.

Harold set the carrier on the entryway tile and opened the cat door.

Thumper shot out like a cannonball and disappeared behind the couch.

Kimberlee's cheeks warmed. Her chest prickled with perspiration. What she must be thinking. Thumper—screeching. Amanda—howling. *I don't think we're making a very good first impression.*

A uniformed nurse stepped out from the library, patting the little white hat perched on top of her short brown hair. She adjusted the spotless white apron that cinched in her ample waistline. She leaned down to grasp Amanda's hand. "Hello, Amanda. I'm Nanny Sally. If you come with me, I'll show you all the new toys." She steered her toward the stairs.

Kimberlee turned to Grandmother. "Wait. Where is she taking—?"

"I've arranged for a nanny to take care of our Amanda while y'all are here," Grandmother drawled. "She's taking her up to the children's room. Don't worry. Your bedroom is just a lick and a promise down the hall."

"I'm not sure I want her… You never mentioned that we'd be separated." Kimberlee wrung her hands and bit her lower lip.

Amanda waved as they reached the turn in the staircase.

"I'll come up in a little while, sweetheart," Kimberlee called after the two, who had nearly reached the top of the stairs.

"Y'all come with me to the patio. You must need a drink. My attorney, Wilbur Breckenridge, is here. He can't wait to meet you." Grandmother gripped Kimberlee's arm and pulled her toward the sliding glass door.

She looked back. Amanda and the nanny were already out of sight as Grandmother led the way to the patio with Brett close on their heels.

They found Dorian already seated in a lawn chair, a glass of wine in her hand and Sam curled at her feet.

"I see you found your way, Dorian. Wilbur, this is my other granddaughter, Kimberlee, and her husband, Brett. I see you've already met the other one."

The other one? How rude to refer to Dorian… Kimberlee caught Dorian's eye.

Wilbur pulled his thin, six-foot frame from his chair and extended his hand. His dark suit, pink shirt with a button-down collar and a narrow pinstriped tie were the height of fashion. The light bounced off his highly polished boots. He wore his bright red hair slicked back on the sides and combed into a wave in the front. He shook Brett's hand and then turned toward Kimberlee. "It's a pleasure, Kimberlee, Dorian." He nodded in their general direction and smiled. His eyes squinted and his freckled nose wrinkled to the side, giving his face somewhat of a sneaky expression.

"Yes, it's nice to meet you too," Kimberlee said. What was it about that guy she didn't like?

Grandmother tipped her martini glass and took a long drink. "They came all the way from California just to visit their ole granny. Wasn't that nice? Brett's an author." She waggled her hand toward Wilbur. "Now you men get acquainted while I talk to my girls. Dorian, come on over here and sit with me on the lawn swing."

Dorian stood and crossed the patio. Sam got up and ambled along beside her.

Grandmother waved her martini glass toward Sam. "That there dog can sit on the patio with us while we're out here. He'll have to stay on the porch when we go inside. I don't allow dogs in my house."

Dorian stopped beside the swing. "But, you said we could bring our pets—"

"I didn't say you could keep him in the house, now did I?" Grandmother clamped her mouth in a firm line. She held Dorian's gaze in a hard stare.

Dorian's face flushed. Her cheeks pinked. A vein throbbed beside her eye. "Grandmother, I can assure you, Sam is a certified Search and Rescue dog. He's well-trained and well-behaved. You'll have no trouble…" She glanced between Kimberlee and Brett, as if pleading for moral support.

Kimberlee dropped her gaze. What could she say? She didn't want to cause trouble. She gripped Brett's hand tighter. Her stomach seemed to slide sideways.

Grandmother waved her hand across the patio. "Dorian, dear. This here is my house and my rules. You're a guest here. I'm sure y'all understand, now don't you?" Her eyebrows lowered and she fixed a glare at Dorian.

"Of course, Grandmother. As you wish." Dorian leaned down, hiding her flaming cheeks. She rubbed Sam's head and stroked his soft golden ears.

Grandmother smiled and rubbed her hands together, ever so much like a praying mantis on a summer day. Was she pleased with the outcome of her first confrontation with both of her guests? With Amanda tucked away in the nursery and Sam relegated to the back porch, Grandmother had managed to put everyone in their place within five minutes, leaving no doubt who was in control. A chill worked its way up Kimberlee's spine. How hard was it to change an airplane reservation from next Sunday to tomorrow? The desire to look for a phone book was overwhelming.

Grandmother blurted out, "Well, now that's settled, what are y'all standing around for? Sit down. What will you have to drink, Brett? We're on our third martini. You and your lovely bride have some catching up to do."

Brett glanced at Kimberlee. He shoved his hands in his pockets and shifted from one foot to the other. "We're really not much in the way of drinkers. Perhaps…just a glass of white wine?"

Kimberlee rolled her eyes from Brett to Dorian and then sat in the lawn chair next to Dorian.

Grandmother pressed a glass of wine into her hand.

Kimberlee reached down and gave Dorian's arm a squeeze. What could they do? They were guests in Grandmother's house. She stared across the manicured grass toward the prairie that seemed to go on for as far as the eye could see. The ceiling fan whirled overhead. A stray cobweb whipped back and forth in the breeze below the fan. She checked her watch again. 3:40, less than three minutes since they'd walked in the door.

Dear God, what had they gotten into? It was going to be a long week if the last five minutes was any indication.

Chapter Four

our white feet tucked beneath his belly and his fluffy black tail whipping, Thumper peeked out from beneath the sofa. He heard voices—Brett and Kimberlee—out on the patio. He sniffed, savoring the unfamiliar smells of hay and horses drifting in from the open window. Another delightful scent wafted across the room and sneaked beneath his hiding place, teasing his nostrils and making the hair on the back of his neck stand erect. The scent tasted familiar and yet…evocative and foreign.

Oh, moment of discovery, sweet love's fantasy revealed. He poked his head from beneath the sofa and lifted his nose, drew in the bouquet, rolled it around his tongue and teeth, seeking to identify the direction of the tantalizing bouquet. After several long minutes, he crept from his hiding place and followed the enticing aroma. *Aha.* The flavor of a feminine flower, not a figment of his furtive fantasy.

She drew him as if by magic—teasing, taunting, beguiling him until his senses reeled. He padded through the house, but to his dismay, was unable to locate this unseen temptress, this invisible goddess, this captivating illusion that occupied his mind.

He followed the fragrance into the library, his gaze traveling up the bookcases where he spied Lillian Braun's *Cat Who* series and a complete collection of *Rita May Brown and Sneaky Pie Brown.* Kimberlee often displayed the titles in her store window, examples of inspired modern day mysteries for ailurophiles.

Their eyes met as the fascinating creature peered down from the top of the bookshelf, her front toes curled beneath her breast. The sun streaming through the window shimmered off her silken ears. Her fur, like rows of buttercups set in a field of marigolds, shot through a summer sunset. Her eyes, midnight slits peeking through golden moons. Her sensuous tail coiled around her nose, rising and falling in a hypnotizing rhythm, matched the thud of his heart.

Electricity crackled through the library. She was not a gossamer dream, but a lissome feline goddess. She stared down from atop the shelf with total insouciance—a living, breathing challenge to his masterful art of *woomanship.*

During his bachelor days at Fern Lake, he had always preferred a darker-colored girlfriend as opposed to the lighter tabby-marked variety. His interest in this golden-haired vixen with stripes the color of marigolds was both perplexing and titillating.

He'd had his share of lady friends, though he was not obsessed with romance. He fancied himself a diplomatic lover, not given to one-night stands, but more discerning in his treatment of female companions. He disliked the idea of *love em' and leave em',* having heard tales of his father's abandonment issues following mother's whirlwind romance. Mother had shared stories of her lonely nights on the fencepost, waiting in vain for his father's return. Thumper vowed he wouldn't be that kind of cat or cad. But, this enticing, exotic creature was something a cat could sink his teeth into. This lady begged a more committed long-term relationship.

Now, to put his best foot forward…but which foot? All four of his nimble black legs ended in elegant, snowy white feet with multiple toes. He stretched out his front legs, raised his rear to display his muscular posterior and tight gluts. He then twisted into a three-point pretzel-like position and licked his inner thighs. These contortions were calculated to demonstrate his strongest attributes and yet reveal a willingness to concede control, a maneuver that he had perfected. It had never failed in his effort to impress a lady cat yet.

"Howdy, stranger. New in town?" The sound of her voice, like the thrum of a hummingbird's wings, sent shockwaves through his heart.

He stared into her enchanting face—the angle of her teasing

whiskers—the slant of taunting ears—her tantalizing eyes, tinged ever so slightly with green, glittered in the sunlight. Her tiny pointed teeth—perfection.

She breathed a sigh and twitched her tail in a seductive manner.

Okay, you're up, Thumper. Remember, you don't get a second chance to make a first impression. "Thumper's the name. Brought the family to visit the grandmother for a few days. Care to show me around?" He licked his bib into a conflation of black and white, turned and stared out the window. "Not that it matters one way or the other if you do or don't, you understand. Just sayin'." *Please say yes, oh please, please, say yes...*

"Thumper? What kind of name is that? Sounds like a rabbit."

His heart crumpled at the distain in her voice. There it was again, that silly name. Thumper—like the bunny. How many times had he wished that Amanda would have named him Butch or Cruncher. Or even Felix. But no—since Kimberlee came into his life, he had to go through life as—Thumper. His dream of a romantic fling with this straw-colored vixen had as much chance now as a balloon at a porcupine's birthday party. He sighed.

Might as well leave before things get ugly. He hung his head, turned and shuffled to the door.

"Wait."

He stopped at the sound of her velvet voice. His ears perked, whiskers taunt. He glanced back. "Yes?"

She stood and rearranged her sumptuous body on the top shelf. No question. All her curves were in the right places. "Don't go yet, Thumper. I like rabbits."

Hallelujah! Hallelujah!

Perhaps something blowing through the desert air made her receptive to his advances. Perhaps it was his calculated humbleness and winning personality, or perhaps it was just destiny.

In no time at all, he learned her name. *Noe-Noe.* Even her name was poetry and song. Within the hour, he not only coaxed her off the bookshelf, but promising lunch, had her half way across the lawn to the large gurgling fountain beneath the willow tree in the back yard. Tiny birds swooped down to bathe in the spray bouncing from the fountain into the grass.

Thumper and Noe-Noe crouched beneath the tree, inching in microscopic spurts toward their unsuspecting victims. The birds bathed with wild abandon, unaware they were the entrees on the lunch menu.

Thumper's eyes darted from subject to subject, assessing the banquet. "*Umm…* I think I'll have the light tan bird with the red head hopping on the outside edge of the spray. Have you made a selection, lamb-chop?"

Noe-Noe lowered her eyes, the tip of her tail gently swaying with indecision. "Go ahead and choose for me. I can't seem to make up my mind."

Thumper's tail jiggled in anticipation. "Are you ready?" His whiskers twitched and he uttered an almost inaudible sound. *Eh eh eh eh.* "I'll flank to the port side and draw their fire. You bear starboard and catch one as it tries to make an escape. We'll share the booty *al dente.*"

Thumper's rear end rocked for traction. "Now!" He sprang to the left.

Noe-Noe sprang right. Their heads collided in midair.

The birds rose as if with a single mind, circled overhead and landed in the willow. Mad twitters erupted from the trees.

Thumper and Noe-Noe lay in a heap. Two pairs of startled eyes peered out from a mass of fur, eight paws intertwined; black and white fur twisted with stripes the color of mustard.

Noe-Noe disentangled her legs. *Humph!* She huffed off toward the barn.

Thumper bounded after her. "Wait. What happened? I told you to flank starboard. Starboard! You went port instead of starboard. Haven't you ever been on a boat?"

"It's not my fault. It could happen to anybody." She lowered her ears. "What's a boat?"

Kimberlee ceased to pay attention as Grandmother continued to hold court on the patio. The minutes ticked into an hour. Kimberlee shifted uncomfortably in her chair.

The attorney wore a perpetual smile and jumped at every opportunity to make a fawning remark. "Mrs. Lassiter, can I pour you another martini?" His demeanor, one of humble subservience.

Grandmother smiled and nodded, wiggling at the attention like a love-starved puppy.

"The wind is coming up, Mrs. Lassiter. Perhaps an afghan for your knees?" Leaping to his feet, Wilbur's ingratiating tone belied the coldness in his eyes.

Was Grandmother actually buying this crap-a-doodle?

Wilbur's delicate hands flailed the air. "How do you persuade such enormous blooms from the wisteria?" His fascination with Grandmother's gardening prowess was over-solicitous and sounded insincere. "You've done wonders with the yard."

Doubt he's ever snipped a wisteria vine in his life.

"Oh, pshaw. It's nothing at all." Grandmother beamed under the obsequious remarks.

Kimberlee shifted on the lawn swing. She wrinkled her forehead. Wasn't it strange, why Wilbur fussed so much over Grandmother? He already had all her business.

By the third platitude within as many minutes, Kimberlee leaned toward Dorian and whispered, "Is he spreading it on a little thick, or what?"

"Like butter on hot toast," Dorian whispered back, covering her mouth with her hand.

Grandmother's head whipped around. "Girls, do you have something you wish to share? It's quite rude to whisper in mixed company."

Kimberlee ducked her head and folded her hands in her lap just like she had in the fifth grade when she was caught passing notes. She and Dorian exchanged glances and giggled.

"Now, let me tell you about the ranch." Grandmother droned on, waving toward the prairie. "It runs this-a-way from just outside Eagle Pass and up against the mountains there in the east and about two miles that-a-way to the border of the Kickapoo Indian Reservation. It stretches clear over yonder and butts up against the Rio Grande, which, you know, is the border between Texas and Mexico."

For the next hour, Grandmother recited a monologue, extolling the expansive history of the ranch, the history of Texas and numerous anecdotes that ranged from the Mexican-American war to a fist fight behind the barn last New Year's Eve.

Brett had long since lost interest and buried his nose in an *Equestrian Today* magazine.

So much for her concern that Grandmother would be a sophisticated business woman in a purple pantsuit. Kimberlee was sure her head might explode if she sat there another minute.

She stood and ran her hands over her wrinkled slacks. The wrinkles were sculpted in place and permanently molded from perspiration and prolonged inactivity. "Grandmother, I have a raging headache. Please forgive me. I must lie down for a while."

"Of course, dear. I'll have the housekeeper show you to your room. Imelda?"

Imelda appeared in the doorway. With her dark hair pulled behind her ears, a black cap on her head and a white apron tied around her middle, she was the epitome of the perfect Hispanic housekeeper, efficient, motherly and no doubt, an excellent cook to boot. "Yes, ma'am?"

"Show Miss Kimberlee to her room."

Imelda nodded. "If the miss will follow me, *por favor*."

Grandmother's voice followed Kimberlee as she left the patio.

"Now, when my first husband and I, God rest his soul, bought the ranch back in 1962…"

Imelda led Kimberlee up the stairs. "Come this way, miss."

"Where is Amanda's room, Imelda?"

"Right down the hall." She indicated the second door on the left.

Kimberlee nodded. "Thanks. I'll check on her after I rest a bit."

"Here is where you will stay. It was Miss Melody's room." Imelda shoved open the bedroom door. "You will have a nice view of the stables."

"This was Melody's room? Dorian's mom?"

Why on earth hadn't Grandmother given this room to Dorian?

Chapter Five

Elegant Victorian era furniture decorated the bedroom. Kimberlee glanced at the heavy dark claw-foot dresser. Her suitcases were neatly stacked at the end of the dark four-poster bed with the tall carved headboard. *Yikes. Shades of the Knights of the Round Table.*

"Missus Lassiter thought you and your husband would be more comfortable in the larger room. The bathroom is just down that way, to the right. Your little girl is just down the hall."

"I see. Wasn't that thoughtful of her." She nodded at the housekeeper.

Imelda bobbed a little curtsey. "Will that be all, miss?"

"Yes. Thank you, Imelda." Kimberlee closed the door. As she turned, she caught just a glimpse of a woman with shoulder-length hair on the opposite side of the room. Her hand flew to her mouth. "Oh, I didn't see you there. Who are you?" *Melody's ghost?*

The startled reflection of her own face framed by a mirror with carved flowers stared back. She put her fingers to her chest to calm her pattering heart and laughed. *It's you, you goofball. You're looking at a mirror.* It must be the headache, making her see things.

She moved to the end of the bed and ran her fingers over the engravings on the bedpost. Could this have been Grandmother's furniture when she first married? How many times did she make love in this bed? For that matter, is it possible her grandfather died in it?

She and Brett had to sleep in here all week! She shivered and rubbed her throbbing temples. The images she had conjured up would not get rid of a headache. If anything… Maybe a bit of fresh air would help.

She poured a glass of water from the tumbler on the dresser and swallowed a headache pill, then tiptoed down to Amanda's room. She turned the knob. The door was locked. She tapped on the door. No answer. Turning to leave, the door opened a crack and Nanny Sally stuck her head out. "Yes?"

"Oh, there you are. I thought I'd stop by and see—"

"She's sleeping. You'll have to come back later."

"I just want—"

Nanny Sally slammed the door with a bang.

Kimberlee put up her hand to knock again. Voices at the foot of the stairs! The guests were moving into the living room. If they saw her, they'd expect her to join the conversation downstairs. That was the last thing she wanted to do right now.

She hurried down the squeaking back staircase, through the kitchen and onto the back porch where Sam lay curled on an old blanket. "You poor thing." Kimberlee snapped her fingers. "Come and keep me company. Dorian would want you to get outside and do your business."

Sam scrambled up from the blanket, his flowing tail waving. He ran ahead of her down the porch steps.

Kimberlee strolled behind Sam, across the barnyard toward the paddock where a stable boy led a beautiful black mare through an exercise routine. Grandmother had talked at length about the breeding program, how they broke the horses to the saddle, their special diet, how to train a winner for the show ring, and the many complications of running the ranch. Just thinking about it made her head ache. Was the woman trying to impress them with the complexity of running a successful ranch?

"If she meant to scare me off, she did a good job," Kimberlee mumbled to Sam.

She climbed onto the rail fence to watch the young stable man in the paddock. The mare reared and pawed the air. In the next paddock, an agitated stallion trotted just beyond the rail fence. The stable man brought the prancing mare under control and back into a slow circular walk. He made it look so easy. Kimberlee climbed down off the fence, waved and gave him a thumb's up. *I could never do that, not in a million years.*

Her headache was lifting with each breath of clear desert air. "Come on, Sam, let's sneak away for half an hour and go for a walk. I doubt Grandmother even misses me, she's so busy running her mouth." Kimberlee giggled and patted Sam's head. "That wasn't very nice, was it? My bad!"

With his tail wagging, Sam ran ahead, sniffing the ground as they crossed the yard.

She sighed. What had happened to the pleasant vacation she'd dreamed of? Things had gone wrong from the moment they arrived. Amanda, being put into a nursery. Sam, now banished to the back porch. Grandmother's insensitive remarks and unreasonable demands to Dorian. The prospect of sleeping in a room that felt haunted.

Kimberlee stopped to get her bearings about a quarter-mile from the ranch, noting the surrounding landmarks. Three jagged rock formations on the distant hills stood just beyond the ranch house. She glanced at her watch. 5:00 P.M. At least an hour before dinner. "We can't venture too far, Sam. Considering the first impression we made and bailing on Grandmother's boring lecture, I don't think getting lost on *day one* would do my image any favors."

Sam's lolling tongue and waving tail suggested that he agreed.

The prairie blazed with color—flowering shrubs, rocks and varying shades of grass. Fluffy clouds drifted across the sky casting fingers of shadows, pointing first at a flame colored bush and next to a craggy rock formation.

Kimberlee swallowed a lump in her throat. The beauty of the desert stirred her heart.

A red and green striped lizard raced across the path. Sam lunged and followed in mad pursuit.

"Sam, come on back, boy. That's far enough."

Sam turned and raced back to her side. "Good dog."

She pulled sunglasses from her pocket and gazed across the prairie to the distant rocky cliffs. The sky had turned from blue to a faint shade of pink and yellow. A thrill tickled her spine. Waking every morning to a pink sunrise and completing each day with a red and golden sunset held a sudden appeal. Maybe they should consider the ranch, should Grandmother offer it to them.

A jackrabbit loped up the path, stopped to nibble a blade of grass, and then disappeared behind a bush. His head popped up above the greenery. He spied Sam and took off, zigging and zagging across the prairie with Sam close behind. "Sam! Don't go too far."

If Grandmother offered the ranch to Dorian, Sam wouldn't have any complaints, either, spending the rest of his life here.

In the distance, a flurry of dust rumbled and curled across the prairie. A kaleidoscope of moving colors coalesced into a herd of wild horses. The rumbling grew louder as the herd galloped nearer, the black stallion racing at the head.

Kimberlee froze, lest a single movement on her part should frighten them away. Her heart raced as the herd skidded to a stop, not thirty feet from where she stood. Had they come over to inspect this strange creature invading their territory?

Quantum took one step toward her and then another and another, his neck outstretched, nostrils quivering.

She held her breath and ever so slowly, stretched out her hand. How amazing that he would bring his harem so close. Her heartbeat raced and the hair on the back of her neck tingled.

Quantum huffed. His breath warmed her palm. The scent of sagebrush and dust clung to his coat. Their eyes met, and for a magical moment, her spirit joined with this wild creature of the prairie.

The mares turned away from their leader, sensing no fear. They milled around, then began to graze on the short clumps of grass scattered among the shrubs.

Moments later, as suddenly as they appeared, Quantum wheeled and raced away with his harem at his heels.

Kimberlee stood transfixed in wonder until they disappeared in a cloud of dust—the spell broken.

She walked on, lost in the glory of the few moments she shared with the herd. The experience almost pushed away the dismay she felt since meeting her grandmother.

Sam? *Where is he?* She scanned the horizon. "Sam? Come on back, boy." She whistled and tipped her head to listen for his answering bark. No response. He'd been out of sight since before the herd came so near. Where could he be? *That's just great.* Now she'd lost the dog.

A chilling clacking near her foot… A snake! All thoughts of Sam or Grandmother or even the wild horses vanished. She halted in mid-step. Only her eyes moved as she sought the snake. Heat coursed through her chest and chill-bumps speckled her arms. *Where? Where?*

Not three feet away, the creature lay coiled with its head erect, its bright red tongue *snicking* in and out. Its eyes locked onto hers in a hypnotizing stare. The snake shook a warning meant to terrify and paralyze its victim. It was working!

Whatever you do, don't move, Of course, there were rattlesnakes in the hills around Fern Lake. They usually gave ample warning and could be avoided. No such luck today. The startled reptile must have been sleeping when she came upon it.

Dear God, what was she going to do? She held her breath. The seconds ticked by. Beads of perspiration trickled between her breasts. Already lightheaded, she couldn't wait much longer to decide. Run or wait to see what the snake would do? The snake had the advantage. In about thirty seconds she'd faint right on top of the thing. Her tennis shoes and light clothing wouldn't be much protection, especially, way out here, alone on the prairie.

Brett, Amanda, What would they do without—

Ruff! Ruff! Ruff!

Sam! Coming back. She shifted her gaze from the snake to search for the dog. *Don't come back, Sam. Not now.*

The snake tasted the air with its forked tongue and turned toward the dog, its head lowered, still rapping out a warning.

Now. Kimberlee lunged backwards, stumbled and fell. *Dear God, help me.*

A shrub shook nearby as Sam burst through the bushes with a crash and grabbed the reptile behind the head.

Kimberlee gasped for air.

Sam and the snake thrashed on the ground. The rising dust made it difficult to clearly see the pair. The snake twisted and jerked, wrapped its body around Sam's legs. Sam fell and then regained his feet, snarling and growling, shaking the snake.

Kimberlee raised a broken branch over her head. If she struck, she might hit Sam.

Almost as quickly as the battle started, it ended. Sam stood panting, saliva dripping, his damp fur bristling around his neck. The snake lay still on the ground, bright red blood pooling in the dust, oozing from teeth marks in the back of its head.

"Oh, Sam." Kimberlee sank to her knees beside the dog, tears pricking her eyes. She ran her hands over his heaving ribs, searching for any sign of a bite. "Are you okay? Thank God. Dorian would never forgive me if anything happened to you."

She sat on a nearby log to catch her breath and calm her pounding heart. Sam lay at her feet, resting his head on her knees. He rolled his big brown eyes toward her, tongue lolling, a silly dog grin curling his lips.

"Yes, you know you're a wonderful dog, don't you?" She stroked his head. "Yes, you are."

Kimberlee rose from the log and kicked her would-be attacker. "It's good and dead. Good dog." She wiped the perspiration from her forehead with the back of her hand. "Let's go back, Sam. I've had about as much of Mother Nature as I can stand for one day."

Living on the Texas prairie could mean sharing magical moments with wild horses and golden sunsets, but it also had its fair share of life and death experiences.

Chapter Six

ust humiliating! That's what it was. Downright humiliating. Thumper rose and shook his long black coat. *So much for lunch beside the water fountain. Crashing into each other and knocking her into a heap—how embarrassing. She'll think I'm a California country-bumpkin.*

Thumper wracked his brain. How was he to re-ingratiate himself back into Noe-Noe's good graces? Since cruel fate had interfered with a demonstration of his hunting prowess, perhaps he'd be better served by impressing her with his bod. "Wanna' go for a walk, *mi amour?*" He stretched out his front legs, enhancing his rippling shoulder muscles. *That should do it.*

Noe-Noe blinked, tipped her nose and sniffed. "Roast swine."

The hair on the back of Thumper's neck bristled. "Alright, so things didn't work out like I planned and we didn't get *capon al dente* like I promised. At least I tried. There's no need to call me names." He turned toward the barn where men and women from a local catering service scurried like scalded ants between the kitchen facility in the barn and the picnic area. Just a hint of the aroma of roasted pork drifted across the barnyard from the barbecue where fat dripped off the spit, sizzling and popping as it struck the hot coals.

Thumper wiggled his nose. "Oh... Roast swine. Got it." Once again, he'd stuck all six toes of his snowy white foot in his mouth. His whiskers warmed. Was there no end to his humiliation with this female?

Noe-Noe minced forward on her golden feet. "I could show you the barn. It's quiet inside. We could be alone and…talk. There might even be mice near the feeding troughs, but be careful around the horses. If they step on you, you're toast." Noe-Noe stopped to scratch her ear.

Thumper paused to wait for her. His whiskers twitched as he admired her fetching figure. *What a babe.*

Noe-Noe stopped scratching and glared at him, her ears bent back. "No. I don't have fleas. I have allergies!"

"Hadn't entered my mind, my little butterball." Thumper leaped into a pile of hay just outside the barn door. "Let's stop here. It looks so inviting. I love to nap in the sunshine."

"Sounds lovely." Noe-Noe climbed to the top of the haystack and kneaded the straw into a soft bed. She flopped onto her side. "Come on up. There's room for two."

Thumper scampered up the hay. He lifted his head and sniffed. "We can watch the caterers from here and monitor the progress of the main course. Smell that tantalizing aroma …which reminds me …" He stretched out beside her, nudging her shoulder. "Perhaps you'll join me for dinner and a *tete-a-tete* later?"

Noe-Noe tipped her head to the side. The pupils in her eyes dilated. "Dinner? You wouldn't try to take advantage of an innocent country girl, would you?"

Thumper flicked his ear. The skin beneath his mustache tickled. "A gentleman would never ask a lady to go beyond the lengths she wished to go."

"So, you're telling me, you're a gentleman?"

"I'm shocked and appalled that you'd think otherwise." Was he that transparent? *My nonchalant meter must need a tune-up.*

"A lady wouldn't turn down an invitation from a gentleman who professed such honorable intentions. Dinner and *umm*…would be lovely."

A tune danced through his head. *Oh, sweet mystery of life, at last I've found you…* What a wonderful song… Half asleep, Thumper kept a watchful eye on the barnyard proceedings in general and the barbecue spit in particular. He leaned his shoulder gently against Noe-Noe's ribs.

So, this is what love feels like. Yowwza!

The scrunch of footsteps and voices invaded his reverie. One eye popped open. *What yonder blackguard presumes upon my wooing?*

"That's Mrs. Lassiter's attorney, Wilbur, and Harold, the stable master," Noe-Noe whispered.

The men wandered toward the barn, deep in conversation.

Harold paused beside the haystack and pulled a pack of cigarettes from his shirt pocket, lit one and took a puff. "I hope you know what you're doing. I'm concerned about these visitors. What if they figure out what's going on—"

"My decision, not yours." Wilbur pulled a lighter from his pocket, turned from the wind and lit his own cigarette. He snapped the lighter shut and shoved it back in his pocket. He took a drag and exhaled through his nose.

"I'm really uncomfortable with Mrs. Lassiter bringing the girls into this." Harold's cigarette bounced with each word. "They'll be asking questions and sticking their noses into everything. What if they figure out what's going on?"

Wilbur snorted. "In that case, one less grandkid to compete for the old lady's money wouldn't be a bad thing, would it?" He blew a puff of smoke over his head.

"So, you'd rather have the sheriff poking around because some damn city kid is dead? How stupid can you get?"

Wilbur wrinkled his brow. He threw the cigarette down and ground it into the dirt, muttering. He straightened his tie, turned on his heel and stomped away.

Harold wiped his forehead with his handkerchief and stuffed it back into his overalls. "Damn fool and his cockamamie ideas. Why did I ever get mixed up with him in the first place?"

He glanced up at the cats, picking his front tooth with a fingernail. "So, you've got a girlfriend already, *huh*? Nice work, kitty." He grinned, took another puff and blew the smoke toward the cats in the haystack, and then crushed out the cigarette under his boot.

Thumper's whiskers pulled back as Harold disappeared into the barn. He coughed and jumped to his feet, "Noe-Noe, wake up. They were talking about Kimberlee and Dorian. What's he mean about something *going on*? What's going on? Are my *persons* in danger?"

"Not if they don't stick their noses where they don't belong and stay out of Wilbur's business." Noe-Noe rolled over on her back and closed her eyes. "Now, don't ask any more questions, *mi amour*. The day is too beautiful to discuss it any further."

Thumper's stomach lurched. The aroma of roasted pork mixed with cigarettes and danger was enough to spoil anyone's appetite.

Chapter Seven

Margaret opened the kitchen door and gazed across the prairie. With the sun high overhead lighting the crags and valleys, the ragged hills looked almost blue in the distance. She never tired of the sight.

The succulent aroma of roasted pig drifted across the yard. She lifted her head, sniffed and sighed. One of the stable boys slowly cranked the handle of the spit, and the golden pig rotated, feet up, head down, and then its head came into view again. She nodded. Things were progressing well with the main course.

Off to the side of the barn, caterers scurried about—tack room to the serving stations and back again. Sure, they were expensive, but it was all part of the atmosphere she hoped to create. Her granddaughters must be impressed, well fed and oblivious to the real purpose behind her invitation to visit the ranch.

She sniffed again, savoring the aroma, then closed the door to the kitchen where Imelda pulled a pineapple upside down cake from the oven.

"*Mmm*. Smells good. Where are the girls, by the way?"

"Your guests have retired to their rooms until dinner." Imelda jerked her head toward the stairs.

"Good. Is everything ready, Imelda? The rest of the guests should arrive about 6:30 P.M."

"Everything's under control. I just serve the cake. The caterers will take care of the rest."

"*Ah.* Good." There was just enough time to make a quick trip to visit precious Amanda while everyone else was out of the way.

Margaret grabbed a couple of week-old chocolate chip cookies from the bottom of the cookie jar and hurried up the back stairs. A grin crept across her face. The idea had come to her several months ago, gaining momentum the more she pondered the plan. Enticing the grandchildren to Texas with the promise of inheriting her fortune was the easy part. While they were here, she'd strategize on the best way to keep Amanda, over Kimberlee's dead body, if she had to, figuratively speaking, of course...

The idea of having another child to carry on the family traditions—her own blood descendent and rightful heir—sent a rush of warmth into her chest. She stopped on the stairs to catch her breath. She'd made too many mistakes with her own children, Mark and Melody, and lost both of them. If she had another chance to raise a child...

From the first glimpse of Amanda, she knew she'd made the right decision. She couldn't wait until Kimberlee was gone and she'd have Amanda all to herself. This time, things would be different. *Shall I have her call me Mama?* Perhaps that was too much to ask right away. Better to wait a while until Amanda felt more at home on the ranch and forgot her mother.

Margaret had wasted the better part of the afternoon talking to Dorian and Brett. It took every ounce of discipline not to rush off to the nursery to see Amanda, especially after Kimberlee left the patio. A migraine, indeed. All the more obvious, Kimberlee wasn't fit to raise a child. All the expense and the planning it had taken to arrange this week would be worthwhile once she got rid of Kimberlee, even if it meant putting up with the lot of them for a few days. The only reason they came in the first place was because of the promised inheritance. As if she'd trust her precious ranch to either one of those foolish girls.

She tiptoed down the hall toward Amanda's room, patting the cookies in her pocket. What would it be like to raise a little girl again? No doubt, little girls were sweet, with hair ribbons, dolls, tea parties and frilly dresses, but they did grow up. Then you had to deal with the teen years.

Melody had never been interested in those girly things and always wanted to wear overalls and chase after her brother. Too bad children didn't come with written instructions or a guarantee of how they'd turn out. Girls could break your heart. Melody had certainly done that, running away at the age of seventeen to marry that no-good guitar player, what's his name? Dilham? Dildong? Dilman.

But, first things first. All those tears when Amanda first arrived. Clearly, Kimberlee had babied the child—made her timid and weak. She'd have to buck up around here. Life could be tough on the prairie. A girl had to be tougher.

She'd keep Amanda on a tighter rein than Melody. This time, she'd make all the right decisions. Dance classes, proms, college and the girl would marry a doctor or a veterinarian from Eagle Pass and they'd live right here on the ranch.

She tiptoed past Dorian's room and stopped to listen at Kimberlee's door. Inside, she heard the murmur of voices, but no discernible words.

Margaret opened the nursery door and peeked inside.

Amanda pushed a little train around a track on the rug, while the nanny flipped through a magazine nearby.

"Nanny Sally. Go on down to the kitchen and have some coffee." Margaret gestured toward the stairs. "I'll stay with our little darling for a while."

"Oh, thank you, ma'am." Nanny Sally scurried out the door.

Margaret slid open a cupboard and snapped on the tape recorder hidden inside. She closed the cupboard and leaned against it. "Now, Amanda, come to Nana and give me some sugar. Nana has brought you a nice chocolate cookie."

Amanda hopped up from the floor and ran to her.

Margaret knelt down and pulled her into her arms. "So, tell me, Amanda. What do you like best about the ranch so far?"

Amanda drove the little caboose through the air. "Oh, I like the horsies. We saw ponies in the park one time." She frowned. "There was a spotted pony, but Mama said we didn't have time to ride him."

"That doesn't sound very nice." Margaret wrinkled her nose. "Your mommy isn't very nice to you, is she?" *Let's set some ground rules right up front.*

Amanda put her finger in her mouth. "Mama's nice, but—"

Margaret gripped Amanda's shoulder. "But, what? What does she do that isn't nice?" Just as she thought, if you ply a child with cookies and the right question, you can get them to say anything. Ammunition to use another day.

"Mama has headaches and takes lots of naps. Sometimes she says she doesn't feel good and can't play with me."

"I see. And, pills. I'll bet she takes lots of pills…for the headaches." Amanda nodded.

She's a drug addict, just as I thought. Not a fit mother. "Does your daddy ever play with you?" Margaret pulled the second cookie from her pocket and waved it in front of Amanda.

"Daddy Brett's not my really daddy. My really daddy lives a long ways away. Daddy Brett works on his computer, so sometimes when I ask if he wants to play Candyland, he says he's too busy."

"*Ah,* I see. Isn't that awful? Imagine a mommy and daddy too busy to play with you. If you were my little girl, I'd never be too busy to play with you." Margaret ran her hands over Amanda's brown curls. "Does your Mama spank you when you're naughty?" If she could record Amanda saying her mother spanked her, it wouldn't be hard to claim child abuse. The taped evidence would speak for itself.

"Mama says it's naughty to feed Fumper at the table when I'm 'spose to eat my chicken, but she never spanks me." Her brown curls bounced. She picked up the train caboose and drove it through the air over her head.

Margaret snatched the caboose from Amanda's hand and tossed it on the floor. She puckered her lips and gave Amanda's shoulder a shake. "Pay attention when I'm talking to you."

Amanda's eyes flew open.

Margaret bit her lip. *Watch it, Margaret. Don't frighten the child.*

She smiled. "It's alright, dear. I'm sorry. Who is *Fumper*, dear?"

"You know. My kitty. We bringed him with us in the car." She looked around the nursery. "Where's Fumper?"

"Fumper. Of course. How silly of me to forget. He's probably downstairs. Why do you call him Fumper?"

"'Cause when I was a little girl, he *fumped* on the door, so I letted him come in. Mama said his coat was soft as a bunny, so I named him Fumper, like in my Bambi book."

"Oh! Thumper! How quaint." Margaret sniffed. "Now, tell me, does your Mama and Daddy ever quarrel and make you scared?" She made *boogieman* fingers in front of Amanda's face. A claim of child endangerment added to child abuse and drug use should do the trick.

Amanda shook her head. "Nooo."

Margaret's smile slipped. "*Huh.* That's hard to believe." She ran her hand over her mouth, wiping the frown from her lips. "So you like ponies, right?"

Amanda bounced up. "*Uh-huh.*"

Margaret struggled to get up from the floor and pulled Amanda into her arms. "Well, it's too bad your mother won't let you live with me, because I would never, never scold you or spank you. You could have cookies every day and I would buy you a pony of your very own. What do you think of that?"

Amanda wrinkled her forehead and then nodded.

"Let's ask Harold if he can find a pony just the right size for you to ride tomorrow."

Grandmother shuffled to the intercom by the door and punched the button to the kitchen. "Nanny Sally. Come back upstairs this instant." She stood by the open door, tapping her foot.

One should never underestimate what you can learn from a child. This conversation hadn't yielded much, but she had all week. Nanny Sally had instructions to ask leading questions and would run the tape recorder all day. Before the week was over, Margaret counted on getting something she could use against Kimberlee in a custody battle.

Kimberlee had divorced Amanda's father. Perhaps there was something related to the divorce she could work with. *Ah, not a bad idea.*

Margaret scowled as Nanny Sally hurried up the stairs. "I'm sorry, ma'am. You said to go to the kitchen. I didn't think—"

"That's right. You didn't think. I don't pay you to hang around the kitchen gabbing. Your agency should have taught you better. Now, don't forget what I told you about changing that tape every—"

Amanda came up to the door holding the cookie.

Nanny Sally brushed past her.

Margaret patted Amanda's head. "Good bye, darling. Nana will see you tonight at the barbecue."

As she pulled the nursery door closed, she caught a glimpse of Amanda stuffing the whole cookie into her mouth. *Greedy little pig.* Just another bad habit she'd have to break, once Kimberlee was out of the way.

Margaret hurried to her room and flopped onto the edge of her bed where Noe-Noe lay napping. The scene was set, the hook baited and she had eyes and ears on Amanda.

Noe-Noe chirped a greeting and rolled over, her feet in the air. Without a thought, Margaret stroked Noe-Noe's tummy, in answer to the unspoken demand. "Now! What else can I do to discredit Kimberlee?"

Noe-Noe purred and twisted onto her side, ducking her head into Margaret's hand.

"I've got it." Margaret reached for the telephone and dialed information in Santa Barbara. Why hadn't she thought of this sooner?

"Information, how can I help you?"

"I'm looking for a reputable detective agency. Can you recommend someone in the Santa Barbara area?" Margaret drummed her fingers on the nightstand, keeping time with each throb of blood in her head.

"I'm not able to recommend anyone, ma'am. I can only provide a phone number."

"*Damn it,* then just give me the number of the first detective agency listed in the phone book." She scowled and shook the phone. Each heartbeat thumped in her ears.

"Yes, ma'am... That would be the Ableman Detective Agency. The number is 555-0147. Do you wish me to connect you?"

"What do you think I called for?" Margaret flung a throw pillow across the room. "Of course, I want you to connect me." *Blast!* Everywhere she turned, she had to deal with idiots.

Noe-Noe jumped off the bed and ran toward the closed door.

Margaret patted an invitation back on the pillow. Noe-Noe ignored her.

The phone rang, once, twice, three times in Margaret's ear. *No answer.* She started to hang up, when a gruff voice came on the line. "Ableman Detective Agency." A thick hacking cough spewed through the receiver. "'Scuse me."

Margaret closed her eyes, pushing the disgusting sound from her mind. "This is Mrs. Lassiter from Eagle Pass, Texas." She wrinkled her nose and stuck out her tongue at the phone. "I need some information about a woman who lived in the L.A. area this past year. Is that something y'all can help me with?"

"Yes, ma'am. Our specialty is confidential investigations. Now, before we begin commencing, let me explain some of the *technicals* to you. I'll need a $500 fee retainer, to get started, you understand. Our customary fee charge is $100 an hour to commence investigating and we'll give you the first initial report within 48 hours. Is that acceptable?"

Margaret's shoulders slumped. She reached toward the pillow to stroke Noe-Noe's head but she wasn't there. *Where did she go?* Margaret glanced around the room. Noe-Noe still sat by the door. She patted the bed again. "$100 an hour? That sounds a bit pricey."

"Not when you consider the benefactual recompense of my investigation, so to speak. Can I get your credit card number?" The detective wheezed.

"My credit card? Don't you think you should find out who—"

"Ma'am, I've come to cogitate that it's a good *idear* to collect the fee retainer up front and find out the *perticalers* after. Sometimes we don't deal with such honest folks, such as I'm sure you're one of…if you grasp my meaning." His chuckle ended in another wheeze.

Margaret pulled a tissue from the nightstand and dabbed her forehead. "I suppose I can see your point, but I'm not comfortable giving my credit card number over the phone." She shook her head. "I'd rather not—"

"And in addition to your credit card, ma'am, I'll *requite* your phone and fax number, so's I can fax you a contract. We can start commencing on your *perticaler* problem as soon as I receive the signed contract and your fee retainer charges clear your credit card…*heh heh.*"

"*Umm.*" Margaret glanced around the room. What had she gotten herself into? She sighed and gave the requested information.

Noe-Noe tiptoed across the rug, jumped on the bed, turned in a circle and lay down again, leaning against Margaret's hip. She tipped her head back and peered into Margaret's face.

Papers crinkled. "Now that we have all that out of the way, let me complete this intake form. To whom do you want us to perform our investigation on?"

Margaret rolled her eyes. *An English major, no doubt.* She patted Noe-Noe's head. "Kimberlee Clarke, my granddaughter. She divorced her husband several years ago, name of Douglas Larson. They lived somewhere in the Los Angeles area, and…and…she has a child, but I think she's an unfit mother." Her cheeks tingled. She hunched her shoulders.

"And this Clarke dame…I mean, your granddaughter, *heh heh.* Tell me what in *perticaler* you're looking for?" The detective snickered. "She a blonde? I'll bet she's a looker. A slut, you say?"

Margaret shuddered. She imagined him reaching for his groin. She put her hands over her eyes and shook her head. Was she actually having this conversation? "What? Don't be impertinent. I don't see how the color of her hair, or whether she's… Now pay attention. She's got a little girl, Amanda. I want information that would convince a judge… I mean, any information about her divorce from Mr. Larson. You know. Like, was she involved with affairs, drugs, debt, questionable associates, anything to prove she's, well, she's not... Do you understand or not?"

"*Uh-huh,* I get it. Sexual affairs, no doubt. You wanna' know like if she ever registered at a motel, or had any indiscreet *ron-dez-vows,* and so forth." His words gushed in a sing-song rapid stream and his heavy breathing ended in a gurgle. "*Ahh...hhh.*"

Margaret's cheeks flamed. "Now, see here. Don't get the wrong impression. I'm the child's great-grandmother, and my only concern is for her welfare. I want to know why Kimberlee and her first husband got a divorce. She's married again, but who knows what kind of influence a stranger might have on my child, er, rather, her child. I'm afraid she's being neglected. Or abused. You do understand, don't you?"

"Of course, Mrs. Lassiter...*heh heh.* I understand all right. Yessiree. I'm sure I can dig up something, er...discover the truth. If it's out there, we'll find it. Everything you want to know. Let me fax that contract right over. Just fill in all the blanks and sign it and send it back and we'll get to work this afternoon. We won't let this slut...*heh. heh...* I mean your, *umm...* abuse that poor child for even one more day. Now, just a little more information... Let me get your phone and fax number. Sexual affairs, you say? Yessiree...*heh heh.* You wouldn't happen to have a picture of the slu...*um...*Mizzuz Clarke, would you?"

Margaret verified the requested information and hung up. She put her head in her hands, imagining a fat, bald man sitting in a smoky room with his dirty shoes on the desk, the butt of a cigar clamped in his teeth, and several weeks' grime under his fingernails. *What have I done?* Well, too late now. Why had she made such an arrangement with a man who earned his living searching through garbage cans, promoting scandals and selling dirt to the highest bidder? She could almost see his twisted smile... his hand busy at his zipper... His words echoed in her head. *Bet she's built...a slut, you say.*

Margaret pinched the bridge of her nose. *I'm not going to cry, I'm not.* She pressed her face into Noe-Noe's fur and wept.

Chapter Eight

Kimberlee opened the tall armoire door and pulled a hanger off the pole. She hung up Brett's shirts, and then turned toward the bed. "That's when I heard the snake. It about scared me to death. I was so far from the ranch house. Thank goodness Sam was there." She shook her head and tucked underwear and tee shirts into the top drawer of the Victorian dresser.

Brett's rocking chair squeaked as he leaned forward. "What were you thinking, going out there alone? I wish you'd asked me to—"

"And what difference would that have made?" Kimberlee whirled around, hands planted on her hips. "A snake's a snake. It could have bit you just as easily as me. I can take care of myself. Everything worked out okay, didn't it?" She snapped the lid on the last suitcase and shoved it under the bed.

"Honey, you misunderstood. I want you to be safe. I'm just saying you shouldn't have gone off by yourself, that's all. You don't know anything about the prairie. If Sam hadn't been there, it could have turned out a lot different. I don't even want to think…"

She lowered her head. Her cheeks warmed. "I know. I'm sorry for snapping. It's just, everything is so awful. Grandmother's acting so… so… And Dorian's having a fit. She said she should have left Sam with Jack. Who knew Grandmother would treat him like a dog?" She had to smile. Humor pops up in the most awkward ways.

The mattress squeaked as she flopped onto the edge of the bed. She gazed around the room. "And just look at this room." She nodded toward the towering dresser. "This old furniture gives me the heebie-jeebies. What do people see in this stuff? The place could be haunted."

Prickles raced up her forearm as she thought of the woman she'd seen when she first came into Melody's bedroom. Silly girl. Scared of her reflection in the gilded mirror. *It was me… wasn't it?*

"Oh, I don't know." Brett ran his hand over the carved arm on the rocking chair. "Imagine how long a craftsman worked to carve this." He pointed up toward the headboard. "And look at the workmanship on those roses—all carved by hand."

Kimberlee glanced up. "If you say so." She sighed, leaned back against the headboard and closed her eyes. "So, what did Grandmother say after I left the patio?" She snickered. "Did you hear all about how she and her husband settled the Old West?"

"Grandmother's attorney kept up more of his nonsense. When he wasn't complimenting her doilies, he couldn't stop talking about The Children's Benefit Society. He's so proud of himself for founding the program."

"*Umm.* The what?"

"Apparently Wilbur had convinced Grandmother to leave her estate to the children in this program he started. The sudden decision to change her beneficiary to one of you girls isn't sitting very well with him, the old skinflint. To hear him tell it, if she doesn't endow the charity, 300 kids will starve to death. As if—"

"I've never heard of The Children's–whatever. What is it?"

Brett shook his head. "He says they provide after-school care, hot lunch for preschoolers and camping trips for the boys, stuff like that. It's just in a couple of local towns. I'd like to learn more about it. Shall we drive into Eagle Pass tomorrow and check it out? You could do a little shopping while we're there."

Kimberlee opened her eyes and leaned forward, her expression brighter. "I'm sure Grandmother wouldn't mind if we got out of this dungeon…I mean, do some sightseeing. Lord knows it will be a cold day in *you-know-where* before I come back here again."

Brett laughed. "The way I see it, if Grandmother changes her beneficiary, the financial support to Wilbur's charity is likely to stop.

I'd hate to see a worthwhile program end because one of you girls… you know."

"You're right. If it's a worthy cause, it shouldn't stop. I'm sure Dorian would agree. We could bring it up at the next Fern Lake Merchant's Association meeting. They're always looking for worthy projects."

"Maybe we could get the Association to continue funding it. Let's make a day of it. Eagle Pass. Sightseeing. Lunch, the works. Shall we take Amanda?" Kimberlee glanced toward Amanda's suitcase, sitting by the bedroom door.

"Grandmother mentioned that she'd rented a pony this week. She plans to take Amanda riding tomorrow. She'd be disappointed if we took her. I think Amanda will be alright here with the nanny."

"Which brings up another subject. If I'd known Grandmother was going to put us in separate rooms, I don't know… Maybe I would have thought twice about coming."

Kimberlee punched a pillow and stuffed it higher behind her head. "I stopped in to check on Amanda when I went out for my walk. The nanny said she was napping, but I swear I heard her voice. It's one thing to have separate rooms and quite another to be told to buzz off when you go to visit your child."

Brett peeked out the window at the caterers hurrying around the yard. "We'll see her in a little while at the barbecue. They're going to have fireworks after dinner." He let the curtain slid back. "I'll take her suitcase over in a few minutes. I can speak to the nanny about it if you want me to." He stood, and then sat on the edge of the bed, reached for Kimberlee's hand. "Honey, I don't think Grandmother's trying to upset you. She probably thinks a caregiver for Amanda will free up your time to have more fun."

"I'm sure she has our best interest at heart. She's gone to a lot of expense. I'll forget it now and see how it goes." Kimberlee smoothed the coverlet on the bed. "Listen." She unbuttoned the top button on her blouse. "We're alone is this gorgeous Victorian haunted mausoleum.

Maybe we should take this opportunity to...you know." Kimberlee winked at Brett.

Brett peeled off his shirt and pulled her into his arms. "Maybe this is exactly what Grandmother had in mind. Maybe she wants another great-grandchild."

"You goofball."

He nuzzled her neck, covering it with kisses.

Chapter Nine

No one could ask for a more remarkable sunset to brighten Kimberlee's mood. The sun dipped behind the hills, creating a gorgeous red and orange sky—beautiful to see, but with just a touch of chill in the air. No question about it, the prairie was putting on her best show for the out of town guests.

Kimberlee's heart was near overflowing, surrounded as she was by the golden sunset, filled with contented bliss following her *afternoon delight* with Brett, the promise of good food, good friends and family. Even Grandmother had come through with a call to her neighbor and the unexpected arrival of the rented pony—a day ahead of schedule. At that moment, life was good there beneath the trees. She sighed.

Grandmother sat next to her, lounging in a wicker lawn chair brought over from the front veranda. Dorian sat on her other side. "Bet you don't have sunsets like this in California." Grandmother unscrewed the lid from her thermos bottle and poured the cap full. "Would you care for a drink? It's my favorite. Whiskey and soda." She waved the thermos toward Kimberlee.

Kimberlee shook her head. "Not just now, thanks. This is fine." She lifted her diet soda and nodded toward the plate of cheese and salami balanced on her knee.

Dorian leaned over, reaching for the thermos. "Why, I believe I'd like a drink."

Grandmother turned away from Dorian toward the yard where Harold led Amanda around the yard on the pony. She took a sip from her cup.

Dorian's face flushed. She glanced toward Kimberlee.

What just happened? Hadn't she heard Dorian, or was Grandmother ignoring her on purpose? Awkward! Goose bumps popped up from Kimberlee's elbows to her shoulders. *Oh, no you don't, Granny. You're not going to spoil my good mood with your nonsense.*

She rubbed her arms and cleared her throat. "Didn't you say you wanted a drink, Dorian?" Kimberlee peeked up through her eyelashes to see what affect her remark made on the old lady. Now, would she offer the thermos to Dorian?

Seeming unaware of the comments directed her way, Grandmother's gaze was locked on Amanda circling the yard on the spotted pony.

Apparently not. What has she got against Dorian?

Dorian shook her hand. "No…no. Never mind. I've noticed a sudden chill in the air. How about you?"

Kimberlee grinned. "We should have thought to bring our sweaters." She glanced back at Grandmother. Still no response.

Grandmother nodded toward Harold and the pony. "Looks like Harold made a hit with Amanda."

Harold gave the reins a tug and started the pony in a trot.

Amanda wiggled and squirmed in the saddle, and then giggles burst from her lips.

"Yes, she's certainly enjoying herself." Kimberlee's eyes crinkled as the pony passed close by. *My angel.* "I think she wishes she had a grandpa. She took to Harold right away when they carried Thumper into the house." Growing up without a father or grandfather had left a hole in Kimberlee's own heart. If she hadn't wanted more for Amanda, she wouldn't put up with Grandmother's slights and unreasonable demands.

Aunt Martha used to say, 'sometimes one has to deal with life's lemons to make lemonade for the young-uns.' This vacation was shaping up to be a week-long sentence in a lemonade stand.

"Harold is such a nice man," Grandmother simpered. "I'm so lucky to have him. I don't think I could run the place without him." She hiccupped and dabbed her eyes with her hankie. "He's been my rock since my husband passed away, God rest his soul." She tucked the hankie back into her ample bosom and reinserted a stray bobby pin into the crown of curls on the top of her head.

Who did she think she was fooling with that bright orange hair? *Shame on you, Kimberlee.*

"He reminds me of someone," Kimberlee said. She had an odd sense of *dèjá vu,* like she knew him from another place, another time…and then it was gone. "I can't put my finger on it. It's been on my mind ever since he picked us up at the airport. What's his story, Grandmother?"

A smile crossed her wrinkled face. Her head turned, following Amanda and the pony plodding in a circle behind Harold.

"Grandmother?" Kimberlee touched her arm. "Did you hear me? I asked about Harold."

"*Huh*? Oh, yes, Harold. I lost my husband about ten years ago." She sipped her drink and set the thermos cup back on the tray beside her chair. "I put an ad in a trade magazine for an experienced stable master. Harold called from the Cayman Islands and asked about the position. He told me he knew your father, Kimberlee. They roomed together in a military hospital in Germany. He said Mark had talked at length about Lassiter Farms. That's why the ad caught his eye. I was inclined to give him the job because he knew Mark." Grandmother leaned forward.

"Harold didn't have much ranch experience, but he was a quick learner. I've never regretted hiring him. You should try to visit with him while you're here. I'm sure he'd be happy to share some of his stories about your dad."

Harold stopped the pony and checked Amanda's stirrups. He ran a hand over her curls. "Isn't that sweet?" Grandmother giggled. "He always loved children. He and Imelda never had any of their own. Imelda's his wife, you know."

A shiver ran down Kimberlee's spine. Did she really want to talk to Harold about her father? She'd had migraines and nightmares all her life and only recently realized she had witnessed her father's murder when she was a toddler. Would talking to Harold start up the nightmares again? "I'll try to look him up and talk with him." She rubbed her temples. *Or not. Probably not.*

"Is your headache back?" Dorian touched Kimberlee's hand, a look of concern in her eyes.

Kimberlee folded her arms across her chest and rubbed both arms. "It's nothing, really. I was just thinking about my father. And I'm a bit chilly."

Dorian pulled her sweater from the back of her chair. "Here! Take my sweater. I'm naturally hot-blooded." She winked and waggled both eyebrows.

Kimberlee shoved her arms through the sleeves and pulled it up around her neck. "Thanks. That feels better." She shifted in her chair to face Dorian. "I can't tell you how grateful I am for Sam rescuing me this afternoon. He's my hero." Kimberlee reached down and patted the golden retriever lying at Dorian's feet.

Dorian stroked Sam's head. "Yes. He's always been my hero. Aside from you and Brett, I think he's about my best friend."

Thumper circled Kimberlee's chair, taking a wide berth around Sam, his eyes glued to her plate of cheese and salami. He stood on his hind legs, pawed at her knee with his big foot and uttered a pathetic, *mew...mew.*

"*Aw*. Poor baby. Are you hungry?" Kimberlee pinched off a bite of salami and held it out. "Here you go. You act like you're half-starved. It always works back home on barbecue night, doesn't it?" Thumper dropped to the grass and nibbled the slice of meat.

Grandmother's cat sidled closer, watching Thumper munch his snack. She turned golden eyes toward Grandmother's plate balanced on her lap. The cheese slid precariously back and forth as Grandmother shifted her weight. The sleek amber-colored cat stood on her hind feet, snagged a chunk of cheese off her plate and dashed up a nearby tree.

"Noe-Noe, Shoo. Scat. That cat, I can't tell you how many times

I've scolded her for sneaking something." Grandmother shook her fist at the tree. "Now you know how she got her name."

Kimberlee lifted an eyebrow. "What's her name?"

"That's her name. Noe-Noe."

Dorian giggled. "No-no?"

"Yes."

Kimberlee set her soda in the chair slot. "I'm confused. Is her name Yes or No No?

"Yes, it's Noe-Noe."

Kimberlee shook her head. Leave it alone. She wasn't going to play the Abbott and Costello game any longer.

Thumper raced up the tree after Noe-Noe. The two cats crouched on the low branch directly over the women's heads.

Dorian stroked Sam's head. "Why do you think it's cute when Noe-Noe is naughty? Sam would never steal food." The pout on her lips spoke louder than words. She was obviously still miffed that Sam was banned to the porch.

Kimberlee pointed toward the branch. "Thumper was just as greedy. They both grabbed the treat and ran. He was just polite enough to ask first. They're two of a kind."

"They should be," Grandmother said. "They're cousins, you know."

Kimberlee raised an eyebrow. The whiskey and soda must be clabbering her brain cells. "What do you mean, cousins? We live a thousand miles from here."

"Well, it's a long story." Grandmother turned toward the barbecue pit, and then cast a conspiratorial glance between her granddaughters and the cats perched on the branch over their heads. "I guess I have time to explain before dinner."

Thumper leaned down, as though intent on hearing the tale.

Grandmother sipped her drink. "Shortly after your father died, Dorian's mother moved her family to Fern Lake. Melody was convinced she was psychic and could help solve her brother's murder. She offered her services to the Fern Lake police, but they wouldn't have anything to do with her." Grandmother snorted. "She decided to investigate for herself. Foolish girl."

Kimberlee's fingers tingled. Her cheeks felt cold. She glanced toward Dorian. Melody? A psychic, investigating her father's murder? Dorian never mentioned it before. From the look on her pale face, this was news to her, as well.

Dorian lifted her shoulders ever so slightly and shook her head, her eyes wide.

Grandmother leaned toward Dorian. "Can you imagine, learning one day that your daughter was killed by a hit and run driver and the next day, you receive a letter from her? It's so hard to believe she's really gone. Sometimes I look out my window and I swear I see her walking across the yard, just like when she was a girl."

Kimberlee shook her grandmother's arm. "What did her letter say?"

Grandmother flinched. "She said she'd been asking questions at the Fern Lake Lodge, next door to where Mark was killed. She said she met the boy who worked there. He showed her a litter of kittens. She planned to bring one home to you, Dorian."

Kimberlee looked up at the cats in the tree. Thumper's ancestors. She bit her knuckle. "That would have been our friend, Jack. He's worked at the lodge since before my father died. Go on. What happened next, Grandmother?" This story was better than any she'd seen on television lately.

"Melody's letter said she overheard the lodge owner talking about disposing of a body. She said she was going to report it to the authorities, but she never had a chance. She was killed the next day by a hit and run driver. They never found the driver."

Kimberlee's hand flew to her mouth. The lodge owner? Ted Herman. Only last year when she returned to Fern Lake and met Brett, they'd investigated her father's murder—to no avail. One of the suspects was Ted Herman, but without proof… Hadn't Ted Herman caused her enough grief? Now to think he might have been responsible for Melody's death, too? Thank God the evil man had died years ago. Tears prickled and stung her eyes.

Dorian touched her grandmother's arm. "I'm so sorry."

Grandmother stared across the yard. She waved her hand, as though dispelling the disturbing memory. "I sent a copy of her letter to the police, but I never heard from them. I suppose they thought it was more of her crazy talk. I've always thought there was some connection to her death. Maybe I'm wrong, but…" She whipped the hankie from between her bosom, swiped it under her nose and blew.

"I don't suppose you kept Mother's letter?" Dorian gripped the arms of her lawn chair.

"Why, I believe I did. It was the last communication I had with her, you see, so I put it in my sewing basket. Perhaps we'll find some time to look at it another day, dear." She dabbed her eyes with the soiled hankie and sniffled.

Kimberlee shivered. "Was Melody really psychic? Like, when she was younger? Or just after my father died?"

Grandmother looked up at the cats, crouched on the tree branch over their chairs. "Now that you mention it, I believe back in high school, she might have had *visions,* or whatever you want to call them. She used to tell me a friend was coming. Sure enough, before the day was over, someone showed up at the door."

Grandmother drained the last gulp from her cup and screwed it back on the thermos bottle.

Up in the tree, Thumper perched on the branch, ears tilted, studying the women.

"Grandmother, about the cats… I still don't understand. You said they're cousins. How is Melody's death connected to Thumper and Yes-No?"

"Noe-Noe. N.O.E-N.O.E?" Grandmother laughed. "We were talking about the cats, weren't we? Well, you see, after Melody's funeral, I tracked down that young man Melody told me about. I wanted that kitten she planned to bring home. She'd named her Spook." Grandmother twisted the damp hankie in her lap. "I know it's silly, but Melody loved that kitten. I had to bring her home with me. She was marked similar to your cat, Kimberlee, black with white feet and lots of toes. Over the years, all the cats on the ranch were descendants from Spook. So I guess she and Stomper must be related too."

"Thumper," Dorian and Kimberlee said in unison.

"That's what I said. They're sort of cousins, aren't they? Sharing an ancestor? Maybe that's why Stumper is so taken with her."

Dorian raised her hand and opened her mouth. Kimberlee shook her head. She glanced up at Thumper and *what's her name*. He straddled the branch like a jungle cat, his eyes riveted on Grandmother's face. "Look at Thumper. He looks like he's listening to the story of his relationship to N-O-E-N-O-E."

"Noe-Noe," Grandmother said.

"Oh, I get it." Kimberlee laughed. "Or maybe he's just smitten by Noe-Noe's great big gold eyes." Her heart warmed toward her grandmother. Bringing home a kitten just because her daughter loved it. Only a very special person would do such a thing. Maybe she'd been unfair and judged her too harshly. Maybe Grandmother put up a cold front to hide a soft heart. Maybe—

A stable boy clanged the dinner bell. The chef's giant carving knife glinted in the receding light as he carved the succulent pig.

Grandmother heaved herself from the wicker chair and tottered toward the barbecue. She clapped her hands, grinning at all the guests who had gathered. "Come on over everyone. Time for din-din. All you vegetarians—back of the line. *Ha-ha.* Come and meet my precious grandchildren."

The folks from neighboring ranches wandered from the barn and around the yard where they had gathered in little groups, and headed toward the food tables.

Kimberlee grabbed Dorian's arm before she could stand, and whispered. "Can you meet me and Brett in the library about 11:30

P.M., after everybody goes to bed? We need to talk about all this."

"Good idea. I feel like my head could explode any minute. Are you ready? I'm hungry." Dorian stood and moved toward the tables.

Grandmother stopped beside the barbecue. She shielded her eyes from the setting sun and called. "Kimberlee, we're waiting. The least you could do is come and eat dinner with your own child. You haven't spent a minute with her since you got here. What kind of a mother are you?" Grandmother spun on her heel and grabbed a paper plate.

Thumper's claws sunk deeper into the branch. In all probabilities, Dorian's mother, Melody, had overheard something that got her killed. A memory stirred in his mind—images from twenty-five years ago...

As though seeing through his ancestor's eyes, Thumper felt he was back at the Fern Lake lodge on the very day Grandmother mentioned. There was Black Cat, his great-great grandfather, the resident lodge cat, bathing on a pile of crates stacked on the pier.

Jack's new friend, Melody, had stopped to stroke his back. He leaned into her caress. The young woman moved away from the crate. Black Cat's eyes narrowed to slits as he watched her stroll down the pier. He resumed his bath.

Two men's voices carried from a boat moored nearby. "Stop worrying. I'll take care of everything. He won't make any more trouble after tonight."

Melody stopped dead still and stared at the boat.

Black Cat's tongue stopped mid-lick. *What did he say?* He cocked his head toward the boat, straining to hear.

"I'll take him night fishing. Leave it to me. No one will ever find his body, but you have to make sure we're not seen leaving together." The chilling words could mean only one thing. The men were plotting murder. But, who was the intended victim?

Melody heard the men talking. Her hand flew to her mouth. She stooped behind a box. Only the top of her ponytail was visible from the end of the pier where Black Cat watched.

Black Cat's hackles rose, his gaze riveted toward the containers where Melody crouched. *Careful, girl. Get away from there while you can.* If the men found her there...

He jumped off the crate and dashed down the pier toward the girl.

A voice from the boat snarled. "Don't I always watch your back? I'll have Jack put up the *wet paint* sign about 7:30 P.M. That'll keep everyone off the dock. No one will see you leave about 8:00 P.M."

Black Cat's ears twitched. How much longer would Melody be safe behind the crate?

"There can't be any evidence of him staying here, either," the voice went on. "I don't want the authorities tracking him through the motel's registration book."

"My wife always fixes the books, so there's no trace."

Black Cat stopped half way down the pier when he recognized the voice.

Ted Herman, the lodge owner.

Melody peeked around the box, and then hurried back down the pier, each step clicking against the wooden slats. Nearing the end, she looked back.

Ted Herman and the other man climbed off the boat onto the dock.

Melody ducked behind another pile of crates. Black Cat zipped over and crouched beside her. He rubbed against her knee. *Shh. Melody. Don't move a muscle.*

Melody closed her eyes. She put her head on her knees and clasped her hands. "Please God, don't let them find me here," she whispered.

Two pairs of boots clunked closer, closer to where they hid. Black Cat lowered his head. His heart thumped against his chest like a cuckoo clock wound too tight. He was safe enough. He was just a cat. But, Melody? If they found her hiding here, they'd know she'd overheard them. She could become another candidate for their projected midnight swim.

Black Cat's hair bristled. His muscles tightened. What could he do if they grabbed Melody? He flexed his sharp claws, determined to fight for her if they found her. Tiny though he might be, and doubtful he could make much difference against two men, but they would bear his marks before this fight was over.

The deep voice said, "Did you have any trouble with the last one?" There was no answer.

Melody held her breath. Two silent fear-filled minutes passed. Where did they go? She peeked out from behind the crate. The dock was empty. "They're gone! They must have turned in at the Bait Shop." She jumped up.

Black Cat watched as she ran the length of the dock toward the street. Stepping off the pier onto the lawn, Melody collided into Mrs. Herman. "Watch where you're going, young lady." The older woman stumbled and caught her balance.

"Sorry." Melody raced across the lawn. She jumped into her car, gunned the engine and rushed away.

"Well, I declare. I'll bet that young woman was up to no good. Probably shoplifting in the Bait Shop. I'm going to speak to Ted about her." Mrs. Herman shook her head and had moved on down the dock past Black Cat...

The hair on Thumper's neck stood upright. He scanned the empty chairs beneath the tree where moments ago his *persons* had sat. He shook his head to clear the sinister memory from his mind. Melody's hit and run death took on a more menacing possibility, if Mrs. Herman told her husband that Melody had been on the dock.

Across the barnyard, Grandmother, Dorian and Kimberlee lined up by the picnic tables.

Amanda frolicked around Kimberlee's legs, neighing and whinnying, pretending she was a horse.

Noe-Noe stretched up against the tree trunk and scratched at the bark. "Are you staying up there all night? Come down. I have something to tell you."

Thumper leaped off the branch and landed at her feet. "What is it, my little popinjay?"

She dropped to the ground and tapped her orange striped paw on the grass. "I thought you should know. I overheard Grandmother on the phone this afternoon. She called a private investigator, and—"

"Whatever for?"

Noe-Noe lifted her nose, sniffed and half-closed her eyes. "If you'll stop interrupting, I'll tell you. She wants Amanda. She's going to try and take her away from Kimberlee, that's what for." She spun on her heels and headed for the barn.

A flash of pain behind Thumper's eyes blurred his vision. Grandmother? Trying to take Amanda? So that's what this is all about. Not the inheritance at all—just a devious plot to steal Kimberlee's child.

He gazed across the barnyard where Grandmother scooped chili beans and potato salad onto her plate. A growl rumbled through his chest. Maybe Ted Herman was responsible for Melody's death twenty-five years ago, maybe not. Nothing he could do about that now. Grandmother's plan to steal Amanda? That was a different barrel of fish. No way would he stand by empty-pawed and let that happen.

He lowered his ears and hissed. Just like great-great grandfather Black Cat, he would risk tooth and claw and fight to the death to protect his loved ones.

Chapter Ten

"Good. Glad to see you guys finally made it." Dorian grabbed Kimberlee's arm and pulled her into the dimly lit library.

Kimberlee jerked as her heart skipped a beat. "Dorian! Don't do that. You scared the *be-jammers* out of me." She'd giggled when they sneaked past Grandmother's closed bedroom door, feeling their way down the dark staircase. Dorian jumping out from the shadows didn't help her nerves, still more than a little on edge.

Light streamed in from the hallway and illuminated the library, creating a conspiratorial atmosphere to their clandestine meeting. Kimberlee glanced at her wristwatch. "I told you 11:30 P.M. You're early." She shoved her handbag under the library table next to the fireplace and settled next to Brett on the sofa.

Dorian flopped into a sofa chair across from them. "So, what's on your mind?"

"Okay, so am I the only one who feels like Dorothy in the Land of Oz? What do you think about all this?" Kimberlee leaned toward her friend.

"Which *all this* did you have in mind? About hearing that my mother investigated your dad's murder, or the *zuit-suit* attorney, or dear Grandmother Schizophrenia?" Dorian's pink nightie peeked out from her bathrobe. She adjusted the neckline on her robe. Her brow furrowed.

Kimberlee squinted at her friend in the semi-darkness. With her make-up scrubbed off, dark circles under her eyes and blotches on her cheeks, Dorian looked her age. Not the model stepping out of a magazine ad tonight, but a troubled forty-something woman. *She's as unhappy as I am.*

Brett snickered. "Well, I guess, all of it." He nodded toward Kimberlee. "Before I forget, we wanted to tell you we're sorry about Grandmother's attitude toward Sam."

"Yeah. Live and learn. I should have left him home. I guess what she meant by 'bring your pets' was really, 'pets welcome, unless it's a dog.'"

Kimberlee nodded. "Well, thank goodness you did bring him. What would I have done today if he hadn't been with me?"

Dorian waved her hand, as if it was nothing. "And, as far as Grandmother… It's all too clear now why my dad didn't keep in touch with her after Mom died." She smiled. "I guess she means well, but, what she said about my mother… It really shook me up. I knew my mother died in a hit and run, but I didn't know she moved us to Fern Lake to investigate your father's death. And I sure didn't know anything about her being psychic." She shook her head. "I always wondered why… Sometimes, I feel things too, like… I think—"

Kimberlee touched Dorian's shoulder. "Welcome to my world. Now you know where I've been this past year. It's like one morning you wake up in a twilight zone. Believe me, I understand. Do you think your mother was killed because of what she overheard that day on the dock?"

"Mom's letter said that she heard something about *disposing of a body*. Maybe they were talking about a neighbor's dog or something." Dorian twisted her fingers.

"Yeah, right, and I've got a gold tooth I'll sell you for a buck. You don't really think they were going out on the lake at night to dispose of a dog." Brett stood and paced the rug.

Dorian shrugged. "I guess not." She looked down at her twisting hands and slid them under her hips.

"Your mom was killed the day after she heard someone plotting murder. That can't be a coincidence," Brett said.

"But a body never washed up on shore. At least, none that we know about." Dorian pulled her hands from under her hips and began to twist her fingers again.

"Listen. There's not much point in worrying about it now." Brett shoved magazines around on the coffee table. "Even if Ted Herman was planting guys in the lake and was responsible for your mother's death, he's been dead for twenty-five years. Last summer, Mrs. Herman told me he died in the Cayman Islands but they never found his body."

Kimberlee gasped. She put her hand to her cheek. "He died in the… He…"

"What? What were you going to say, honey?"

"Something Grandmother said. It's been bothering me all afternoon, but I couldn't put my finger on it. She said the stable master… Harold something-or-other?"

Dorian nodded. "Harold Marlowe, the bearded guy who picked us up at the airport. What about him?"

"She said Harold was living in the *Cayman Islands* before she hired him..." Kimberlee stared across the dark library. The scene beneath the trees this afternoon popped into her head. The feeling that she had known Harold before…before…

"Oh Brett, it couldn't be him, could it?" Chilly bumps raced up her arms. "You always said you thought Ted Herman might have faked his death." Kimberlee grabbed a pillow and hugged it to her chest. Waves of nausea struck her stomach. Her ears buzzed. Her head felt full of cotton balls. She put her hand to her forehead. Was it possible? Ted Herman. Still alive? It couldn't be!

Brett put his arm around her shoulder. "What are you saying? You think Harold could be Ted Herman? You don't think…"

Dorian shook her head, her eyebrows raised. "Nice old Harold? That's ridiculous. If he really was Ted, why would he come back here? He—" She clutched her fist to her breast.

"It's been twenty-five years. He's about the right age and with the gray beard and if you add thirty-odd pounds, I guess it's possible."

Kimberlee flung the pillow on the floor. There's no way she'd recognize him now. She was only four years old when her father—

Brett's voice cut into her thoughts. "Let's think about it a minute. What if Ted was considered a person of interest in your father's murder back then, but there was no proof to connect him to the murder. Then, your dad's sister, Melody, was killed under suspicious circumstances not long afterward. What if Ted heard the police were adding apples and oranges? To keep from being indicted, or just to get away from Mrs. Herman, he—"

"Couldn't blame him for that." Kimberlee rolled her eyes.

"Let me finish." Brett waved his hand dismissively. "False documents aren't that hard to produce. It's easy to get a copy of a baby's birth certificate—let's say a baby named Harold Marlowe—who died the year Ted was born. Ted assumes his name. He goes to the Cayman Islands, fakes his death on the fishing boat, has some money stashed in a numbered account and everyone thinks he's dead. End of two murder investigations. End of bitchy wife. End of Fern Lake Lodge financial burdens and whatever was going on out on the lake with that other guy."

Dorian pulled her legs up into the chair and bounced forward. "So, now he's Harold Marlowe and he lives in the Cayman Islands. Years go by, and then maybe he gets into a jam over there. He wants to return to the States, or—"

"I know. I know. Let me." Kimberlee grabbed Brett's arm. "*Harold* lives in the Cayman Islands. He sees Grandmother's ad in the magazine and remembers the name of the ranch from when he knew my father. He manipulates Grandmother with a sob story and gets the job here on the ranch. It's not likely he's going to run into anyone from Fern Lake here in Texas. It could have happened—"

Squeak.

The library door edged open. Light from the hallway crawled, inch by inch, across the floor toward the sofa. Could Harold, the possible impostor, have been listening outside the door?

Kimberlee's eyes opened wide. Her hand flew to her mouth as drops of perspiration popped out under her arms. She gasped. They'd just accused Harold of committing murder—maybe twice—maybe three times! If Ted-Harold killed her father and Melody, and the guy out on the lake, and created a false identity to hide his crimes, how far would he go to protect his secret?

Tomorrow morning when Imelda came in to dust, would she find three dead bodies strewn around the room, blood soaking into the carpet and spattered over the sofa, a kitchen knife driven into her throat? Her hand went to the back of her neck.

The door creaked open further. The patch of light leaped across the bottom of the sofa, swept up her body and into her face. Kimberlee squealed and buried her face in Brett's shoulder.

Meow?

Kimberlee lifted her head. *Meow?*

Thumper put his head around the door and shoved it open.

"It's Thumper," Dorian whispered. Had she been imagining the worst, too?

Kimberlee's breath whooshed out in a gasp. She giggled and rubbed her fingers while the blood crept back into her tingling extremities. What a crazy notion. Blood soaked bodies, indeed. Where had that come from?

"What's wrong? Who did you think it was? Harold?" Brett laughed.

"Of course not, silly. He just startled me."

Thumper padded across the library, jumped onto the couch and rubbed against Kimberlee's arm.

She touched her trembling hand to his head. "Thumper, you about scared me to death. If you had been… Never mind." Kimberlee started to hum *I Left my Heart in San Francisco*. She turned toward the fireplace and studied the clock on the mantle. 11:55 P.M.

Nice clock.

Art Deco.

Thumper stretched and yawned, turned in a circle and flopped on the sofa, next to her hip.

Kimberlee rubbed his back. His rasping purr vibrated through her hand, hastening the blood flow into her tingling fingers. She lowered her face into his fur and whispered, "Sweet boy, good kitty. Don't do that to me again."

"Okay, okay. Earth to Kimberlee," Brett said. "We all love the cat, but come on back. We were talking about Harold." He reached over and gave Thumper's head a pat. "Before we let our imaginations carry us away and make accusations, we need facts. If Harold really is Ted Herman, does it really matter and if so, what can we do about it?"

Dorian shifted in her chair. "I think the whole idea is ridiculous. You guys are just—"

Still shaken from her crazy thoughts about Harold, Kimberlee watched Thumper lift his head, his fur puffed out on his back, his gaze riveted on something across the room. *Oh no, it's not my imagination. He hears something too.*

Thumper oozed off the edge of the couch, padded toes landing on thick carpet without a sound, as slick as syrup sliding off buttermilk pancakes.

Thumper's ears lowered. He skulked across the carpet. In an instant, his whole persona changed. The pussycat snuggling by Kimberlee's hip, disappeared. Gone was the docile companion napping on the sofa, exuding adoration and love with every rasping purr. In an instant, he was a marauding killer, bent on dismemberment and murder…or so it seemed as he slunk across the floor, belly low to the rug, ears flattened on his head. What did he see? What kind of horrors lurked in the corner of the library? A rat? Another snake? "Brett. What is it?"

No answer.

"Brett?" Hadn't he heard her? Why didn't he answer?

Kimberlee gasped and pulled her legs onto the couch. As if in slow motion, Thumper hunkered on the rug, wiggled his rear to gain traction and leaped—at Kimberlee's purse. He wrestled it out from under the library table and kicked it into submission with his back feet. His rout a success, the vanquished purse collapsed in defeat as the latch snapped open. Thumper reached in with his big white paw and fished out the *target*—her wallet. But wait. Not yet willing to surrender, the wallet fought on. Thumper pitched the rebellious wallet over his head, caught it, and streaked around the room, shaking it until it was near senseless.

"No, Thumper. Stop. Brett, do something." Her voice sounded fuzzy and far away, like she was shouting in a tunnel. She flapped her hands. Nothing could stop Thumper from carrying out his deadly *Black-OP's mission.* He lunged onto a chair, the vanquished wallet clutched in his jaws, then up on the table and back onto the floor. At last, the subjected wallet snapped open, spewing its secrets onto the rug.

Brett moved in slow motion and made a grab for the culprit, but Thumper leaped away. As abrupt as his purse-attack had begun, it ended. Having completed his objective and the target dispatched, the assassin aborted his mission. He slunk into a dark corner, leaving the carcass of his kill, or in this instance, Kimberlee's purse, upside down on the hearth, the battlefield littered with casualties. Like the aftermath of a hurricane, credit cards, dollar bills and photographs lay strewn across the rug.

"Honey. Are you okay? You're as cold as ice. What's wrong?" Brett smoothed Kimberlee's hair from her face.

She shook her head to erase the images of the envisioned battlefield. Her cheeks tingled. She clutched her knees, drawn up to her chin. Brett's face slid back into focus, the slithering walls straightened and stood still. "I...I'm fine. Just a little dizzy, I think. Everything happened so fast." The tingling in her fingers subsided and a warm sensation crept up the back of her neck.

"Oh, really, Kimberlee. First, you imagine *Harold,* and now you're upset about this?" Dorian shook with giggles. "Look at you. What did you think it was? A mouse?"

"I guess I still had that snake on my mind. I thought—"

"*Shoosh.* You guys. Not so loud. You'll wake everyone." Brett stooped and scooped the scattered money and photographs into a pile.

"Thumper must have raided the catnip. I've never seen him like this." He shoved the wallet and lipstick back into Kimberlee's purse. He picked up a faded photograph and slanted it toward the light. "*Hey.* Here's that picture of your dad and Ted Herman with the deer. The one I snitched from Mrs. Herman's house last year. Remember? Thumper bit holes in it." He handed the photo to Kimberlee.

"Let me see. Oh, my God. Has that been in my wallet all this time?" She jiggled her finger toward the desk. "Look over there and see if you can find a magnifying glass." They had thought Ted was a suspect in her father's murder. If the picture could settle Harold's questionable identity, she might put Ted back in his watery grave where she'd kept him for the past year. She laid the photo on the coffee table.

Brett clicked on the desk lamp. Beneath a clutter of pens and notepads in the top drawer, he found a small magnifying glass. "Here's one. Come and look at this." He passed the glass over the photo.

Kimberlee peered over Brett's shoulder. In the photo, her father and Ted stood cradling their rifles, standing on each side of a deer suspended from a tree.

"It's not a very good photograph," Dorian said. The holes from Thumper's teeth marks made Ted's features difficult to recognize. She handed the photo to Kimberlee. "It looks like Thumper sort of did a number on it, like his performance just now. What do you think? Could it be Harold?"

Kimberlee turned the photo toward the light. "Ted does resemble Harold somewhat, doesn't he? It's so hard to tell. I don't really remember him." She laid the photo back on the table.

"Kimberlee. Call Jack in the morning and ask him if he can do some research for us. See if he can find out where Harold was born, where he grew up, something that will shed light on his life before he went to the Cayman's. We could do it here on Grandmother's computer, but I don't want anyone to know what we're doing."

Kimberlee nodded. "What if Jack's search proves we're right? What if we're convinced he really is Ted Herman? What then?"

Dorian reached for the photo. "In that case, we let the authorities decide what to do about him. They can question him if they have anything linking him to your father's murder."

Kimberlee rubbed her hand across her forehead. Things were moving out of control. Like Thumper's tear through the library, leaving the contents of her purse askew, their peaceful lives were turned upside down. Here she was, stuck in the desert with the Wicked Witch of the East, wondering if her worst nemesis had risen from the grave. How was she supposed to go around like nothing happened? Oh, and by the way, were they having fun yet?

"All this talk about Harold is scaring me." Kimberlee pulled one foot under her hip. "I'm sure Amanda will want to ride the pony with Harold again tomorrow. It'll raise all kinds of red flags if I refuse to let her go out to the barn. Maybe we should keep her with us tomorrow."

Brett took Kimberlee's hand. "You'll just have to trust that he wouldn't hurt Amanda. If Harold is just a nice old man with whiskers, there's no problem. If he really is Ted, well, you told me he always took good care of you when you were a baby."

"Wait, if he's Ted, that means he's—"

"Don't even go there, Kimberlee." Brett's eyebrows squinched together. He shook his head. "This isn't the day to ask that question. Not now. We could be wrong, you know."

She lowered her eyes. "I won't go there."

Kimberlee stared into the dark corners of the library. Memories washed over her. She shook her head and closed her eyes. *I don't want to go there.* Too late. The images from a thousand nightmares flashed through her mind.

She crept down the staircase, one step at a time. At the foot of the stairs, blood soaked the flowered carpet beneath her father's head. She turned and saw a figure in red rush out the door. Was it the same checkered coat in the photograph? Ted Herman's coat?

Dorian stood and pulled her robe tighter around her waist. "We better get back to bed before someone hears us and comes to investigate."

Brett helped Kimberlee to her feet. "Let's go."

"Dorian. We're going into Eagle Pass tomorrow. Do you want to come along?" Kimberlee rubbed her knee, still a-tingle from sitting on her foot so long.

Dorian shook her head. "Sounds good, but I made arrangements for a riding lesson tomorrow. And Grandmother said she planned a hayride and a picnic down at the river. We better not all leave. I'll stay and keep an eye on Amanda. You guys go on and have fun. What's up with Eagle Pass?"

"We're going to town to snoop around, I mean, do a little shopping." Brett grinned. "We think we should check out Wilbur's children's program. He'd likely lose his funding if Grandmother changes her beneficiary. If it's a worthy project, we might consider funding it in her honor, maybe through the Fern Lake Merchant Society."

"That's a good idea. I agree."

Kimberlee took Brett's arm. "We should get to bed. Though I doubt I'll get much sleep in Grandmother's House of Horrors bedroom, not to mention with all this on my mind."

Brett peeked out the library door. "All clear. Let's go." He placed his hand on Kimberlee's shoulder. "Good night, Dorian," he whispered. "We'll see you at breakfast."

"Good night." They tiptoed toward the stairs.

Thumper crouched beside Noe-Noe beneath the hall table as the three left the library and climbed the stairs. "That all went quite nicely if I do say so myself." His ear twitched toward the stairs.

"You mean, there was some method to your madness with the wild purse thingy?" Noe-Noe mewed, "Whatever for?"

Thumper yawned. "I knew she still had Mark and Ted's picture in her wallet. I wanted them to look at it and start thinking about Harold. It worked, didn't it?"

Noe-Noe turned her head. "So, are you saying that Harold might really be Ted Herman in disguise, after all these years?"

Thumper shrugged. "Not sure, but it's possible. There is a resemblance."

"Well, guess what? For your information, I could tell you things that would make your tail kink, if I were so inclined, which I'm not. My ancestors are from Fern Lake, too, don't forget."

Thumper patted Noe-Noe's paw. "You? You never said you had the memories."

"You never asked. There are plenty of things I haven't told you."

"What do you know? Is Harold really Ted Herman? Was he responsible for Melody's hit and run?" Thumper dropped his head and then peeked up, squinting one eye. "Do you know who killed Kimberlee's father?" His pupils slid into little black slits.

"Questions. Questions. Maybe, someday when I have the time…" She yawned, displaying her sharp little teeth, all aligned in a perfect semi-circle. "Maybe someday, I'll give you some answers, but not tonight, smarty britches." Noe-Noe hissed and stalked up the stairs towards Grandmother's room, her hips swaying seductively with each step.

"*Um, um… Just sayin'*—"

Chapter Eleven

Several miles from the ranch house, Sitka, the mountain lion, crouched on an overhanging rock formation near the canyon wall. The fur on her shoulders shimmered like strands of gold and silver threads in the early dawn. Twenty feet below, a white-tailed deer grazed on an outcropping of dry grass.

Sitka hunched, every muscle tense, her gaze locked on the deer.

The deer took several steps closer.

Sitka sprinted across the rock and leaped onto the deer's back. With one powerful crunch, she broke its neck. She dragged her kill into the shrubs where she ate her fill, then scratched grass and brush over the carcass to camouflage it from coyotes and vultures. Over the next several days, she would return to feed until it was gone.

Sitka's two, three-month-old cubs waited in a rocky alcove den nearby, safe from enemies and protected from the hot sun and chilly nights.

She jumped onto the rock where her cubs waited, wild-eyed as she came into the den. She lay down and rasped her rough tongue over the kittens as they kneaded her belly to hasten the life-sustaining milk. Satiated from her breakfast and content that all was well on the home front, she dozed.

A noise from the nearby canyon brought her fully awake. Sitka scanned the plains. Nothing moved within her view. The only sound was the cry of a small creature in the distance, perhaps the victim of another predator. She closed her eyes and slept.

With breakfast completed and Amanda back in the nursery getting dressed for her pony ride, Kimberlee waited by the front door, anxious to leave for town. A full ten minutes ago, Brett had hurried back to their room to change into his walking shoes, promising he would return in a jiffy. She checked her watch. What could be keeping him?

She glanced toward the kitchen door, thankfully closed. She had no desire to run into Grandmother again. The scene this morning was all too fresh in her mind. Amanda having a melt-down over a crooked ear on a Mickey Mouse pancake and Grandmother's stony glare when she heard they wouldn't be available for her hayride this afternoon. *Yikes,* Drama!

She opened her purse and checked the date on their airline tickets, then read for the umpteenth time, the brochure from the travel agency. Six more fun-filled days of frolicking under Texas skies, moonlit horseback rides and prairie dog serenades. Apparently, Ajax Travel Agency never met Grandma.

Where was Brett? Maybe she had time to call Jack again. She dialed the Fern Lake lodge on her cellphone.

"Herman's Motor Lodge. How can I help ya?"

"Jack, you dear. I called a couple of times and left a message."

"Sorry. I was down ta the dock, working on a motor. I left my phone up here in my jacket. I'm here now, so what's up?" A dog barked in the background. "Chance says 'hi'."

A smile crinkled her cheeks. "Tell her I said, 'hi.' I wonder if you have some time to do some research for me. You're such an expert with the internet." Kimberlee nibbled her lip. Jack would do anything she asked. She had no need to butter him up, but it never hurt to spread a little sugar before you asked for a favor. Aunt Martha always said, 'You catch more flies with honey'—

"Sure. What do you need?"

"It's about the stable master." Kimberlee glanced around to make sure no one was listening. Grandmother was still in the kitchen. She lowered her voice. "We're thinking there's something fishy about him."

"What's fishy—"

Kimberlee walked to the foot of the stairs and looked up. No Brett in sight. "It's a long story. The guy says his name is Harold Marlowe, but we think… Are you ready for this? We think he might really be Ted Herman," she whispered.

"You're kidding. Our Ted Herman? From the lodge? He's been dead for years."

"That's just it. That's what we always thought. But now we're not so sure."

"That's a pretty far-fetched theory. What makes ya think he's our Ted?"

She relayed all the gory details about the conversation in the library the night before and the picture Thumper found. "See what you can find out about Harold Marlowe. *M-a-r-l-o-w-e.* He'd be about sixty-five. Background, school, you know. He claims he was in the hospital with my dad and he spent some time in the Cayman Islands. That's about all we know about him. I hope we're wrong, but—"

"I'll make a trip to the library this morning. Let me get back to you. Other than that, are you guys having—"

"Oh, Brett's coming. Gotta go. We're headed for town. Thanks, Jack. "

Brett trotted down the stairs. "Ready?"

Kimberlee waved and jiggled the phone. She mouthed the word, "Jack."

"Jack? Tell him hello from me." Brett nodded toward the door.

"Brett says 'hi.' Gotta' go, Jack. Thanks. Bye." She clicked off the cell phone, smiled, and picked up her purse. "Let's get out of here before we run into Grandma."

Ahhh... Kimberlee leaned toward the open car window where the wind blew through her hair. Just the right number of agave cactus and sagebrush on the ragged hills to suggest that she was in Texas. She closed her eyes. Better yet, no grandmother to get in her face.

Twenty minutes of driving brought Kimberlee and Brett to the outskirts of Eagle Pass. The small community baked under the hot Texas sun. A few shade trees and fewer flowering shrubs clung to life in front of various homes and businesses.

Brett slowed Grandmother's van at the edge of town. "Read me the address of the Children's Benefit Program."

Kimberlee checked the address again as they passed several faded buildings. "Supposed to be right on Main Street." Only minutes now until she'd see Wilbur's charity in action. She had her camera loaded and ready to photograph the children. "I talked to Dorian this morning at breakfast. If the Children's Program works as well as Wilbur says, we might start another like it in Fern Lake.

"I mean, whoever Grandmother chooses to inherit, we'll have the funds. We want to use the money to give back to the community. The Children's Program could—"

"Now, don't get ahead of yourself. Promises are cheap. Your grandmother told Wilbur she'd leave the money to his charity and then changed her mind. She could change it again, just as quick."

"I know. But we can't help but think about it." She pointed to a building just ahead. "There it is. On the corner. The Children's Benefit Program." A faded sign hung over the door of the crumbling stucco building. Chipped paint around the entrance threatened to tumble off at the slightest touch.

"Doesn't look very impressive, does it?" Brett switched off the motor and set the brake.

"No." Her heart sank. All last night she'd imagined a quaint stucco building with a donkey-planter in front and a potted cactus by the door. Or a cactus garden with birds skittering around a carved birdbath. Anything but this.

Kimberlee scanned the surrounding neighborhood. Faded buildings with aluminum roofs flanked the Children's Benefit building.

"This is it? I don't know… Where is the building Grandmother said Wilbur was putting up this year? I don't see any new construction."

"Maybe it's at another location." Brett opened Kimberlee's door. "Let's go in and see what they have to say."

The bell over the door jingled as they stepped inside. Several cases of toilet paper, pork and beans and coffee were piled against the far wall. A middle-aged Hispanic woman reached across her desk and turned down the screeching Mariachi music on an old radio as she beckoned them inside. "Come in, come in. My name Maria."

"We're the Clarke's from California," Brett said. "My wife is Mrs. Lassiter's granddaughter. Is this the Children's Benefit Program?" He looked around the office.

Kimberlee followed his gaze. The only thing that suggested children was a faded kitten calendar behind the desk still open to December from the previous year.

Maria smiled and pushed several ledgers aside, creating a path between her and Kimberlee. She motioned toward the chairs facing her desk. "Please. Sit. Sit. Yes. This the Children's Benefit Program. I am bookkeeper. Mr. Wilbur—he very kind man. He makes nice places for childrens to play. How I can help you with?"

Brett raised an eyebrow and sat in the indicated chair. Kimberlee placed her hand on his arm. "My husband and I want to learn more about the program. What services do you provide?" She glanced around the office. "Where are the children?"

Maria looked from one to the other and tipped her head. "Oh, no childrens here. Other towns where childrens are. They make nice lunch and games. Sometimes sleep outsides all night." She nodded, sending the hair piled on top of her head swaying.

"Where are the other programs located? How many other town… towns?" Kimberlee's cheeks warmed. She cleared her throat and crossed her legs. This conversation was spiraling downhill fast. Concentrate. What was she saying?

Maria counted on her fingers. "San Antonio, Crystal City, Carrizo

Springs, Gardendale, Laredo, Del Rio, several down by Rio Grande City. I think must be in *ocho, nueve, diez.* Nine or ten towns."

"How many children are involved in each program in the different towns?" Kimberlee slid an ash tray further from the edge of the desk. The air in the office was stale enough without the addition of cigarettes right under her nose.

Maria shrugged. "I do not know all how many in each towns."

"So, no children here in Eagle Pass? You're just stuck with paying all the bills, *huh*?" Brett chuckled, gesturing at the ledgers on her desk.

"Oh, no! I take care of writings down the numbers in my books." She patted the stack of ledgers and bobbed her head to the side. A hair pin tumbled to the desk. Maria retrieved the pin and shoved it back into her wad of hair. "Each town program have its own book. Mr. Wilbur, he writes the checks and gives me numbers for writings down. Like food and rent and lights from each places."

Her forehead wrinkled and then a smile brightened her face. "Oh, yes. One more important duties what I can do. On some times, Mr. Wilbur give me list of supplies and I order big, big boxes of...of things." She pointed toward the dusty cases stacked by the wall. "Mr. Wilbur comes on sometimes in his truck and takes the boxes to the each childrens places."

Kimberlee glanced at the stack of boxes, then to Brett and back to Maria. "Wouldn't it be more efficient if the supplies were sent directly to each facility instead of sending them here before redistribution?"

Maria blinked several times. Her cheeks reddened. "My English not so good. I don't know these words you say. effish...redis... I think maybe Mr. Wilbur takes the boxes to each childrens places for to play with the childrens."

She glanced around the office and slid the penholder back and forth. Her hand trembled as she picked up her coffee cup and took a drink. She set the cup down and picked up the telephone. Her mouth drew into a straight line. "I have no more time. I think maybe you talk to Mr. Wilbur for ask more questions. I call him on telephone."

"No, don't bother him, Maria." Brett fixed his big blue eyes and bewitching smile on the flustered woman.

"We're staying out at the Lassiter ranch. Wilbur will be dining with us tonight. I'm sure he can answer all our questions this evening."

The wrinkles in Maria's forehead smoothed and moved to crinkles around her mouth when she smiled.

Brett stood and leaned his hands on her desk. "Say, would you happen to have a list of addresses for the different programs? We'll be driving through Texas later this week. We'd love to stop at some of the other facilities." Leave it to Brett to finagle a woman into doing just exactly what he wanted.

Maria nodded and set the receiver back on the phone. "That would be more fine." She rummaged through the papers on her desk and then opened one drawer after another. "Ah, yes, here it is." She pulled out a wrinkled sheet of paper, smoothed it with her thumb and handed it to Brett. "Here is a list of the childrens places."

"Thanks, Maria. You've been a big help." Brett opened the front door for Kimberlee and then called back to Maria, "We'll send a donation as soon as we get home. Don't say anything to Wilbur. We want to surprise him, okay? See you later."

Maria nodded and waved, then reached for the phone. "*Muchas gracias. Buenas dias.*"

The front door closed with a jingle. "Well. That was…interesting." Kimberlee scanned the block. "There's a Denny's across the street. Shall we get some lunch?"

"Sounds like a plan."

Several doors down, Brett stopped in front of Vince's Music Store where a red Yamaha electric guitar held center stage in a window display of musical instruments. "Look at that."

Kimberlee took his hand and dragged him away. "Come along. Your birthday's not for another three months."

"Yes, my queen."

Hand in hand, they dashed across the street and into the restaurant.

The waitress seated them at a table, handed Brett a couple of menus, spun on her heels and left.

Kimberlee scanned the menu. Hamburger with jalapeno peppers and cheese on a hoagie roll. *The office had cartons of pork and beans and coffee stacked in the corner.* Roast beef on rye with a side of potato salad. *She had ledgers on the desk for each facility?* Open range chicken on a sesame seed bun. *A bookkeeper that barely speaks English and doesn't keep books?*

"Honey? What did you decide? I'm going to have the bacon-cheeseburger."

"What? Oh. Sorry. My mind was a million miles away."

The waitress hovered, pencil in hand.

"I'll have the same. Cheeseburger and a diet cola, please."

The waitress nodded and left.

"Did you ever see a business run like that? What do you think?"

Brett shrugged. "It was odd, wasn't it? Maria's English skills are limited. Maybe she's not capable of handling the whole bookkeeping process. Though, why would Wilbur pay the bills and just have her record the data? Doesn't make sense. Why would he even need her?"

"Maybe he's just giving her a job because she needs the money. I'm disappointed there are no children here. I was so hoping to meet the kids. If Dorian and I decide to start a similar facility in Fern Lake, it would be helpful to get an idea how it's run."

Brett pulled Maria's address sheet from his pocket and spread it out on the table. "Carrizo Springs isn't too far away. We could drive over there before we head back to the ranch. You can see the kids there."

"I'd like that. Let's stop somewhere along the way and pick up some fruit and candy for the children. I hear they grow red mulberries and persimmons in this part of Texas. We can take some back to Amanda. She's never tasted that fruit before."

Throughout their lunch, she and Brett talked about the hot lunches, after school programs and camping trips Maria had described.

An hour later and fifty boring miles of bad road south of Eagle

Pass, they arrived at the outskirts of Carrizo Springs. Bags of fruit and small toys covered the back seat. The aroma of over-ripe persimmons filled the car.

A bullet-ridden sign at the edge of town read *Welcome to Carrizo Springs-population – 6,000.* Ragged palm trees lined the road. Unattended shrubs, near dead from lack of water, poked jagged stalks upward like praying hands. Among the few dreary houses, lawns lay brown and dormant, likely only green during the short-lived rain of winter. Water seemed a luxury, not to be wasted on mere landscaping.

Several blocks later, they passed a man crouched on the sidewalk near the liquor store, taking advantage of the meager shade from scraggly trees. A young girl with a baby astraddle her hip, gawked as he drank from a paper bag. He grinned and held up the bag.

Bile rose in Kimberlee's throat. "Did you see that? The girl with the baby..." Kimberlee pointed. "Can you believe it? She can't be more than thirteen." *I wonder if that's her baby.*

The girl spun on her heels, giggled and scurried into a sparsely landscaped park where barefoot children played on a broken swing set and others dug in a half-empty sand box.

Brett slowed the car just in time as a tumble weed rolled across the street. It came to a stop against a spilled refuse container where a mangy dog dug through the garbage.

Kimberlee shook her head and sighed. Children without shoes. Playgrounds with broken equipment. Refuse containers overflowing in parks without grass. Where were the civic-minded citizens in this town? Didn't anybody care? Was this Texas, USA, or some *third-world* country where social consciousness meant keeping beggars away from the tourists? "I can't stand to think how blessed we are, compared to these kids. Can't we do something to help? The least we can do is donate to Wilbur's charity. Thank goodness he had the good sense to put it here in Carrizo Springs. These children need his help far more than in Eagle Pass."

She glanced at the list of addresses. "The local facility is on Dimmit

Street. There. Pull into that Sonic Burger and ask for directions."

Brett pulled the car up to the drive-through window where loud mariachi music from inside defeated any hope of normal conversation. He leaned toward the window to make his voice heard and shouted. "Can you tell me how to get to Dimmit Street from here?"

The pimple-faced teenager pointed up the street. "Dimmit Street runs north and south. Take a left about two blocks off the main intersection. Can I get you anything?"

"We'd like two diet colas, please."

Within a few minutes, sipping sodas through paper straws, they were on Dimmit Street checking numbers on the dismal buildings. It was hard to imagine, but these buildings looked even worse than those on Main Street.

Brett ducked his head and scanned the addresses on the right side of the street. "It's going to be on your side. 2801, 2793..."

Their car crept past several decrepit houses with overgrown shrubbery and dead lawns squatting between tall buildings. On a deserted warehouse, between boarded up windows, the faint outline of a vintage tobacco advertisement still clung to the brick wall. Kimberlee squinted to make out the print. *Horseshoe Tobacco–Best in the West.*

Brett stopped the car in front of a clapboard house next door to the warehouse. A tattered tarp covering an abandoned vehicle in the driveway exposed a rusty blue station wagon with four flat tires. On the end of the porch, a numbered placard dangled from a rusty chain. "This is it? 2575."

Goosebumps prickled Kimberlee's arms as she stared at the house behind the weed filled yard. "Surely this can't be right." She glanced back at the paper. "2575 Dimmit Street." The first tiny shreds of doubt tickled the back of her mind. Why would Wilbur put his program in this dumpy house? Or did he...

"It's the right address." Brett's jaw tightened. He turned off the motor and opened his door. "Come on. I don't like the looks of this. Let's go find out what's going on."

They hurried up the cracked sidewalk to the weather-beaten front door. Brett knocked.

No answer.

A cobweb stretched between the windowpane and the dirty blinds inside. A spider jiggled in the swaying web as the blinds bent down. Two fingers and a pair of eyes appeared between the dirty slats, and then the blinds snapped back. The spider scurried to the center of its web.

Kimberlee shivered. How long since anyone had cleaned the blinds? From the size of the cobweb, maybe never?

Brett knocked again and shrugged. He shoved his hands in his pockets and rocked back on his heels.

The door creaked open. A cigarette bounced between the woman's two thin lips. "Whatcha want?" Ashes clung tenaciously from the tip of her cigarette.

"*Umm…I...*" Kimberlee concentrated on the woman's faded orange hair, almost the same shade as Grandmother's. Was this the standard color of choice for every Texas woman over seventy? She could imagine the sign at the local Piggley Wiggley.

Hideous Hair Dye–On Sale–This Week Only.

The woman jerked her head upward. "I said, whatcha want?" Ashes tumbled down her wrinkled housecoat.

Kimberlee held out the sheet of paper. "We're looking for the Children's Benefit Program. We have the address right here, 2575 Dimmit Street?" She forced a smile, licked her dry lips and tried again. A more natural smile this time. Would her quivering eyelid give away the fact that she felt like a religious zealot going door-to-door?

"This is 2575 Dimmit Street, but I don't know nothin' about no children's whatcha call it." The lady of the house pulled the cigarette from her mouth and flicked the ashes on the porch. "My kids is all grown up and gone. They never got no benefit from livin' here, to hear them tell it." She put the cigarette to her lips and took a drag. A cough from deep in her chest suggested the cigarettes had already taken their toll and her days were numbered. "I said, whatcha want?"

"We're sorry to bother you," Brett said. "The Children's Benefit Program is an after-school program. We must have the wrong address. Do you have any idea where they're located?" He took a step back and looked up and down the street.

The woman took another pull on her cigarette and blew the smoke up and over the deep furrows in her forehead.

Kimberlee's gaze followed the smoke up beyond her orange head until it curled like a mushroom cloud beneath the porch roof.

"Never heard of no such after-school thing." The woman stepped back into the house, pulling the door half-way closed behind her. "You might check with the Chamber a' Commerce." The door slammed with a bang.

A chip of paint fell from the door frame onto the dirty threshold. Kimberlee reached for Brett's hand. In the window, a helpless fly beat its wings, entangled in the cobweb. The spider rushed toward his latest victim.

Kimberlee closed her eyes. "Let's get out of here." They hurried back to the car. "How can this be right?" She flapped the paper. "We have the address right here."

Brett drummed his fingers on the steering wheel as they drove slowly down the street. "We can call the Chamber of Commerce, just to be sure, but I wouldn't be surprised if Wilbur's whole program is a scam to get Grandmother's money. There's a phone. I'll look up the number and make a quick call."

Brett stopped the car and went into the phone booth. Within three minutes, he slammed down the receiver, stomped back to the car and shook his head. "News flash. Information says there's no Children's Benefit Program listed in Carrizo Springs."

"So, where do we go from here?" Kimberlee scanned the cluttered sidewalks. "If there are no children in the Eagle Pass facility and this address is a fake… Is there really a Children's Benefit Program at all? Maybe we should call the sheriff and report what we've found."

"Before we do that, we'd have to check every address on Maria's list. There could be some explanation, though at the moment, I sure can't think of one. Let's check out the Crystal City address before we head back to the ranch." Brett made a U-turn at the next block and headed back to the freeway. He pulled onto Highway 83, heading north.

Kimberlee watched out the window, fighting back the tears stinging her eyes. Another disappointment. Nothing in this Texas hell-hole would surprise her at this point. And what were they going to do with fifteen pounds of mulberries and persimmons?

A freeway sign up ahead read:

Crystal City–8 miles

Site of Japanese Internment Camp–World War II

Kimberlee pulled a folded paper from her purse. "That sign reminds me. I picked up a brochure at Denny's. It says here they had over 3,000 internees in the camp from 1942 to 1947." She looked down at the brochure. "I hate to think what our Japanese-American citizens went through."

"Under the circumstances, what else could the President do? We were at war. The camp was intended to protect us from them as much as it was to protect the Japanese-Americans from retaliation from our citizens."

"That's just putting a better spin on it. There's no excuse for all the injustice."

Brett nodded. "Let's hope there's never an opportunity to find out what we would do again, given the same circumstances."

"From your lips to God's ears." Kimberlee folded the brochure and put it back in her purse. They rode in silence.

"I have an awful feeling we're not going to find anything different in Crystal City than in Eagle Pass or Carrizo Springs," she said. "The whole Children's Program sounds like a fake. Grandmother trusted Wilbur with her legal affairs. He's taking advantage of her. Like the Japanese-Americans who trusted the country to take care of them. How betrayed they must have felt, imprisoned and having their properties confiscated because of their nationality. It was so unfair."

Brett kept his eyes on the road. He didn't answer.

"You know what? If this whole Children's Program is a scam… If Wilbur suspected we were getting ready to blow the whistle on him… Brett, this is beginning to scare me. I'm going to call Dorian. She needs to know what we found."

He turned toward her. "What good will it do to call her now? We'll be home in a couple hours."

"At least she can keep an eye on Grandmother." Kimberlee opened her cell phone. "I've only got one bar. Hope it holds out long enough." She dialed Dorian's number. "Hello, Dorian... yeah, hi. Listen…" She told Dorian what they had found in Eagle Pass and Carrizo Springs. "We're headed for Crystal City now. Probably won't find anything different there than in the first two places."

"I was suspicious of that old scoundrel right from the start," Dorian said. "All his whining and begging. I'll call Jack and have him look into the Children's Benefit Society."

"Poor Jack," Kimberlee laughed. "He won't have time to run the lodge what with all the research we've given him." Weren't they fortunate to have a skilled *techie* willing to help with such unpleasant tasks?

"Kimberlee. While you're in town, why don't you buy Jack a nice pair of hand-tooled leather boots? He deserves a reward for all this work."

Kimberlee laughed. "Probably something he should buy himself. I'll look for something nice, though. As far as Wilbur's charity, I hope we're wrong. Listen, I better go. We're just pulling into town now. See you later." Kimberlee clicked the cell phone off.

Brett slowed the car at the outskirts of Crystal City. In the center of town they stopped in front of a six-foot high statue of Popeye the Sailor Man, the popular character in the cartoon strip in the 1920s and 30s. The placard beneath the statue declared him the city mascot. Crystal City produced more than eighty percent of the nation's spinach crop.

Everyone knows how Popeye loves spinach.

Kimberlee wasn't surprised when the address given for the Crystal City Children's Benefit Program turned out to look like one of the WWII abandoned internment camp—an empty lot surrounded by barbed wire.

Brett rolled down his window. "Well, there you have it." He waved at the deserted wind-blown lot. "A phony headquarters in Eagle Pass, a bag lady in Carrizo Springs, and an empty lot in Crystal City."

"That about sums it up." Kimberlee nodded toward the barbed wire. "We should head back to the ranch. I'll call information and get the number for the Chamber of Commerce, just to be sure." Kimberlee turned away, hiding the tears in her eyes. "All our good intentions of continuing the Children's Program—all down the drain." She held the cell phone, reluctant to make the call, but knowing it had to be done.

"How is your grandmother going to take this?"

Kimberlee shrugged. "I'm sure not looking forward to telling her."

Within half an hour, they were headed back toward Eagle Pass. "The lady at the Chamber never heard of the Children's Program. Grandmother is going to be devastated. Wilbur has had control of her affairs for years. What else do you suppose he's done?"

"Hard to say. He could have manipulated stock and transferred assets into his own account, or any number of devious things."

Kimberlee sighed. She sat quietly as they drove out of town, and then turned to Brett. "I've been thinking. How did he think he could get away with it, especially after Grandmother said she was changing her will?" She rearranged the bags of fruit in the back seat that had fallen over. "Didn't he think Grandmother would eventually find out what he was doing? How long could he lie to her about the Children's Program?"

Brett shook his head. "Maybe he figured, she's old, she'll die soon, and then he'd get control of the whole estate before anyone got wise. He must have had a fit when he heard we were coming."

He pulled onto Highway 89. It was early afternoon by the time they retraced their path back through Carrizo Springs and Eagle Pass, heading back to the ranch.

"I'm going to call Jack again. He'll be sick of me calling so often." She reached for her phone and dialed his number at Fern Lake. "Hi. It's me again. How's it going?"

"What's up? I haven't had much time—"

"I know. That's not why I called. I've got another job for you." She took a deep breath and looked out the window. "I don't know which is more important. Looking into Harold's story, or this new problem."

"Yeah, Dorian called and told me about the Children's Program. Sure sorry."

"Maybe you should also see what you can find on Wilbur Breckenridge. He's probably the CEO of the program. He lives in Eagle Pass."

"Sure will. Let's see. Harold Marlowe, Children's Program, Wilbur Breckenridge. I'll let ya know what I find, if I ever get off the computer."

"Thanks Jack. I knew we could count on you."

"Kimberlee, you guys better watch yer back, do ya hear me? If you're right about Harold's identity or Wilbur's embezzling, and they get wise to you asking questions—"

A shiver crinkled down her backbone. "That's why we asked *you* to look into it. Hopefully, they won't know we're asking questions. Besides, what're they going to do, silly, go after all three of us?" Kimberlee pulled down the vanity mirror and wiped a smudge of lipstick from the corner of her mouth.

"Listen to me," Jack's voice cut into her dark thoughts. "It wouldn't be hard ta arrange an accident out there in the Texas desert."

Goose bumps crawled up her arms. "Thanks, Jack. Gives me something else to worry about. We'll be careful." She closed her eyes. *Why did he have to say that out loud?* Bad enough, she'd thought it in her own mind.

Chapter Twelve

uite a beautiful sight, no matter how many times I see it. Margaret gazed out the kitchen window across Star's paddock and onto the prairie. In the distance, blue-gray mountains stood outlined against a brilliant blue sky. Clouds, resembling Indian smoke signals, peeked over the top of the ridge. A billow of dust gathered at the base of the hills. Maybe Quantum's wild herd?

She'd lived with these things for the past sixty years. How many times had she ridden across the prairie with her husband, watching the sunset? How many cattle round-ups, riding through the rain, sleeping on the ground? How many foals had she pulled into the world in the middle of the night, shivering in the cold, blowing on her hands to warm them? It all seemed so long ago, but now, the hardships that seemed so overwhelming at the time had become precious memories.

She was young and attractive back then, or so she was told, not like now, wrinkled and old. Amanda would change all that. Life would be beautiful again once she had the child in her life. She'd have a second chance. This time, she'd do things differently. This time, everything would turn out right.

Her gaze wandered to the paddock by the barn where Nanny Sally led the pony in a circle and her little darling bounced in the saddle, squealing with delight. She smirked. With Brett and Kimberlee gone for the day, she had the child all to herself. Just the way she wanted it.

Over by the side yard, Thumper and Noe-Noe crouched beneath the willow tree watching little red-headed sparrows splash in the fountain. The cat's ears lay low and their heads jerked from one bird to another. What do cats dream of? Fricasseed sparrow served on a bed of catnip drizzled with cream? Margaret smiled.

Dorian and Sam stepped out of the barn. He scooted across the yard toward the house. Margaret pushed open the kitchen door. "Dorian, dear, do y'all have time to come and chat with me?" *Little hussy with her high and mighty ways. I'll take her down a peg if it's the last thing I do.*

Dorian waved. "I'll be right there, Grandmother."

The cats turned at the sound of their voices and raced toward the porch. The screen door slammed behind Dorian, just missing Noe-Noe's tail.

Margaret waited in the kitchen. "Come up to my room. With everyone gone, this is a good chance for us to get better acquainted."

"Let me put Sam on the porch and grab a bottle of water. I'll be right up."

The cats raced ahead and wove between Margaret's legs as she climbed the stairs.

She had just enough time to hang up her sweater before Dorian tapped on her door. Margaret greeted her granddaughter with a smile. "Come on in. Have a seat." She pointed to the rocker and stepped to the window. In the distance, a tractor droned, leaving the field dotted with bales of hay strung out like Morse code—dots and dashes stretched across the pages of a giant book.

Thumper and Noe-Noe jumped onto the bed and slumped against the pillows.

Margaret sat in an overstuffed chair beside the window. "This is one of my favorite places in the afternoon. I can see the whole ranch from this window. Sometimes I just sit here for hours, watching the men work the horses. It's very relaxing."

"Just beautiful. I can see why you love it."

"Can you slide that window open a bit and let in some fresh air, dear? It's a mite stuffy in here." She fanned her face with her bare hand.

Dorian lifted the window and then settled back into the rocker.

"Now you've been here for a while, what do you think of the ranch?

Are you having a good time, dear?" Margaret picked up a crocheted lap robe and spread it across her knees. *Make her comfortable. Gain her trust. Don't forget to smile.*

"It's so peaceful and quiet here, it's almost like stepping into another world. Quite a surprise. It's not at all what I expected."

Margaret stared at Dorian. *Might as well give her a good show. It will throw her off the track. Yes. This would be a good way to begin.*

She smoothed her hair back behind her ear and folded her hands in her lap. She took a deep breath. "I'm pleased that you're so happy here. What would you say if I told you I'm thinking of making you my beneficiary? Would you consider staying on and running the ranch?" She grinned. *Not so cheery. You'll look like the Cheshire cat.*

Dorian started. Her face turned pink. "Me? You're offering me the ranch? I don't know what to say. I'd have to give it a lot of thought." She stared wide-eyed out the window and then back to her grandmother.

"What are you thinking, dear? Tell me." *Fool girl's taken the bait. Now, to pull her in and get her on my side. Might come in handy down the road a piece.*

"It would mean so many changes," Dorian murmured. "I've always wanted to travel. It would be nice to have money."

"That's true."

A little wrinkle creased Dorian's forehead. "And, I won't deny that I've thought about what I'd say if you chose me. But, it's one thing to think about living on a Texas ranch with wild horses and golden sunsets. It's quite another to consider the major changes I'd have to make in my life."

"That's true too." Margaret nodded. "What's the down side? You could do all sorts of things you can't afford now. Clothes, vacations. If you have a charitable bent, you could fund a number of organizations or provide scholarships to underprivileged children."

"I'd have to leave my friends and my job at the Fern Lake Police Department and move to Texas. I'd have to uproot my father from his home and move him out here. He's getting on in years and might not even want to come. It's a lot to think about." She stared out the window.

"Well, girl, everything you say is true. But, I'm waiting for an answer. How much time does it take to accept a fortune?"

"I don't know what to say." Dorian wrung her hands. "I never seriously thought you would choose me. I don't know anything about running a horse ranch."

"Oh, pish. What's to know? That's what stable hands are for. They do all the hard work. Harold would be here to manage all the hired help. You wouldn't exactly have to shovel horse crap yourself, you know."

Dorian giggled. "Harold would stay on? Of course, he would. I was wondering." She leaned toward her grandmother's chair. "Tell me more about him, his background, that sort of thing. What kind of a man is he?"

"What? Why do you ask?" Margaret glanced down at the crocheted robe in her lap. "I don't understand young people today. Can't keep your mind on a single thought to save your life." Margaret threw up her hands. "I've just offered y'all a six million dollar ranch and you ask questions about the stable master?" The crocheted piece slipped to the floor.

Dorian patted Margaret's wrinkled hand and smiled. "It's not that I don't appreciate your offer, or even that I wouldn't seriously consider living here. You'll have to give me time to think it through before I give you an answer." She retrieved the robe and laid it over her grandmother's knees.

Margaret's cheeks warmed. She sank back in her chair. "Oh, I see." That hadn't gone quite like she planned. Dorian should have jumped at the chance. *Guess she's not as greedy as I thought.*

"What's wrong?" Dorian peered into Margaret's flushed face. She took her hand. "You don't look well. Do you feel all right?

"You surprised me. I thought you'd be delighted with my proposal."

"Wait. Now that I think about it, you didn't exactly offer me the ranch. You said, 'What would you say if I offered you the ranch.'" Dorian raised an eyebrow. "Perhaps you didn't really offer me anything.

Perhaps you just wanted to get my reaction before you decided. Am I right?"

Margaret lowered her eyes and twisted her hands. "You're smarter than I gave you credit for. You guessed my little secret. I'm rather brash, you know. I like to take people by surprise and hear what they say before they have time to come up with what they think I want to hear."

"*Ahh.* So, now that I'm on to you, answer my question. What more can you tell me about Harold?"

Back to Harold again? What gives, here? "I've already told you everything I know. He said he was a friend of Mark's and I hired him. Beyond that, I didn't question. And why on earth should you care one way or the other?"

"It's not important now, Grandmother. You see, I'm a little brash, too. I wanted your gut reaction before you had time to say what you thought I wanted to hear." Dorian chuckled.

Margaret glanced at her wristwatch. "You should run along now. We'll talk more about this later after we've both had time to think. We're leaving on the hayride down to the river in half an hour. It's an off-shoot of the Rio Grande, you know, right on the Mexico border. It's quite beautiful and it's a good place to instruct Amanda about Texas geography." *And get her used to me as her guardian, while her mother is out carousing, no doubt.*

Dorian stood and gave Thumper a pat. At the door, she turned. "I'm sure she'll be fascinated. Particularly, coming from someone as knowledgeable as you."

Was she being sarcastic? She'd have to watch that one. Dorian had more going for her than she had first thought. Was that going to be a problem?

Chapter Thirteen

eek-a boo! Thumper peered out from beneath the haystack on the wagon. Noe-Noe lay so close, her whiskers tickled his nose. With each bump in the road, Dorian, Sam, Nanny Sally and Amanda bounced on top of the straw. The hay wagon hit a dip and lurched to the side. It righted itself and bumped on to its destination, the picnic grounds by the river.

Amanda squealed as Nanny Sally grabbed her arm to keep her aboard.

Wilbur drove ahead of the wagon with Grandmother in his 1945 restored Jeep, loaded with coolers, the picnic basket and folding chairs. He turned to look back at the hay wagon. His face darkened and his scowl deepened with every bump in the dirt road.

Thumper leaned over and gave Noe-Noe's face a lick. "I say, my little caramel creampuff. Check out Wilbur's face. I don't think he's having a good time. *Tch-tch.*"

"Do ya think?" Noe-Noe returned a lick across his ears.

He sneezed. From a sprig of straw, or Noe Noe's whiskers? "Bless you, my sweet."

The mini-caravan came to a stop near the river, next to the picnic tables. Child, dog and women tumbled off the wagon.

Wilbur pulled the Jeep off the road and jumped out. He gave the vintage rifle scabbard on the fender an affectionate pat, walked around the Jeep and offered Grandmother his hand as she lumbered onto the grass.

Thumper gave a little snort. "Wilbur would rather be hunting jack rabbits, than hanging out with Granny."

"Tough noogies. He's probably trying to keep an eye on her and the grandkids so she doesn't give away the farm…so to speak." She gave her gold-ringed tail a switch.

With what looked like supreme effort, Wilbur painted a grin on his face as he carried the lawn chairs into the shade where Grandmother and Dorian waited.

Amanda led Nanny Sally to the nearby meadow to pick flowers.

Thumper hopped down from the wagon and shook his magnificent coat. Bits of straw flew in all directions as the muscles rippled across his shoulders and down his back. "Race you." He streaked to a nearby willow tree. Up he flew, claws skittering against the bark until he'd settled on a satisfactory branch. Was Noe-Noe watching? Had he impressed her with his shining coat, muscular body and feline agility?

Beneath the tree, Noe-Noe sat, her languid eyes half-closed, licking the straw from her seductive golden chest, apparently oblivious to her companion's high-jinx. She didn't appear to give a flying fig about his magnificent physique. Or was the little minx playing hard to get? Noe-Noe looked up. "Oh. There you are. Wondered where you got off to." With three leaps, she was beside him.

Look at her svelte shoulders and lithe hips as she moves up the tree. She practically oozes across the branch. Thumper's whiskers pulled back. Hey. That isn't the way that was supposed to work. He was supposed to impress her when he climbed the tree, not the other way around. *Females!*

Harold unhitched the horses and led them beneath the willow tree where the cats hovered. He tied the horses to a low branch and placed a bucket of water nearby.

Meow!

Harold glanced up. "Hi, cats. So you guys hitched a ride, did ya? Now don't get lost when we head back." He walked back to the Jeep where Wilbur struggled to pull the heavy ice chest from the back.

Wilbur rubbed his hands together, then ran one hand over his unruly red hair. He reached again for the unwieldy ice chest.

"Need some help?" Harold grinned and took hold of the ice chest, pulled it out of the Jeep and set it in the grass.

"I can manage. I don't need your help." Wilbur grabbed one end and hefted. *Ummph.* A damp ring circled his pearl-buttoned, checkered shirt collar. A fine layer of red Texas earth dusted his highly polished and sculptured boots with silver toe guards.

"Sure you do. Here, take the other end." Harold took hold of the opposite side and together, they carried it into the shade.

Perspiration beaded Wilbur's forehead and trickled onto his freckled nose. His face resembled a grinning Halloween mask as he wiped the sweat from his brow. "There you go, Mrs. Lassiter." His face crinkled with a huge grin. "Thought I'd bring you the cooler, in case you ladies want a cold drink."

"Thank you Harold, Wilbur. We just might do that," Grandmother said.

Stepping away from the ladies, Harold slapped Wilbur's shoulder. "What's up with you? You're grinning like you just won the lottery or something."

"Fat chance. Come with me. We need to talk." Wilbur's pretentious smile returned to its customary scowl. He glanced back toward the women, clutched Harold's arm and dragged him toward the river.

Noe-Noe scrambled down the tree.

Thumper jumped off the branch and grabbed her around the neck. They rolled, locked in quasi-mortal-combat, kicking and squirming. She lowered her ears, hissed and swiped her paw at him. He leaped sideways and scampered toward the river. "*Ha.* You missed. Bet you can't catch me."

Noe-Noe followed in hot pursuit. Halfway down the trail, they raced past Harold and Wilbur and reached the riverbank ahead of the men.

Thumper hunkered behind a log. *The forward guard approaches. I'll lie in wait, prepared to do battle to the death. I shall leap at my unsuspecting enemies as they come down the trail. Death to the scoundrels.* Thumper crouched lower as the men approached, his back feet treading the ground for traction. What fun. He'd scare the be-jammers out of them.

The men ambled nearer, deep in conversation, until Wilbur's voice could be heard over the sound of rushing water. They paused near Thumper's hiding place.

Noe-Noe slipped up on little cat feet and lay down beside him, shoulders touching.

"…done something before these damn kids showed up. If only the old woman had died before she decided to change the Trust." Wilbur struck his palm with his fist. "She says she's going to choose one of them this week."

"What are you babbling about?" Drops of perspiration popped out on Harold's forehead. He wiped his face with the back of his sleeve.

"Unless something happened to her first," Wilbur mumbled. "It would have to look like an accident." His hand trembled as he pulled a cigarette from his pocket, lit it and took a drag.

All thoughts of good-natured war games and pretend Black Ops vanished from Thumper's head. Grandmother? Were they talking about killing Grandmother? *I don't like her much, but I don't want to see her dead!* Thumper glanced at Noe-Noe, his ears lowered.

Fur raised on the back of her neck. A low growl gurgled in her throat.

Harold took a step back, his face white. "This is nonsense. How can you even think that? Mrs. Lassiter has always been good to us. I don't think—"

"That's the problem. You don't think. What do you suppose happens to our little scheme when she changes the blasted Trust?" Wilbur's face turned a mottled grey.

Leaves crackled under Thumper's feet as he shifted position.

Wilbur jerked his head toward the bushes. "What was that?"

Thumper and Noe-Noe hunkered lower beneath the shrubs.

"I thought I heard something." Wilbur walked toward the shrub and pulled down a branch. "It's nothing. Just those damn cats." He turned back to Harold.

"Screw the Trust." A vein in Harold's forehead throbbed. He shook his grey ponytail and flung his hand back toward the picnic tables. "I don't want no part of this!"

"What's up with you? You wearing mama's lacy underpants today? I just told you. If these kids figure out what's going on with the Children's Program… Well, I'm not the only one going to jail, you can bet on that. We have to do something quick, before the old battle axe changes her will."

Harold wiped his hands on his jeans. "What…what exactly are you suggesting?"

"We'd have to make it look like an accident. You know, at her age, unexpected things happen. On the other hand, we could implicate one of the grandkids, like they knocked her off for the money."

"That's ridiculous. Why would they do that? She's already said she'd leave the ranch to one of them. You're talking crazy." Harold glanced back toward the picnic tables. Perspiration trickled down his forehead.

Wilbur tossed down the cigarette and ground it into the dirt. "That's just the thing. She hasn't decided which. One will inherit, and the other is left out in the cold. If she dies before she declares a beneficiary, they'd assume they'd each get a share. They might think a definite half of a fortune is better than a chance of getting nothing."

"But, she's already named the Children's Program in her Trust. Wouldn't the police suspect you if they figured foul play?" Harold eyebrows looked like two hairy caterpillars.

Thumper's hair stood on end. *Murder most foul.*

Wilbur's jaw tightened. His words rasped through clenched teeth. "The kids don't know anything about the Revocable Trust naming the Children's Society."

At the sound of his words, Thumper's tail thrashed the ground.

"How do you know what they'd think? She might have already

mentioned something about the Trust." Harold whined, sounding like he was pleading a case in Judge Judy's courtroom.

Wilbur lowered his voice. "Point taken. Too many possibilities. Framing one of them is too complicated. Better we should make it look like an accident. Harold, you're smarter than I figured." He reached in his pocket, pulled out another cigarette and lit it. "Now, what kind of accident should we arrange?"

Harold turned toward the river, sighed and shook his head. "Yeah, I'm smart enough to know you've lost your mind. Now, get this crazy idea out of your head and come on back with me." He took Wilbur's arm and pulled him toward the picnic tables.

Wilbur yanked free.

The hair on Thumper's back trembled. He glanced toward the picnic area where his family waited. Water tumbling over the rocks nearly drowned out Sam's bark and Amanda's shrieks as he chased her around a tree. It was a toss-up who was chasing who. Or who was winning.

A soft whistle drew Thumper's attention back to Wilbur. What was he thinking? More devious plots, no doubt.

Wilbur leaned over and wrote his name in the soft sand at the river's edge.

Harold shoved his hands in his pockets. His face was deathly pale. Clearly, he wanted no part of Wilbur's treacherous scheme. But, could he prevent Wilbur from his evil plans? The silence stretched on.

When Wilbur spoke, Harold jumped. "Now, come on, pal. When you've thought about it a while, you'll see that I'm right. You've got as much to lose as I do. You wouldn't want your little wife to suffer, would you?"

Harold's gray face turned white. His head whipped around. His voice was harsh and ragged. "What does that mean? That sounds almost like a threat, Wilbur, old buddy."

"Let's just say you know what needs to be done. It's not like you've exactly been a boy scout all your life, have you? Here's my plan. Have

Imelda put some sleeping pills in Mrs. Lassiter's milk Thursday night before she goes to bed. After the barn dance, when everyone's asleep, I'll take care of everything. You don't have to lift a finger. I'll make it look like she got out of bed and fell down the stairs. She'll have a nice funeral and all the kids can go home, none the wiser."

"So, it's not enough you want to kill Mrs. Lassiter. Now, you want my wife to help you do it?" Harold glared at Wilbur. He shook his head. "She'll never agree."

"Oh, I think she will. Remind her of the mutual funds you've stashed away and the Acapulco trips she takes every year, thanks to the Children's Benefit Program. If she wants to keep up her current lifestyle, she'll cooperate. She's as guilty as the rest of us. We're all in this together."

Harold's face crumpled. "And, if you get caught, we'll all go down together, right?"

"I don't plan to get caught." Wilbur smirked.

Harold shook his head, spun on his heel and started toward the picnic grounds. He looked back over his shoulder. "You're out of your mind, Wilbur. I'm not going to let you do it. I'll figure out a way to stop you, whatever it takes." He hurried down the trail toward the family.

Wilbur snorted. "So that's the way it's going to be, is it? Okay, have it your own way, buddy. You just wrote your own ticket for you *and* your little woman."

Thumper shivered. Cold chills rippled through his body. He leaned into Noe-Noe's shoulder for comfort. "We've got to stop them. What are we going to do?"

Her body shook. She had no answer.

Thumper leaped from his hiding place, his hair standing on end. He streaked down the path toward the shade trees where Grandmother and Dorian sat with Sam curled at their feet. Thumper skidded to a stop and collided with Sam's leg, his fur puffed up twice its normal size.

Sam jumped, hair bristling, then recognizing Thumper, he relaxed. "Don't do me like that, brother. I could have killed you with one snap of my jaws."

Thumper gasped. "As if..." His chest heaved as he caught his breath.

Dorian laughed, "What's the matter, Thumper? You look like you've just met up with the devil."

Grandmother huffed. "Devil, indeed. More likely he saw a snake in the grass."

Dorian shivered and rubbed her arms.

"There's Harold now." Grandmother waved to the man approaching the picnic site. "Yoo-hoo! I wondered where you got off to. I think we're ready to eat. Would y'all be so kind and get the picnic basket out of the Jeep? There's a dear."

Harold hurried to the Jeep, retrieved the basket and opened the lid.

"Thank you, Harold." Grandmother smiled. "What would I do without you?"

Harold's face flushed red as a Christmas tree bulb. "Here you go, Ms. Lassiter, your special drink, nice and cold, just the way you like it." His hand shook as he handed her the thermos bottle and a sandwich.

Thumper crouched near Grandmother's feet, his ears back, glaring at Harold. He tracked the sandwich from Harold's hand to Grandmother.

Harold shifted from one foot to the other. "If there's nothing else, ma'am, I'll go check on the horses." He cleared his throat. "Make sure they didn't kick over the water bucket."

"That's fine. You run along and let us girls gossip."

He nodded, touched his forehead and turned toward the wagon.

"Oh, Harold, before you go, would you tell Nanny Sally and Amanda we have lunch ready? They should come back and get something to eat." Grandmother stood. As she stepped forward, her foot slid sideways on the uneven ground, throwing her off balance. She flung out both arms.

Thumper's gaze leaped from Grandmother's face to the sandwich as she fell toward him. He jumped out of the way just as the sandwich landed with a plop by his head. Grandmother landed on her hip, her left foot twisted beneath her.

"Oh, my God. Grandmother!" Dorian jumped from her chair and stooped down.

Harold ran back and knelt beside her.

"Are you all right?" Dorian ran her hand over Grandmother's left ankle.

Grandmother drew a sharp breath through her teeth. Her cheeks paled. She moaned. Her mouth twisted. Tears sparkled in her eyes. Her ankle took on a dark reddish hue and began to swell.

"Harold, run to the Jeep," Dorian said. "See if you can find a blanket. Her ankle's twisted, but I don't think it's broken. And hand me a water bottle from the cooler."

Harold rushed to bring the requested items.

Thumper squatted on the ground several feet away. What could he do? Powerless, that's what he was. Hearing a murder plot unfold down by the river had been unnerving enough, and now Grandmother lay helpless on the ground. She wouldn't even be able to defend herself against Wilbur if he followed through with his plan and tried to push her down the stairs.

Noe-Noe hurried up beside him. "What happened? I heard all the commotion. Did Wilbur already push her down? Right in front of everybody?"

"No. No. She fell. I don't know why."

Wilbur rushed up, hovering over the family crouched on the ground. "Is she alright? What happened?" An odd smile twitched the corner of his mouth. Did he think Grandmother's injury would make his plan that much easier? Likely, he was right. Wilbur plastered an innocent expression on his face that wouldn't have fooled a five-year-old. He didn't give a royal rip what happened. Probably wished she'd broken her neck when she fell. His feigned concern fooled the family, or maybe they were just too busy to notice.

"Get me some ice and one of those sandwich bags. We'll make an icepack for Grandmother's ankle." Dorian held a water bottle to

Grandmother's lips.

"Can you sit up?" Harold placed his arm around Grandmother's shoulders.

She nodded. He lifted her and wrapped a blanket from the Jeep around her.

Harold and Dorian lifted Grandmother to a chair and applied the icepack to her swollen ankle.

"Here, now, all you young people. Stop this fussing." Grandmother wiped tears from her eyes. Her words came between short gasps. "I'm fine. You'd think I was dead. Just let me sit here for a minute and catch my breath."

Wilbur turned to Harold and lifted an eyebrow. He nodded his head toward Grandmother and winked.

The color drained from Harold's face.

Thumper growled. For sure, Wilbur wasn't thinking of Grandmother's welfare. But, what was Harold thinking? At this point, it was hard to say if he was an ally or someone to be feared.

"Bring the Jeep over," Wilbur said, a smile twitching his lips, his voice soft and full of feigned concern. "I'll drive her home. You can bring the others back later in the wagon."

Harold nodded. "*Umm.* I guess so. She'd probably be more comfortable back home." He turned to Dorian. "Why don't you go with them?"

Wilbur's eyes opened wide. He put up his hand and shook his head, "Oh, no need for that, I'll take good care of her. You don't need to come, Dorian."

"Then maybe I should drive her." Harold stepped toward the Jeep, beads of perspiration sparkling in the short grey hair at his temple and dotting his forehead.

"Harold, you bring the girls back in the wagon," Grandmother ordered. "Wilbur can drive me. I'll be fine. Now, do as I say." She patted her damp face with her hankie, and then wiped it across her bright red mouth, driving bits of lipstick deeper into the wrinkles and lines above her thin lips.

Harold ducked his head and moved toward the wagon. "Yes, ma'am." His shoulders slumped.

Noe-Noe flattened her ears. She hissed and struck at Wilbur's boot.

Wilbur glared at her and stomped his foot. "Scat!"

She skittered away, turned, hissed again and then dashed under the hay wagon where Sam had scurried when all the commotion started.

Thumper followed her to the wagon. He glanced at Noe-Noe, and then nodded toward Sam. "So, you think we should tell Sam? We can use all the help we can get."

She nodded. "Go ahead. The words stick in my throat, I'm so upset."

Sam jerked his head toward Thumper and shook his long gold fur. "Did she say I had a *tick* on my throat? Where? I can feel it crawling on my back." Sam whirled around, bit the fur on his rump, and then kicked at his neck with his back foot.

Thumper shook his head. "Good grief. You've got a stick up your…"

"Thumper! I said *stick*, Sam, not tick… Oh, never mind," Noe-Noe said. "Wilbur plans to kill Grandmother before she can change something. Something about trusting or willing something-or-other, I don't know what. You know how lawyers are. Nothing they say ever makes any sense. If that isn't bad enough, he might try to blame Kimberlee or Dorian."

Sam's eyes grew big and round. "My Dorian?"

Thumper sighed. "Of course, *your* Dorian. How many Dorian's are there?" *How do persons put up with dogs? They're so stupid.* "One of us will have to stay with her, day and night. We'll stick to her like fleas on a fat dog's back. No offense intended, Sam."

"None taken," Sam growled, giving his hip another cursory nip. "I'd like to help, but since I'm marooned on the back porch, don't know how much good I can do. Look. They're getting ready to leave."

Harold and Wilbur helped Grandmother to her feet. "Here, just lean on me," Harold said. "Don't try to put so much weight on that ankle." The men assisted her to the Jeep.

"I'll ride back with Wilbur and help get her settled," Dorian said. "Nanny and Amanda can come back in the wagon with Harold and the animals."

Wilbur frowned. "Oh, don't bother. I'm sure I can manage alone. There's no need for you to come."

Dorian had already climbed into the back of the Jeep.

"Oh all right, if you insist. Let's go." Wilbur huffed, climbed into the Jeep and started the engine.

Harold sighed and turned back to the hay wagon. "Amanda. Nanny Sally. Come on, we're leaving."

Thumper jumped onto the back of the wagon.

Nanny retrieved the picnic gear and tossed Noe-Noe into the wagon next to Thumper and Sam.

"But we just got here, Nanny. Can't we stay?" Amanda whined.

"No, honey. We have to go back. Your grandmother has hurt her ankle." Nanny placed the picnic basket onto the tailgate. "Okay, Harold, we're ready."

Harold patted the wooden seat beside him. "Do you want to ride up front with me, Amanda? We'll take a nice leisurely drive back along the river. We might see some pretty birds or a raccoon on the way home."

Amanda scrambled over the back of the seat and settled next to Harold.

Not too leisurely, Harold. We need to get back and protect Grandmother. He didn't trust Wilbur, even with Dorian along for the ride. No telling what he might do.

Chapter Fourteen

appled streaks of sunlight touched the briefcase on the patio table where Kimberlee set a pitcher of iced tea and a plate of cookies. Once settled into a lounge chair, she checked her watch and drummed her fingers on the table. It could be hours before the family returned from the river. She was anxious to tell Dorian what they'd learned about the Children's Society. The bad publicity would probably put an end to their plans of a similar program in Fern Lake. Whatever the outcome, nothing could be done about it today.

Might as well take this opportunity to just sit and enjoy the peace and quiet before the family returned. She leaned back, closed her eyes and breathed in the scent of the wisteria overhead. The scent made her homesick for her own front porch and her own wisteria. Or maybe just sick of Texas and all things Grandmother?

Half asleep now, the floral scent took her back to last year when she returned to Fern Lake, twenty-five years after her father's death. She had stood in front of the old abandoned house, dismayed at the tumble-down wreck of her former home and awed by the wisteria vine covering the porch, its blossoms hanging through the rotten timber. She wondered how, with no hand to tend it and watered only by the rain, the vine could grow so large as to crush through the roof. Had that been the moment she decided to stay in Fern Lake and restore the old Victorian to its former beauty?

The hum of tiny wings overhead drew her back from her reverie. She opened her eyes. A red and green hummingbird hovered, almost close enough to touch. It sipped nectar from a blossom and zipped across the lawn.

"You awake?" Brett touched her arm. "You were snoozing a few minutes ago when I checked."

"Oh, hi. I must have dozed off. I was thinking about Fern Lake and wishing we were there. Do you want to join me? I made iced tea."

"Sure. Thanks." Brett poured a glass and set it on the table next to Wilbur's briefcase. He flopped into a chair, his back to the table. "It's nice out here. Quiet." The chittering of birds and water splashing in the fountain were the only sounds.

Kimberlee stood and paced the patio. On the third pass, she glanced at her watch. She picked up a magazine, thumbed through a few pages, and then tossed it down on the briefcase. The magazine slid off to the side. She rubbed her arms. "Isn't that Wilbur's briefcase?" Just the sight of the case brought all her concerns about the Children's Society forefront to her mind.

"It looks like it." Brett ran his hand over the tooled leather.

"This business with Wilbur… I feel so helpless." Ice cubes clinked in Kimberlee's glass.

"There's nothing we can do about it today. You might as well relax. You're as jittery as a jumping bean on a hot tortilla. The family won't be back for hours."

"When do you think?" She glanced at her watch again.

"They planned to have dinner down at the river. I don't expect them before dark."

He took a long drink, and then leaned his chair back against the table, balancing on the two back legs. "You're making me nervous. Sit down."

"Okay, okay. I'll sit over here." She leaned back on the swing cushions and smiled. Bright red-headed sparrows darted in and out of the splashing fountain. "That reminds me. Have you seen Thumper? I thought he and Noe-Noe might be hanging out by the fountain, but I don't see them."

Brett gazed around the yard and shrugged. "Not since this morning. They're probably down at the barn."

How nice to have nothing more on your mind than enjoying life. Bird watching and hunting mice were Thumper's favorite pastimes. She shivered. "As long as they don't bring back a mouse and leave it in my bedroom."

Brett twisted in his chair and reached for his glass. The chair legs slid on the tile floor. He lost his balance and fell against the table, knocking it sideways. Wilbur's briefcase hit the floor with a thud. Brett lay sprawled in a puddle of ice tea.

"Are you okay?" Kimberlee's hand flew to her mouth, stifling her giggles. What was it with men and chairs? If they weren't sitting on them backwards, they were trying to balance on the back two legs.

"What happened?" Brett sat up, a sheepish grin plastered across his face.

"You're a goof-ball, that's what happened." Kimberlee dabbed at his pants where an iced tea stain wicked across his lap. Only Brett could make a fool of himself doing something as simple as drinking iced tea.

He grinned, took the napkin from her and got to his feet. He set the table and chairs upright and set Wilbur's leather briefcase back on the table.

"Did any tea get on Wilbur's case?"

"It looks okay." He paused with his hand on the satchel. "Hey, wait a minute. Wilbur's briefcase." He jiggled his eyebrows, Groucho Marx style. "Do we dare?" He stroked the soft hand-tooled leather case, as though it were a work of art and fingered the combination lock. He scanned the patio and yard, whistling softly.

Kimberlee's cheeks warmed. Did they dare? She glanced back into the house, as though even the thought of snooping in Wilbur's case might conjure up the lawyer. Where was Imelda? Probably in the kitchen or over at her own house. "Brett, shame on you. We couldn't peek inside. Could we?"

"Wilbur lied about a charity and who knows how much money he's embezzled from your grandmother in the process? Do you think we should worry about peeking in his briefcase? Maybe there's evidence in there to prove he's a swindler. It's our duty to your grandmother to see what's inside. At least that's my story, and I'm sticking to it." He grinned.

"I guess when you put it that way. Hurry. Open it."

"It'll be hours before the family gets home. We have plenty of time." Brett held the case to his ear, slowing turning the combination dial one number to the left and then to the right. On the third tick to the left, his face lit up. "Bingo." He shuffled through Wilbur's papers, scanning each for a few seconds and then handed them to Kimberlee. "Boring. Boring. Boring. Wait. What's this? There's something here in the side pocket."

"What is it? Show me."

He pulled out a sheaf of papers with a notary seal on the bottom. "It's a Revocable Living Trust. Oh, good grief! Grandmother's named the Children's Benefit Program as her beneficiary!" He flipped it to the last page "But I thought that's why—"

He gave a low whistle. "I had no idea your grandmother was worth so much. Besides the ranch, she has a sizable stash of stocks, bonds, and mutual funds. Apparently Wilbur handles her entire estate. It's quite a portfolio."

He flipped back through the Revocable Trust. "It says here, the majority of her assets will go to The Children's Benefit Program. There's a small provision for Harold and Imelda, but nothing for you or Dorian or anyone else. Isn't that odd?"

"Let me see." Kimberlee scanned through the document. "So, wait. Then why did she bring us to Texas and give us this cockamamie story about choosing one of us as a beneficiary?" She looked up at Brett. "I don't get it."

Brett laid the briefcase on the table. "A Revocable Living Trust is just what it sounds like. You can change your mind and alter the document without a legal hassle. For some reason, now she's decided to leave her estate to one of you girls, instead of to the Children's

Program. No wonder Wilbur kept hammering her about what her money means to the children."

Humph. "What children?"

"A better question is why is she leaving her estate to only one of you and not sharing it equally? Not to mention Amanda or any future great-grandchildren that might be born."

Kimberlee shrugged. "I guess she can do anything she wants. It's her money. It could mean—"

The sound of a motor rumbled in the front yard.

"Someone's here." Kimberlee glanced at her watch. "I'll go see."

Brett stuffed the papers back into Wilbur's briefcase, spun the dial, and tossed the case back onto the table.

Kimberlee slid open the patio door and hurried to the front room. Who would be coming to visit? Grandmother wouldn't have made any appointments, knowing she was going out for the afternoon.

She opened the front door. Wilbur's Jeep pulled to a stop at the end of the sidewalk. Grandmother sat in the front seat and Dorian in back. Why would he bring them home so early? Where was Amanda? Something must be wrong.

Dorian jumped out of the Jeep.

Kimberlee rushed out the front door and down the walkway. "What happened? Is Amanda okay?"

"Don't worry. She's fine. Harold and Nanny Sally are bringing her in the hay wagon with the animals. Grandmother fell and twisted her ankle." Dorian walked around to the far side of the Jeep to help Grandmother. She and Wilbur each put an arm around her waist and lifted her out.

Kimberlee sighed. "Is there something I can do?"

Dorian shook her head.

Grandmother flinched with each attempt to bear weight on the foot. "Perhaps it would be best if y'all helped me straight up to my room. My, it throbs." She clutched Wilbur's arm.

Brett hurried down the sidewalk. "Here, Dorian, let me help.

Wilbur and I can make a seat with our arms and carry her up the stairs."

Dorian stepped away.

"Upsy-daisy, careful now," Brett joked.

Dorian walked ahead, opening doors and moving things to make a wider path for the others.

"Kimberlee, will you fetch Imelda?" Grandmother called from half-way up the stairs. "Have her bring my pain medication, please." Her face paled with each word.

"We'll be right there, Grandmother." Kimberlee swung open the kitchen door. "Imelda?"

Imelda sat at the kitchen table sorting through her recipe cards and sipping coffee. Her head jerked toward the door. Coffee sloshed onto the table.

"I'm sorry, Imelda. I didn't mean to startle you."

"It's okay, Miss Kimberlee. Was that Missus Lassiter coming home already? I thought they'd be gone for dinner. What can I do for you?"

Kimberlee nodded. "Grandmother's hurt her ankle. Can you bring an ice pack and her pain medication up to her room?"

The color drained from Imelda's face. She shoved the cards back into the recipe box and snapped the lid, then hurried to the freezer, pulled out an unopened package of frozen peas and followed Kimberlee. "Is she going to be alright?"

"I don't know the details. We should call the doctor. See if he'll make a house call. I think someone should look at her ankle tonight. It might be broken."

Kimberlee scrunched the bag of peas, wrapped it in a hand towel and laid it across Grandmother's ankle, propped up on a pillow. A glass of water sat beside a prescription bottle on the nightstand. *She probably stepped in the darn hole on purpose, just to keep us here.*

Dorian hovered near the bed, her arms folded across her chest.

Wilbur and Brett stood near the door.

Imelda fluffed Grandmother's pillows and spread a knitted lap robe across her legs. "Missus Lassiter, you should take one of these pills and rest for a while. The doctor said he'd come as soon as he's finished with his last patient."

Grandmother picked up the bottle. "There, there, now, enough of this fussing. You children go on downstairs and leave me be." She motioned toward the door. "Let me rest until Dr. Turner gets here." She leaned back on her pillow, the prescription bottle clutched in her hand.

"Are you sure you don't need one of us to stay with you, Grandmother?" Kimberlee leaned over the bed, straightening the comforter.

Wilbur and Brett scurried out the bedroom door.

"Go away," Grandmother barked. "You make me nervous standing around, staring at me. Y'all afraid I'll die before I decide who gets my money? Now, go on. Get out of here."

Kimberlee's cheeks warmed. *Why, you ungrateful old bat. Why don't you go ahead and die and get it over with.*

She gave her grandmother's comforter a final tug. "Now, don't be that way. You know we're just worried about you." She slid a little silver bell closer to the side of the nightstand. "Ring the bell if you need anything."

Dorian turned toward the door with Imelda close behind.

"I'm fine. Just go." Grandmother spilled out some tablets, tossed them into her mouth and drank from the glass on her nightstand.

Kimberlee pulled the bedroom door closed behind her. "Dorian, wait up." She caught up with her in the hall and grabbed her arm. "Are you sure Amanda's okay with Harold and Nanny Sally? Brett and I could drive out and meet the wagon. Maybe you should stay here, though, in case *Grandmother Most Grateful* rings for something."

Dorian snickered. "I don't think that's necessary." She started down the stairs. "I think I hear them out there now."

Kimberlee hurried downstairs and met Nanny and Amanda at the door. She grabbed Amanda and swung her around. "Did you have fun, sweetheart?"

Amanda smiled. "*Uh-huh.* We comed home too soon. Nanny said." She thrust out her lower lip.

"No naughty face, now. Run on with Nanny Sally. Daddy Brett will take you out to see the horses later, okay? Mama needs to talk to Dorian right now."

Nanny Sally took Amanda's hand. "Shall we play the Candyland game?" She led Amanda up the stairs.

Kimberlee pulled Dorian into the library and closed the door. "You won't believe what we just found on the patio. Grandmother said she was leaving the ranch to one of us, but we found a Revocable Trust in Wilbur's briefcase. Wait for it." She paused and drew a breath. "She's already signed over her estate to the Children's Program."

"Would that be the program that doesn't exist?"

"That would be the one."

Margaret picked at the coverlet. The fall had shaken her more than she wanted to admit. *If I was younger, I wouldn't have been so clumsy.* Not much she could do about it now. Her driver's license said she was seventy-five years old and she'd even lied about that. She was seventy-six.

She never thought of herself as old until she looked in the mirror. Or, when she stepped into a hole.

She held up her hands and twisted them from front to back. How thin and fragile her skin looked. Bluish veins ran like hills and valleys across the back of her hands. When did they get so wrinkled? She closed her eyes and pulled the coverlet over her arms. *I can't stand to look at my hands.* Tears stung her eyes and trickled down her cheeks. Her foot throbbed. She grit her teeth. She'd sure made a muddle of things. How was she supposed to entertain guests this week when she couldn't even walk without help? Would this complicate her plans regarding Amanda?

She grabbed the prescription bottle, shook out the last two tablets and swallowed them. *Think about something else. Try counting sheep or horses. One, two three…*

She lay without moving and counted to fifty. Mark and Melody, her precious children, both gone now. How they had loved the ranch. She'd never forget the summer Mark turned sixteen and his colt won a blue ribbon at the County Fair. He loved the horse shows almost as much as she did. *Sixty-two, sixty-three, sixty…*

She sighed. Now, she raced across the prairie where new foals scampered by their mother's side.

Like turning the page on her favorite novel, the scene changed again to evenings outside the barn, watching a golden sunset streak through the weathervane as it spun in a gentle wind. Life had been good to her.

Seventy-six, seventy-seven…

At last, the medication began to take effect and the pain in her foot eased. She sighed and sank deeper into her pillow. Thank God for pain pills.

The aroma of Imelda's fresh baked bread wafted under her door. She could almost see her bustle around the kitchen, preparing another meal for her guests. Amanda's face would light up with the first bite of Imelda's bread, slathered with butter and homemade strawberry jam.

Sweet Amanda, so full of life, keeping Nanny hopping—dressing her, chasing her around the lawn, bathing her and putting her to bed. Caring for a five-year-old was a full time job.

The faintest shadow of doubt flicked across her mind. Would she be able to keep up with such an active little girl? She dismissed the doubt. Amanda would give her renewed vitality. Of course, she could handle her. Of course, she'd meet the demands of rearing another child. Piece of cake.

Amanda would grow up to be an obedient teenager. She would go to college and get a degree, not drop out of school like Melody. She'd marry a successful man of Margaret's choosing. She wouldn't run away with a guitar player. And, on her wedding day, Amanda would thank her for everything she had done to make her life perfect. *Because everything will be just right, just like it should be, and I'll do it all by myself.*

The pain in her ankle vanished like a magician's rabbit. She'd always liked rabbits. The flop-eared kind, not the white ones. She opened her eyes. The furniture across the room swayed. The colors on the curtains swirled and melted together. *The children are down stairs, thinking—how foolish I am, to step in a hole. I wonder… Are they worried about me? I should go down and reassure them.*

Margaret struggled to sit up. Her eyes were so heavy. She tried to keep them open. Couldn't.

Why was she so weak? Why couldn't she wake up? *Sleep. No, mustn't sleep. How many pills did I take? … need to get up…I need… help…*

"Imelda." Her voice was barely a whisper. *Ring the bell if you need anything.* She reached toward the nightstand. *Need help.* Her fingers brushed the side of the bell. Her hand slid away and the bell skidded to the edge of the nightstand. She fell back on the bed. The bell jangled as it hit the rug.

Chapter Fifteen

est he offend the ladies, Wilbur blew his cigarette smoke toward the open window in the corner of the library. Across the room, Dorian leaned toward Kimberlee and whispered. They both giggled.

Wilbur's stomach lurched. *Matched set of witches*. Not an unusual occurrence when he was nervous, or embarrassed or uncomfortable. They didn't want him here. Most likely, they were whispering about him. He'd have to wait until the doctor arrived, if he was to appear truly concerned. Leaving sooner would seem uncaring about Margaret's injury. Not that he gave a rip one way or the other, but he'd better keep that to himself.

He squashed his cigarette in the ashtray, ran his hand over his slicked down hair and stood. "Since you guys don't seem to notice whether I'm here or not, I'm going to have coffee with Imelda. Call me when the doctor gets here." He thrust out his chin and sniffed. He turned at the doorway.

No one had looked up. They probably didn't even hear him. *Humph*. He stomped out.

Kimberlee's giggle followed him out the door. At the foot of the stairs, Wilbur glanced back toward the library. No one in sight. He climbed the stairs toward the bedrooms.

Wilbur scanned up and down the hall. *They're all too busy downstairs making fun of me.* He stopped beside Brett and Kimberlee's bedroom door and then held his breath as he opened the door into the cluttered room. A wet towel lay over the back of a chair. Brett's socks and underwear lay scattered across the floor near the bed. Wilbur grimaced and stepped over the soiled clothes. *What good is a wife if she won't pick up your dirty underwear?*

Since Harold wouldn't agree to let Imelda put sleeping pills in Margaret's milk, an accidental fall down the stairs was out. He'd have to resort to his first idea of implicating one of the grandchildren. Brett was the most likely candidate. Better that Brett should take the blame and deflect any suspicion from him.

First thing he needed was something of Brett's to use as the weapon. His gaze traveled to the bedside table. There. A metal flashlight sat beside the lamp. That would do nicely.

Wilbur slipped on his driving gloves, carefully picked up the flashlight so as not to smudge Brett's fingerprints. He hurried out of the bedroom and inched the door closed. Now where to hide the flashlight until he needed it? How about the bathroom? He shoved Brett's flashlight behind the towels in the linen closet.

He tiptoed out and crept down the hall, past the little table where Thumper lay napping.

Thumper half rose from his reclining position and stared at Wilbur, the hair on the back of his neck rising. He growled.

Wilbur paused. Wait! Was that a bell? It sounded like it came from inside Margaret's room. He'd just take a peek. Maybe she needed something. He turned Margaret's doorknob and stepped into her bedroom, leaving the door ajar.

Wilbur's grin spread across his cheeks. Didn't need a law degree to figure what had happened. The old woman lay partially off the pillow with her arm sprawled across the bed. A prescription bottle lay tipped sideways on the nightstand. The silver bell had rolled halfway across the bedroom floor.

Wilbur leaned over and touched Margaret's mouth. His heartbeat picked up. Dare he hope? She was still breathing? Barely. He picked up the pill bottle, shook it and placed it back on the nightstand. Empty. She'd taken all the pills. Attempted suicide or overdose? Either way, it didn't matter. What a lucky break. Change of plans.

Never let a good disaster go to waste. Why wait until Thursday when fate dropped the opportunity right in his lap? It wouldn't take much to finish her off now. Everyone would assume she died from an overdose and he'd be home free. Even Harold couldn't complain. No one would suspect he had a hand in it.

Wilbur picked up a pillow and poised it above Margaret's head. *Thanks, Margaret. You've made this so much easier.* His fingers tightened on the edges of the pillow as he lowered it toward her face.

Creak.

Wilbur jerked and turned toward the door. "Who's there?" He dropped the pillow and plastered on a what-luck-I-found-poor-Margaret-at-death's-door-my-goodness-how-could-this-dreadful-thing-happen face.

Thumper shoved the door open and marched across the room, his fur puffed up, his eyes locked on Wilbur's face. He leaped onto the bed. A growl rumbled in his throat.

"Damn it, cat. Don't scare me like that." Wilbur ran a shaking hand across his chin. He picked up the pillow, took a deep breath and lowered it again toward Margaret's face.

Thumper ears pulled back, his fur a-bristle. *Sssitt!* He struck again and again at Wilbur's arm. *Yowwww!* An ear-splitting shriek filled the room.

What the freakin' heck? Wilbur's stomach seized. He jerked away from the wicked claws and dropped the pillow, his heart knocking against his chest like a woodpecker. He dashed from the room and into the bathroom across the hall, slammed the lock, his hand to his chest, catching his breath. They could probably hear the damn cat all the way to the Mexico border. Sure bet the kids heard it downstairs. They'd be coming up the stairs any second to investigate.

Wilbur checked the mirror for any sign of scratches on his face. Thumper's claws had snagged his sleeve but there were no visible marks on his hands. He splashed water on his face, ran a shaking hand over his hair and straightened his tie.

Sure enough, the sound of feet pounded up the steps. Thanks to the blasted cat, he'd missed the perfect opportunity to end this fiasco. Now, he'd have to go through with Thursday night's plan after all. He lowered the toilet lid and sat. In a few minutes, after he caught his breath, he'd go into Margaret's room and proclaim dismay at her terrible accident. Poor Margaret. *Tch Tch. What have you gone and done?*

Kimberlee jumped when she heard Thumper shriek. The cry so horrible, like a knife driving through her brain. She knew in an instant it was Thumper! Something terrible had happened. Her heart skipped a beat. She grabbed Brett's arm. "That was Thumper. Come on." They rushed from the library and up the stairs.

"It sounded like it came from Grandmother's room." Brett flung open her bedroom door. "Thumper?"

There he stood by Margaret's head, his chest heaving, his irises like huge black buttons, hissing like a vengeful warrior guarding the palace gate. Thumper's fur stood on end. His tail lashed from side to side. His ears pulled back.

"What on earth is the matter with..." Brett hurried across to Grandmother's bed.

The bed pillow and silver bell lay on the floor.

Kimberlee stroked Thumper's head. "There, there. It's alright. We're here now. Easy, boy." She nudged him onto the floor and touched her grandmother's forehead.

Grandmother lay as still as death, her face, white as her sheets. "She's so pale. I don't think she's breathing."

Dorian grabbed her wrist. "The pulse is weak, but she's alive." She picked up the prescription bottle from the nightstand and shook it. "It's empty. Weren't there more pills in it? Could she have taken all of them?"

Kimberlee shrugged.

"What's wrong? I heard the commotion." Nanny hurried into the bedroom.

"Nanny, run and ask Imelda to bring black coffee." Dorian threw back the bedcover, grabbed Grandmother's shoulders and pulled her into a sitting position. Her head lolled to the side.

Nanny rushed out, screaming. "Imelda? Come quick."

"Help me get her undressed and into a cold shower. Maybe there's still time." Dorian pulled Grandmother's legs over the side of the bed. Kimberlee put her arms around her other side and lifted her to her feet. "Shall I call 911?"

"The doctor should be here soon. Right now, let's get her blood flowing."

Thank goodness, Dorian knew what to do. Let her take charge.

"I heard all the noise. What's up?" Wilbur spoke from the doorway. He sounded worried. He should be. If something happened to Grandmother, he'd lose a good client... Wait. No, he wouldn't lose anything. Grandmother had already signed most of her assets over to his fraudulent Children's Program. If she died now, before they could prove... Something niggled at the back of her mind, but no time to work it out now.

Thumper pranced across the rug toward Wilbur, arched his back and hissed. His fur stood on end and his ears pulled down.

What on earth? What's he got against Wilbur?

"Can I help?" Wilbur said, shoving his foot at the hissing cat.

Dorian shook her head. "Wilbur. Go on down stairs and try to reach the doctor again. See what's keeping him."

"Right. Let me know if there's anything else I can do." Wilbur hurried into the hallway, shaking his head. "Such a shame..."

Kimberlee stripped Grandmother down to her underwear and helped Brett carry her into the bathroom.

"Set her there on the shower chair. Hold her up." Dorian twisted the cold water faucet. Kimberlee slid into the shower stall and crouched, holding Grandmother steady in the chair. The water sluiced down.

Kimberlee turned her head to avoid water in her face, but it poured onto her arms and chest as she held Grandmother upright in the chair. A chill raced down her spine. Her hands tingled in the cold water.

Dorian called from the shower. "Brett. Go see if Wilbur's had any luck with Dr. Turner. We can manage."

Kimberlee grit her teeth and leaned into the cold water to prevent Grandmother from sliding off the shower chair. Was any of this doing any good? Were they doing the right thing? *Trust Dorian.* She knew what she was doing.

Brett backed out the bathroom door. "Okay. If you're sure you don't need me. I'll check on Nanny and the coffee."

"Stop. No more. I'm cold..." Margaret mumbled. Her head rolled from side to side. She pushed at the hands that held her upright.

"She's coming around. Isn't that a good sign?" Kimberlee rubbed the backs of Grandmother's hands. "I'm sorry, Grandmother. Please don't fight us. We're trying to help you." Kimberlee shivered in the streaming water. Her tears mingled with the shower and dripped from her chin. *Oh, please God. She can't die. I'm sorry I said such mean things about her. Truly, God, I didn't mean it.*

"That's it. Keep rubbing. We've got to get her blood flowing." Dorian massaged Grandmother's arms and legs.

"Hello? What's going on in here?" *Thank God. It's the doctor.*

"We're in here." Dorian leaned toward the door. "Come on in."

Dr. Turner stuck his head into the shower where Kimberlee crouched, her hands covered with chill bumps, holding Grandmother upright against the shower wall. "Imelda let me in. I couldn't understand what she was saying. Something about an overdose? I thought Margaret sprained her ankle."

Kimberlee ran one hand over her face. "Grandmother was resting after her fall. I guess she took too many pain pills. We found her like this." She jerked her head back toward the bedroom. "Did we do the right thing?"

Dr. Turner nodded and opened his bag. "Exactly right. Here, make her drink this." The doctor reached into the shower and turned off the cold water. He shoved a small bottle into Dorian's hand.

Kimberlee held Grandmother's face and Dorian forced Ipecac into her mouth.

Grandmother fought and coughed, but most of the medicine went down her throat.

"Now, put a robe around her and bring her over to the toilet. She'll be vomiting in a minute."

Kimberlee's hands shook as she wrapped a robe around Grandmother. How frail and helpless she looked. Not at all like the witch from yesterday. She half-dragged her to the toilet.

Grandmother vomited the dissolved tablets and the contents of her stomach. *So much for the thermos full of Grandmother's 'special drink'.* Her vomiting subsided.

"I've got her, Kimberlee. Go and get dried off." Dorian gestured toward the bedroom. "You're shaking like a leaf. You'll catch your death if you don't get warmed up."

Kimberlee shook her head. "I'll be okay. You're cold too."

"I'm tougher than you are. Go on. I've got her."

Imelda stood outside the bathroom door, her hands busy on her rosary beads. "I've brought the coffee. What else can I do, Miss Dorian?"

Dorian looked up. "Bring one of her gowns; something with long sleeves and a dry robe. You can help me get her dressed. And more towels."

Imelda produced a long sleeved flannel gown.

It took only a couple of minutes to get Grandmother into dry clothes and into bed. Imelda brought an extra pillow for her head and fussed with her covers.

"I'm sorry to cause y'all so much trouble," Margaret mumbled, tears trickling down her cheeks.

"Don't even think about it. We heard Thumper screaming and came to see what was wrong. Thank goodness we did. You gave us quite a scare." Kimberlee patted Grandmother's hand. She and Dorian left her in Imelda's care and hurried to change into dry clothes.

Within five minutes, they returned to find Grandmother sitting up in bed, still shivering, but alert. Imelda held a coffee cup to her lips. "Here, drink this, Missus Lassiter. Try to drink as much as you can."

"You're a mighty lucky woman, Margaret." Dr. Taylor had wrapped an ace bandage around her ankle. He snapped the clips into place. "That should do it. It's quite a bad sprain, but it'll be better in a few days. Now, taking too many pain pills is another matter. If it wasn't for the quick thinking of your granddaughters…"

"I'm so ashamed," Grandmother mumbled. "I don't know what I was thinking. I felt so sorry for myself and my ankle hurt so much. I just wanted the pain to go away."

"Nonsense! This cannot happen again. Do I have your word, or do I have to hospitalize you?" Dr. Turner raised an eyebrow and tried to look stern. His lips twitched.

Grandmother ran her fingers across the crocheted edges of her sheet. "I'm quite myself now. I assure you. I won't make that mistake again."

"In that case, I think I've done all I can. Your vital signs are stable. The drugs should be cleared from your system before long. I expect you'll be uncomfortable for a few days with that foot and you should stay in bed tomorrow except for bathroom privileges. If it continues to give you trouble after a few days, come on into the office and we'll x-ray it, but I don't think it's broken." He shook his finger. "Nothing more than two Tylenol every four hours. Now, I mean it, Margaret. I'll not have you doing something foolish like this again." He smiled. "Do you know how it would look if something happened to my favorite patient? Why, I'd probably have to leave town."

Grandmother's smile wavered as she looked up at the doctor. "I understand. Please forgive me."

"I'm not in the forgiving business, Margaret. That's between you and God."

Grandmother's face went even a little paler than before. Tears trickled down her cheeks. She looked so small and pitiful, bundled up among all the pillows, Kimberlee almost felt sorry for her. Sorry and a little bit ashamed and a whole lot relieved. Hadn't she wished her dead, not an hour ago? And hadn't she almost gotten her wish less than half an hour ago? Her cheeks warmed. She turned away from the others. *Thank goodness, they'll never know.*

Grandmother nodded and looked from Kimberlee, to Dorian, and Brett, clustered around her bed. "Why, you all look so worried. I don't know how to thank you. If it wasn't for y'all… I guess I'd be…" She put up her hands to hide her flushed face.

"It wasn't just us, Grandmother." Kimberlee lifted Thumper onto the bed. "It was Thumper. He's the one who warned us. You should thank him."

Kimberlee stroked Thumper's head. "What made you do that? You don't understand a thing about any of this. You have no idea you saved Grandmother's life, do you?"

Thumper lay down on the corner of the bed, his toes curled under his breast. He understood what he'd done, alright. He'd done his duty to take care of his family. And even though she was mean as a garter snake and just as ugly, Grandmother was part of his family.

Noe-Noe jumped up and lay down beside him. Grandmother reached over and stroked both cat's heads. Noe-Noe purred, squinting affectionately at Thumper. She kneaded the blanket, her eyes half-closed, and then flopped down beside him. "You're my hero. Thanks for saving Mum-Mum."

Mum-Mum? She's that fond of the old… The endearment made about as much sense as a scorpion named Snookums. Thumper yawned. "Do you remember Will Rogers? He once said, 'We can't all be heroes because somebody has to sit on the curb and clap as they go by.'"

Noe-Noe twitched a whisker. "Now, it's my turn to guard her. This isn't over. Wilbur's going to try again." She craned her neck back and gazed at Grandmother. "They don't have any idea what really happened, do they."

"The pills, yes. Wilbur? No."

"Oh, I just hate this. I wish we could tell them. I do so envy their language skills." Noe-Noe flicked her ear.

Thumper rolled over, showing off his spectacular white tummy to its best advantage. He waved his two front paws. "Our extra toes make us more intuitive than most cats, but I've often wished I had the gift of language. Even without language, cats are far superior to humans."

"How so, dear-heart?"

An unexpected purr leaped to his throat. His heart did a little flip. *She called me dear-heart. Yowzaa!*

"Thumper, dear? You were saying about us being superior. Of course, I agree, but specifically how would you define our superiority?"

"Specifically?" Thumper closed his eyes and pulled his whiskers back. "Well, cats don't covet one another's blankets or toys. We don't kill our mates or abuse our young. We don't wage war on other neighborhoods or consume things that make us lose control of our senses." He rolled back onto his stomach. "Well, maybe a little catnip from time to time, strictly for recreational purposes."

"I see. Your points are well taken, my dear, but I've heard that mother cats will lie on their young if they're sickly or too weak to survive. Of course, I'm sure it's quite by accident."

"Of course."

Chapter Sixteen

Impending tears prickled Kimberlee's eyes. She threw herself across the bed and buried her face in the pillow. *I won't cry.* What's the use? It wouldn't change anything. She squinched her eyes shut, sat up and willed her disobedient tear ducts to behave. She grabbed a tissue from the nightstand and dabbed at the first rebellious drop. "How long must we stay in this purgatory? I wish we'd never come."

Brett picked at his fingernail. He leaned forward in the rocker. "I know. It's not the ideal vacation, is it? I wish we could go home in the morning, too. But, now that we know about Wilbur and the Children's Program, and especially since your grandmother's accident, I don't see how we can leave until she's back on her feet. We have to stay and settle this thing with Wilbur." He pulled off his shoes and socks, stood and reached for his pajamas.

"We sure can't tell her tonight. Not after all she's been through." Kimberlee slid off the bed and paced the room. "We'll talk to Dorian in the morning and figure out a game plan. We can't talk to Grandmother until we see what Jack's learned." She stopped and turned.

Rebellious tear ducts collaborated with runaway emotions and her eyes filled again. She reached for another tissue. "Or, better yet. Why don't we call the local sheriff tomorrow, dump it in his lap, and catch the first flight out of Texas?" A smile tickled the corner of her mouth.

Bone-tired from the trip to town and Grandmother's shenanigans, if she didn't laugh, she'd cry. Hard enough to keep her tears in check.

Brett shook his head. He pulled off his shirt and slacks and stepped into his pajama bottoms. "Then there's the question about Harold. If he's really Ted… Well, at the moment, that little possibility seems to pale compared to the rest of it." He fluffed the pillows and pulled back the sheets. "You coming to bed?" He bounced on the mattress. "Not bad. It's more comfortable than I thought."

"In a minute." Kimberlee set her purse on the bed and unsnapped the hinge. She pulled out her lipstick, mirror and a notebook. "That's odd. I can't find my migraine tablets." She glanced out the window. "I took one when we stopped at the fruit stand. I'll bet I dropped the bottle somewhere in the car."

"Do you need them now?" Brett tossed back the covers, threw his legs over the side of the bed and sat up.

"Not this minute, but after a day like today, I might need one before morning. Don't get up. You're already settled. I'll run down and get the bottle. Do you still have Grandmother's car keys?"

"There, on the dresser. I'll go if you want me to. I can put on my robe—"

"No. No. Never mind. I'll just be a minute. You stay there." She picked up the keys. "Maybe I'll peek in on Amanda and say good night."

Kimberlee walked down the dim hallway to the nursery and turned the knob. *Locked, again. That's odd.* She tapped on the door. "Nanny Sally? It's me. Kimberlee." No answer. She tapped again and waited.

The door opened a crack. Nanny Sally poked her head out. "Is everything alright? Mrs. Lassiter…?"

"She's doing better. I just came to say good-night to Amanda."

"She's asleep. I'd rather you didn't wake her now."

The frustration of the past forty-eight hours welled up inside Kimberlee. Flashing lights and colored dots like a disco ball exploded in her tired brain. Courtesy and reason fled out the door. She'd had about enough of this woman putting up a wall between her and Amanda. Quite enough. *Bring it on, lady.*

"You'd rather I not… Really?" Kimberlee shoved past Nanny Sally. The door slammed against the wall. "Did I say I planned to wake her? Or did I say I was coming to say good-night? And that's exactly what I intend to do, whether you'd *rather* or not."

Nanny Sally's mouth dropped open. She jerked back.

Kimberlee marched across the room to Amanda's bed. "Don't tell me I can't kiss my own daughter good-night."

Amanda's curls lay spread across the pillow, one arm flung out and the other cuddling a teddy bear. A strand of hair on her cheek stirred with each soft breath.

Just the sight of Amanda was enough to calm Kimberlee's spirit. Her heartbeat slowed and the angry wrinkles melting from her forehead were almost palpable. She pulled the coverlet up and tucked it around Amanda, brushed the ringlets off her face and kissed her forehead. "Sleep with angels, sweetheart."

Her temper now in check, she turned to Nanny Sally. "Why was the door locked? Who do you think is going to come into this room in the middle of the night?"

"I…I was just following Mrs. Lassiter's orders, ma'am."

"Mrs. Lassiter's what?" Kimberlee pointed her finger at Nanny Sally's face. "Let's get this straight right now, missy. I am Amanda's mother. I do not appreciate you telling me that she was asleep and I couldn't see her yesterday afternoon. We both know it was a lie. For the duration of this week in Satan's hell-kitchen, I will come into this room whenever and as often as I choose, day or night. If you attempt to stop me in any way or I find this door locked against me, you'll have the wrath of God to reckon with." She shook her finger. "Do we understand each other?"

"Yes, ma'am." Nanny Sally's eyes held a level of loathing that could have stopped a train.

Kimberlee's gaze locked on Nanny Sally's face. She wouldn't be the first to blink.

Nanny lowered her head and looked away. The color fled from her cheeks. Her lips trembled.

"Good." Kimberlee smirked, knowing she had bested the woman. "Then I'll say goodnight." She opened the door, stepped into the hall and closed it softly behind her. *Wow.* That was pretty darn invigorating. She'd wanted to do that from the minute they arrived.

Kimberlee tiptoed down the stairs. The light from the lamp in front of the picture window cast shadows against the far wall. She groped the wall, feeling for the light switch. *Nah.* Forget the light. She could see well enough. Outside, the porch light threw a glow across the lawn toward the barn. Grandmother's car, parked across the yard, stood shrouded in shadows.

Maybe she should go back and get Brett's flashlight. She glanced back at the house. The pallid glow from her upstairs bedroom window cast a lighted square on the lawn. Brett was right up there. It would take less than two minutes to run out to the car and find the prescription bottle. *It's not that far.*

She scanned the dark yard. The trees, waving in the light breeze beyond the picnic tables, so graceful this afternoon, now looked like monstrous arms reaching skyward. Patchy clouds streaked across the moon, created long shadows clinging to the tractor and the hay mower, turning them into grotesque robotic monsters. Everything looked so different at night, almost like a Halloween scary movie. She shivered. Now wasn't that silly?

At the edge of the lawn, she hesitated, again. *Don't be a baby, Kimberlee. Just go out and get your pills.* She squared her shoulders and hurried across the yard toward the car. Something caught her eye over by the paddock. *What was that?* She stopped and peered into the darkness. The shadows moved. Probably one of the mares. Or was it a man's shadow?

Had Maria called and told Wilbur they were asking questions about the Children's Society? What if he was out there in the dark, watching, and waiting for an opportunity to silence her? Or Harold. Maybe Grandmother had told him they were asking questions about his past.

Blood rushed to her face. Her hands tingled. She focused on the fence, willing the dark blob to be a horse or a box or a strip of canvas waving in the breeze. A coyote howled in the distance. Goose bumps erupted on Kimberlee's arms.

Golly-Gee-Jehosephat. Get a grip. She was letting her imagination run rampant, just like in the library when she imagined Harold listening at the door. Was she six years old, seeing boogiemen in the dark?

She reached the car, stuck the key in the lock and opened the driver's side door. *Dark as the inside of a cow.* The light inside the car must have burnt out. *I should have brought that flashlight.* She felt around the floor on the driver's side. Nothing. She stretched across the seat, running her hand over the passenger seat.

Owwwooo!

Kimberlee started. She sat up and stared through the car window toward the barn. A coyote? Coyotes wouldn't come this close to the house, would they? Was this week in hell to end by being eaten by a coyote a hundred feet from Grandmother's door?

She leaned forward and reached down onto the floor on the passenger side to feel around for the bottle.

A sudden pressure on the small of her back felt like someone's knee. Her heart pounded. A hand on the back of her neck shoved her face into the fold of the seat. She squirmed, tried to sit up. The steady pressure on her back and neck kept her pressed into the cushions. She flailed her free hand and tried to scream, but her screams were muffled against the seat cushions. *Can't breathe!* Dizzying lights surrounded her as the air was squeezed from her lungs. *Hold on! Don't faint. Oh, God! Help me!* A zinging sound filled her head. *Brett!*

The odor of alcohol wafted past her nose. A gruff voice behind her head whispered. "Don't keep puttin' your nose into other people's business. You know what I'm sayin'? Terrible things can happen out here."

As sudden as the attack had begun, it was over, almost as though it had never happened. But, the pain in the small of her back was real. She hadn't imagined it. She lifted her head and gasped. A breath of cool night filled her lungs, clearing the fuzzy sensation inside her head. She pushed up with her hands and scooted back until her feet reached the ground. Was he gone? She looked out across the dark barnyard. There was no movement, no sound. She put her hand to her forehead, the pain in her head raging. She twisted her neck and back. Nothing broken. She grasped the steering wheel and pushed to her feet. *Brett!*

She shot out of the car, raced across the lawn, and dashed into the house. Taking the stairs two at a time, she ran down the hall and threw open her bedroom door, her breathing ragged and hair flying.

"Brett?" Kimberlee stumbled into the bedroom. At the sight of him, she began to cry.

"Honey?" Brett jumped out of bed and rushed to her side. She wilted into his arms. He led her to the bed. "What happened? Did you fall?"

She eased back on the pillows and closed her eyes. "No. I…I… I heard a coyote and then someone pushed me down in the car. He said we should stop asking questions! I was so scared... And then...he was gone." Kimberlee dabbed the tears off her cheeks. She forced herself to take deep breaths.

Brett's eyes flew wider. "Someone pushed you down out in the car? There was a coyote?" He pulled her into his arms. "There, there. You're okay now." He laid her back onto the pillows, stood, grabbed for his pants and pulled them on over his pajamas. He slid a foot into each shoe. "Where's my flashlight?"

"What are you doing?" Tears streaked her face. "Where are you going?"

"I'm going out and look around. I'll find the guy and break his neck!" He zipped his pants, and then hopped on one foot, trying to tie his shoe. "Blast!"

"Don't leave me now. I don't want to be alone." She clutched at his pajama top.

"I won't be long. I'll get Dorian to come in and stay with you." He backed toward the door, his hand outstretched.

"Brett. Honey?" Kimberlee knuckled her eyes.

"Yes?" He paused by the door.

"If you insist on going back out there, will you look for my pills in the car?" Kimberlee ducked her head, a half-smile twisting her lips while tears sparkled in her eyes.

Brett grinned. "You goose. I'll just be a minute. Don't worry." He glanced around the room. "Forget the flashlight!" He dashed out the door.

Kimberlee shoved her head under the pillow and pressed it over her ears, trying to block out the scene that replayed in her mind. She took a deep breath. It was all over. She was safe now. The man had only tried to scare them. But who? Harold? Wilbur? Or somebody else who didn't want them looking into Grandmother's business?

It seemed like only a couple of minutes and the bedroom door flung open. *Brett?* Had he changed his mind? She pulled the pillow off her face.

Dorian leaned over the bed, her hair hanging around her shoulders and not a stitch of make-up on her freckled face.

"Are you alright, sweetie? Brett said someone attacked you." Dorian's cool hand caressed Kimberlee's forehead.

Kimberlee closed her eyes. She shook her head. "I'm okay now. He didn't hurt me. Just tried to scare me to death. Someone doesn't like us asking questions."

"All the more reason we should keep asking." Dorian helped pull Kimberlee's shirt over her head. "Get into bed. We'll talk more about this tomorrow. We'll all feel better after a good night's sleep."

Chapter Seventeen

As I live and breathe, if I ruin these shoes out here… Wilbur pranced across the yard, his eyes glued to the ground, careful to avoid the occasional horse pie. Every time he wanted to talk to Harold, he had to cross eighty yards of horse crap. *I swear he does it on purpose.*

Harold leaned on the fence next to Star's paddock, a blade of straw clenched in his teeth.

A green tinted horsefly the size of a gumball dive-bombed Wilbur's face. He jerked back, flapped his hand at the insect and took a quick step to the left. *Squish.* His right wing-tip loafer landed in a *plop* half buried beneath sawdust. He stopped, and scraped his shoe in the dirt. *So much for my $300 shoes.* With an effort that almost cracked his cheeks, he put a smile on his face. "Harold? How's it going? You still mad at me?" Not that it made much difference in the long run, but…

Harold's gaze kept pace with Star, trotting around the corral. He didn't turn.

The mare threw back her head and whinnied as she passed Warrior, prancing along the fence line, just out of reach.

Wilbur smoothed a flyaway strand of red hair off his forehead. "She's a beauty, alright. *Heh! Heh!* When do you plan to breed her to Warrior?" He waited for Harold's reply. Once again, he'd have to *handle* Harold. *If I can't bring him around, well, then, too bad for him.* He didn't really want to hurt Harold. They'd worked well together for several years and embezzled thousands of dollars from Grandmother's accounts between them. He couldn't help but like the guy. Hadn't Harold gone along with all his ideas—setting up the fraudulent Children's Program, convincing

Mrs. Lassiter that the money was going to underprivileged children, verifying many of Wilbur's comments about imaginary construction? A few pictures of skinny kids and meeting Maria in the Eagle Pass office and Mrs. Lassiter's checks started rolling in.

Harold just didn't want to accept reality. Mrs. Lassiter's promise to sign over her estate to the Children's Program meant millions of dollars under their control, not a thousand or two every month gleaned from a gullible old woman.

What a bummer, that these grandkids showed up and Harold had to go all boy-scout on him. Well, Wilbur would give him one more chance and if he didn't come around, then… "Harold? You still mad?"

Harold turned and held Wilbur's gaze. "You still planning to…you know. What we talked about? Mrs. Lassiter?"

Wilbur stepped up on the fence and leaned forward, balancing his arms on the top rail. "What do you think about Mrs. Lassiter's accident? You missed all the excitement."

"Imelda filled me in. Mrs. Lassiter is fine now. Don't try and change the subject."

"I thought Mrs. Much-Bucks was the subject. Too bad, the kids found her in time, *huh*? She could have taken care of our little problem and we wouldn't have to lift a finger. Now, maybe we should move forward with our original plan." Wilbur grinned.

"What do you mean? Our plan? I thought we decided you were giving up the idea."

Wilbur looked down into Harold's face. "Maybe that's what you thought, but *we* didn't decide anything. You just don't get it, do you? When she changes her will, there goes our chance to get control of the ranch. Do you know how much we'll lose if she makes one of those *bitches* her beneficiary? We need to settle this before she ruins everything."

Harold shook his head and stepped up onto the bottom fence rail, his shoulder next to Wilbur. "You know, we've been at this for a long time and we've both made a bundle. Why don't we quit while we're ahead?" Harold's gaze remained locked on the mare circling the arena. "We've been lucky so far. Now that she's talking about changing the will anyway, why push our luck? We don't need her dough. We quit now and nobody's the wiser. If we keep on… Wilbur, I haven't got the stomach for it. She's been good to me—to both of us." Harold's voice cracked.

What came over him? He never used to be such a goody-goody. "You don't understand." Wilbur's beady eyes half-closed. He grit his teeth, his hands tightened on the top rail. "It has nothing to do with the little dab we get from her every month. I need to control the ranch. I've got money problems. I've run up a $50,000 tab at the Indian reservation casino." *Actually, more like $85,000, but Harold doesn't need to know that.* "They've given me till the end of the month to clear it up or they're threatening to break my bones."

Harold put out his hand, started to speak, then dropped it and shook his head again.

Wilbur hopped off the fence and ran his hand across the top rail. Now what was he going to do? He'd gone through his mutual funds and borrowed another $65,000. "I should have known I couldn't count on you. You've always been a weakling."

"Don't get all gung-ho on me. We can work this out. There must be another way."

Wilbur scowled. "I need some time to figure this out." He paced along the fence, trying to close his mind to the conversation he'd had last week with his loan shark, Bunker.

He had just left his office and unlocked his Jeep when Bunker shoved his scraggy beard into his face and a gun in his ribs. He could still smell the fried garlic and onions on his breath. His heart almost stopped when Bunker whispered, 'Look, Wilbur. The boss says you got sixty days to pay off the whole amount of the loan or else. Let's not forget what happened to ole Danny last year when he tried to stiff the boss.'

How could he forget? Ole Danny's dismembered body had

turned up in the desert, partially eaten by coyotes. If he didn't get Mrs. Lassiter's estate tied up pretty darn quick, he would never meet Bunker's deadline. Once the old lady was dead, he could hold off the thug with a promissory note until the estate was settled. Harold could easily blow the whole deal if he got it in his head to talk to the right people. The only way out was to handle this milksop until he could pay off Bunker.

Wilbur sucked in a breath. How would a guy look if he was trying to figure his way out of a tough spot? He gazed at the horses for a few minutes, squinting wrinkles across his forehead, trying to look worried and sincere. He snapped his fingers, pasted a cheery smile on his face, and turned back to Harold. "You know, I've laid awake worrying about this. I don't really want to hurt the old lady. Maybe you're right. We've both put away a nice little nest egg. I was saving my offshore account for a rainy day, but this is probably as rainy as I'll ever see it, right? Just lucky there's more than enough to cover the tab at the casino. I guess I just got a little crazy about losing the estate." He struck his forehead with the heel of his hand. "Yes, I think you're right. It would just cause more problems than I already have, wouldn't it?" He chuckled.

"And Mrs. Lassiter? That whole thing's off, right?"

"Don't worry. I'll take care of everything."

Harold blew out his breath. His face broke into a smile. "So, what if she asks why you don't need her money any more for the Children's Program?"

"I'll say I got a government grant for the program. She's old. She'll buy that."

Harold nodded. "Sounds good. You're okay with this, right?"

"Sure. Didn't I just say so?" Wilbur raised an eyebrow. *At least that's what you heard, wasn't it?*

Harold's face split into a grin. He jumped off the fence. "Probably should tell Mrs. Lassiter about the government grant right away."

"Don't worry. I told you I'd take care of Mrs. Lassiter." They shook hands.

"There now, see?" Harold reached through the rails and stroked Star's nose. "Everything's going to work out fine. And if you need a loan, just say the word. Imelda and I will be glad to help out."

"Why, thanks, Harold. That's mighty big of you. I think I've figured out how to handle the problem." Wilbur smiled. *No thanks to you.*

"Okay, great. See ya later." Harold started across the yard toward the house. At the corner of the porch, he turned and waved, pulled open the screen door and disappeared into the ranch house kitchen.

"I've got it handled all right," Wilbur muttered. "Come Thursday night, I'll take care of everything; Mrs. Lassiter, you and Imelda. None of you will trouble me again."

"Who…?" Kimberlee turned as the screen door opened. Coffee sloshed from her cup onto her hand.

Harold stepped into the kitchen. He wiped his feet on the mat and closed the screen behind him.

"Oh, it's you. I didn't hear you come up the steps." What should she do? Leave the room or stay and talk? Could he be the *shadow man,* who threatened her last night, coming in to finish the job? She glanced toward the library where Brett and Dorian were watching a ballgame on television.

"I'm sorry. Did I startle you?" Harold's face lit up. "Do you have a few minutes? I'm glad you're here. I wanted to talk to you and never seem to find the time."

What did he have to say? She could always scream if she needed help and Brett would come running. She nodded and pulled out a kitchen chair, gesturing toward it. "Yes. We should talk." She picked up the coffee pot. "Would you like a cup?"

Harold nodded and sat.

Kimberlee poured Harold's coffee and placed the pot back on the coffee machine. She slid into a chair across the table from him. She was careful to keep her expression blank. "Grandmother said you knew my father. He was murdered when I was just a little girl. They say I witnessed the murder, but I don't remember much about it." Kimberlee searched Harold's face. If he was really Ted in disguise, her brash statements should get some sort of reaction from hm. No response. He was either not Ted or he was a terrific actor.

"That's terrible." Harold's face paled. "I'm so sorry. It must have been hard for you, growing up without your dad."

"Yes, it was." She nodded. "Mom died when I was young and my aunt and uncle raised me. I didn't learn about Dad's murder until last year."

Harold nodded again. "That's a real shame." His big hand covered Kimberlee's.

She glanced down at his military ring and then pulled her hand away.

"I suppose you want to talk about your dad?"

"Nothing I've learned about him until now is good. It would be nice to hear something different for a change." Kimberlee brought her coffee cup to her lips and peered at Harold over the top of her cup. She watched his eyes, looking for any hint of falseness in his words or expression. Her heartbeat quickened. She glanced at the door that separated her from Brett. He was less than ten feet away. *Okay, I can do this. Steady, girl.*

"Well, let's see. I met your dad in a military hospital in Germany where he and I shared a room with Ted Herman."

Kimberlee's head jerked back. "Ted Herman? You knew him, too? I didn't think… I knew Dad met Ted in Germany, but…" Harold's face blurred and shimmied. A rush swirled through her head. She blinked to clear her vision. *Hang on Kimberlee. Don't let this rattle you. Count to ten. One—two—three…* She clutched the edge of the table so hard, her knuckles turned white.

"Why, yes. The three of us were bunked together in the same wing.

I had a broken shoulder and Ted was in traction for a back strain. Your dad broke his leg practicing parachute jumps."

Harold droned on, telling about the day to day events in the hospital. How her father had spoken so vividly about the Lassiter ranch in Texas, the horses, the sunsets, the hay fields, the barbecues and barn dances and every other conceivable aspect of living on the prairie.

His words jumbled and Kimberlee's brain raced beyond his voice. If he knew Ted in the hospital, then he couldn't *be* Ted. Were they wrong about Harold, after all? Grandmother's explanation made sense. He was just a nice old man with whiskers.

Harold went on, sharing their life stories. He grew up in Rockland, Maine. Ted told about his hometown in Northern California and Mark wouldn't stop talking about his Texas ranch.

Harold's eyes misted over. "Mark made it all sound so real. Before long, I envied every coyote and barrel cactus on his Texas horse ranch."

Harold's tale carried Kimberlee back to his days in the hospital in Germany. She could almost see her father, his leg trussed up in a sling. She could almost smell the antiseptic.

"We promised to keep in touch. But, you know how things go. Time and distance came between us. After a few years, we only sent occasional Christmas cards and then, even those stopped."

Harold stood and poured himself another cup of coffee. "Refill?"

Kimberlee shook her head. "But, if your hometown was in Maine, how did you get here on Grandmother's ranch?"

Harold twisted his ring. "Well, I'll tell ya. They say you never forget your war buddies, but after a while, the memories grow dim. It was some years later, 1990. I was working with a construction company in the Cayman Islands. One night I goes to a saloon for a belt and who should be sitting there at the bar but my old hospital buddy, Ted. Imagine my surprise?"

"You saw Ted again? In 1990?" This story was getting curiouser and curiouser.

"Yep. It was Ted, alright, but he called himself Teddy. I hardly recognized him. He had a mustache and his long hair pulled back. I guess they called it a mullet back then." Harold grinned and ran his hand through his own gray ponytail.

"That doesn't make sense. We heard that Ted died…or did he?" Maybe she should call Brett in here. He needed to hear this.

Kimberlee's thoughts raced. If Harold's story was true, then Brett's suspicions about Ted were right. He was still alive. Then again, maybe Harold's story was supposed to alleviate any suspicions that he was really Ted in disguise. It was all so confusing. She shook her head and turned back to Harold. "I'm sorry. My mind was wandering. What happened next?"

"Me and Ted spent a couple nights drinking and recollecting the good old days back in the hospital. Ted said he bought a lodge in California when he got out of the service. He told me your dad bought a house next door, got married and had a little girl. Guess that was you." He smiled. "Apparently they were all real buddies. He showed me a picture in his wallet of him and your dad together with a deer they shot."

Kimberlee started. "I know that picture. I've got one like it." Why would Ted keep it so long after her dad died? Had Harold been listening at the library door, after all? Maybe he knew they were looking at the picture. Otherwise, why would he even mention it? Or was it just a coincidence? It was enough to make her head spin. At this point, she wouldn't be surprised if the Cheshire Cat and the White Rabbit marched right through the back door.

"We talked about Mark, but he didn't tell me about the murder. Maybe he didn't want to share the bad news. Ted said he eventually got a divorce, sold the lodge and came to the Cayman's to—"

"That's a filthy lie!" Kimberlee shoved her chair back and paced the kitchen. "He ran away after my dad was murdered. His wife believes he died in a fishing boat accident."

In her mind's eye, she saw Ted lying on a beach in the Cayman Islands while Mrs. Herman grieved and her own mother wandered from pillar to post, dragging a little girl, trying to move past her husband's murder. "That sneaking chicken-rat was living in the Cayman Islands all those years, while everyone believed he was dead."

She stamped her foot and put her hands over her eyes. She took a deep breath. "I don't know why this upsets me so much. It's nothing to me whether he's dead or alive. Not that it changes anything, except..." It must be true or she wouldn't be so upset. Harold was telling the God's truth about everything.

Harold shrugged and looked embarrassed.

She slumped into her chair. "I'm sorry. I interrupted you. You still didn't say how you came to Texas. Please, go on." Harold's face blurred as the sound of his voice faded in and out. She clasped her hands together and blinked to bring him into focus. *Concentrate. Remember everything and tell Brett.*

Harold glanced nervously around the kitchen. Was he looking for an escape route, should she become more agitated? She made an effort to control her emotions. She couldn't let on that she might doubt the truth of his story.

"There's not much more to tell. The third night, Ted and I made it up to meet at the bar, but he never showed. I didn't put much stock in it. About that time, I spotted an ad in an Equestrian magazine. Stable master—Lassiter Farms, in Texas, of all places. I'd just been reminiscing with Ted about Mark's Texas ranch, so it was fresh in my mind, all them sunsets and fine things Mark used to gush about. I took it for a *sign*, that it was the right thing to do.

"I answered the ad. Sure enough, when I dropped Mark's name, Mrs. Lassiter offered me the job and I came lickety-split to Texas. Met Imelda, got married. The rest is history. I've been here ever since." Harold leaned back. His face beamed.

Kimberlee nodded. "I see."

"I hadn't thought about Mark or Ted for years. Then you showed up this week. Mark's little girl. We sure had us some laughs, those weeks in the hospital. And Mrs. Lassiter gave me a chance even though

I didn't know jack-diddly about horses." Harold's smile wavered. He pulled out his handkerchief and wiped his eyes. "Sorry. I guess all this reminiscing has me a little misty." Harold stood and hurried to the back door. "I gotta get back to work. I'll see you later, okay?"

Chapter Eighteen

imberlee shoved open the swinging door between the kitchen and the library and stepped into the middle of a television baseball game. The announcer's blow by blow account of the last play nearly drowned out the crowd's cheers.

Kimberlee hesitated and then raised her hand. "Hey guys, listen. Guess who caught up with me in the kitchen? I've just been talking to Harold."

Brett pushed the television mute button. The ball players leaped across a silent screen.

"What did he have to say for himself?" Dorian set her cup on the coffee table.

"He told me the story of how he met my dad. They shared a hospital room in Germany with Ted Herman. All three of them, together. Can you believe it? So, I guess we've got our answer. He's not Ted."

"Really?" Brett glanced over at Dorian. "So, you're convinced he's telling the truth? Nothing personal, honey, but we need more proof than just his word."

"You don't believe him?" Kimberlee raised her eyebrows. Her gaze flicked from Brett to Dorian. "Okay. I'm probably not telling it right. Let me explain everything the way he said."

Kimberlee related her conversation with Harold. "So you see? He confirmed everything Grandmother told us. They all met originally in Germany. Some years later, he saw Grandmother's ad and came to the ranch." She spread her hands wide, smiled and nodded.

Brett and Dorian stared at the floor. Neither spoke. Dorian twisted her hands and glanced between Kimberlee and the window. Outside, a tractor rumbled past the house and veered toward the barn.

"Well? Why don't you say something? What's the matter?" Kimberlee's voice rose. She put her hand to her forehead. "You're giving me a headache."

Brett stammered. "*Uhh*...okay. It sounds very convincing, but let's think about it. If it's true, it only confirms what we suspected all along—that Ted didn't die in a fishing accident in the Cayman Islands. None of it disproves that he's not Ted and he created a false identity. He could have made up the whole story."

"Well, yes, I guess, but... What about you, Dorian; do you feel the same?" Kimberlee turned toward her. *Please? You understand, don't you? Brett's just being a poop.*

"*Umm*...well, I have to agree with Brett for the time being. We should wait and hear what Jack has to say before we completely dismiss the possibility of... You know... You must agree, don't you?"

"Well, I don't. You guys never give me credit for having a brain in my head. If you'd heard what he had to say, you would understand... Oh, just forget it."

"Why are you reacting this way?" Dorian stood and stepped toward Kimberlee. "You act as though you want to believe him, even if there might be proof to the contrary. I don't get it."

Kimberlee's shoulders slumped. She stared at the floor. Neither one of them understood. She took a deep breath, tears stinging her eyes. "Let me explain. Last year when we investigated Dad's murder, we suspected Ted was involved. Believing he was already dead made it easier, somehow. Now, you say he might still be alive, living right here on Grandmother's ranch all these years...while both my parents are... It would mean that all these years, Ted got away with... Harold seems like a very nice old man. I just don't want to believe he's really Ted. That he'd be capable of the things we suspect."

"Of course, I see what you mean." Dorian touched Kimberlee's hand. "I hadn't thought of it like that. And my mother... Ted could have been responsible for her death, too." She sighed. "I guess, to be honest,

I agree with the way you feel." She looked into Kimberlee's eyes. "Sweetie, what we *want* to believe doesn't change what *is*. We still need to be sure. If he is Ted, someone should know. The matter needs to be more fully investigated by the authorities. We have to be sure."

"I spoke to Jack earlier this morning." Kimberlee wiped the back of her hand across her face. "I'll call him back and tell him what Harold said about living in Maine. Maybe there are some official records to prove it one way or the other. If you'll excuse me, I'm going up to my room for a while. I need to lie down. And I want to check on Amanda." She dashed from the room.

Upstairs, she slammed her bedroom door and sat on the edge of the bed, knuckling her eyes. Her stomach churned. Nausea washed across her belly. Her chest felt like an empty hole where her heart should be. She put her hands over her eyes. "I believed him. I was so sure."

Once again, Ted Herman or just the memory of him turned her world upside down. Now, her head was full of doubts and suspicion again. She shook her head.

Surely, Jack had found something by now. She dialed his number. "Hey! Jack. It's me. How's it going?" She blinked, clearing her vision.

"Oh, hi. Yeah. I found something, alright, but you're not gonna like it. I found a Children's Benefit Program website on the internet. So far, though, nothing about your Harold-guy."

"Try Rockland, Maine. He claims he grew up there." She stood and started down the hall toward the stairs, carrying the cell phone. "Give me the internet address. I'm headed for the library. Brett and Dorian are there. If I lose you, I'll call back."

She hurried down the stairs, and entered the library. Empty. Where did they go? She peered out the window.

Brett and Dorian leaned on the fence next to Star's paddock. Sam raced along the fence, keeping pace with the mare as she trotted back and forth. Dorian threw back her head, probably laughing at Sam. At least Sam was having a good time. Good thing. She sure wasn't and there weren't any prospects on the horizon.

"You still there, Jack?"

"Yeah. Right here."

"Give me a minute. Gotta wake this thing up." She held the phone with one shoulder and jiggled the mouse. "Okay, got it. Let's have that URL." She typed in the web address. The Children's Benefit Program website popped onto the screen in vivid color. "Okay, I've got it, Jack. Hold on. I'm reading it now."

Ten Children's Benefit Programs across Texas provide hot lunches and after-school care to under-privileged children, as well as camping trips, counseling and a mentoring program for troubled teens. Your pledge of $20.00 a month will provide food and after-school care to one child. Won't you donate today?

The masterfully designed website crammed with pictures of adorable big-eyed starved-for-love children had a minimum of three *Click-Here-to-Donate* opportunities on every page. Kimberlee rolled her eyes. "Oh, good heavens." She moved on to the *About Us* page. It held a purported interview with Wilbur Breckenridge.

Mr. Wilbur Breckenridge, CEO of the Children's Benefit Program, is confined to a wheelchair. Despite his need for oxygen, provided through a portable tank, Mr. Breckenridge stated, "My only goal is to bring a little sunshine into the life of a deprived child." Mr. Breckenridge spends his few remaining days devoted to the dear underprivileged children of Texas. Won't you donate generously? A photo of a silver-haired gentleman in a wheelchair, breathing through an oxygen mask dominated the lower right-hand screen.

Kimberlee gasped. She tried to speak and choked on her saliva. "I can't believe this…this...pack of lies." She ran her hand over her forehead where pain mounted an invasion across her brow. "I have to go now, Jack. I…I…can't read this. I just want to scream. The man is despicable. What are we going to do?"

"I'm sorry. I just looked up what ya told—"

"Of course, it's not your fault. I didn't mean anything… Thanks for all your help, Jack."

"You know I'd do anything ta help ya. I'm just sorry about— Oh! Gotta run. Chance is barking at something outside. Catch you later."

"Thanks. See you." She clicked off the cell phone and went to the door. "Brett. Can you guys come in here for a minute? I need to show you something." She waved the cell phone at them.

"Be right there." Dorian and Brett hurried across the yard. Sam followed at their heels. At the front porch, Dorian patted Sam's head. "Stay, Sam." He flopped onto the doormat as she came through the door.

Brett walked in behind her. "What is it, hon? You feeling better?"

"Come here and take a look at this." Kimberlee tapped the computer displaying the Children's Benefit Program website. "I just talked to Jack."

Dorian sat at the desk and scanned the website. Her cheeks turned crimson as she read the screen. She shook her head. "I can't believe… I wonder what my friend, Virgil found? I called him last night."

"Your friend, in the police department?"

"He said he'd call some of his contacts and look into Wilbur's program." Dorian stood, closed the library door and dialed his number. "I'll put him on speaker."

"Hello? Virgil? It's Dorian. I've got Kimberlee and Brett here with me. Did you have any luck with The Children's Benefit Program?"

"Hey! I was going to call you later. Yeah. I called in a few favors. Found out quite a lot. On the surface, everything looks on the up and up. He files an income tax form and claims small donations every month from the website, but not enough to light up the IRS radar. His expenses are about equal to his donations, plus a small stipend for himself. He pays Worker's Comp and withholding taxes on one employee there in Eagle Pass. Apparently the workers in the other facilities are volunteers. Hard to say how much money he really rakes in over the year from the website, though. In a lot of cases, people send cash, you know, and no way to track that. He doesn't claim to be a 501C corporation, so no discrepancy there. You sure he's not legit?"

"Virgil. I told you last night. Brett and Kimberlee went to the addresses where he claims his programs are located. They're either nonexistent or empty lots. You figure it out. He may look okay on paper, but he's as phony as a soybean hotdog. Did you look at his website?"

Virgil laughed. "Seriously! A website's easy enough to fake. Have Brett notify the Eagle Pass Police Department and tell them what you suspect. Let them do the investigating. I don't want you mixed up in this. Once they look into it, the FBI will get involved, since the website is soliciting money across state lines. They'll make short work of Mr. Breckenridge.

"What a creep. Taking money from gullible old ladies who think they're helping little kids. I've got half a mind to fly out there myself and punch this guy's lights out."

"Now you're just being silly, though I agree with the sentiment. We'll handle it from here. Let me know if you find out anything else."

"Will do. When you coming home? I miss your tootsie-wootsie—"

"Never mind what you miss. I'll call you when I get home. You can tell me all about it then."

"*Tell* you? I'd rather *show* you—"

"Good-bye Virgil. Thanks." She clicked the phone and shoved it in her pocket. With her cheeks a rosy shade of red, she turned toward Kimberlee. "Guess you heard. Brett? Should we call the Eagle Pass police?"

"I think it would be better if I drove in and spoke to someone face to face. Do you want to go into town, honey?"

Kimberlee sighed. Which would be less pleasant? Convincing the police to look into Wilbur's transgression or telling Grandmother about her swindling attorney? Choose. Door number one with the gorilla… Or door number two with the tiger. "I don't think so. I'll stay with Dorian. We should probably speak to Grandmother."

"I'll leave that up to you guys. I'll drive in by myself. The sooner we get the police in on this, the better. Mind if I take Sam along for company?"

Dorian shook her head. "Go ahead. He loves to ride."

Brett leaned down, gave Kimberlee a kiss and waved.

"Bye, hon." Kimberlee turned to Dorian. "I'm really dreading this. It's going to be a terrible shock for her to learn what Wilbur's doing."

"I was up there this morning. She's not feeling very well. Imelda is with her. Maybe we should hold off until we hear what the police are going to do. She's so fragile right now, after the fall and last night. She won't take this news lightly. No one likes to think a friend would do such a thing. She's trusted Wilbur for quite a while."

Kimberlee drummed her fingers on the coffee table. She stared out the window. Brett was just pulling out of the driveway with Sam in the front seat next to him. "You know what I've been thinking. Wilbur's game plan was actually a good one. It could have been a financially sound charitable organization."

"What do you mean? His whole plan was outrageous."

"No. Listen. That's not what I mean. The Children's Benefit Program was supposed to provide hot lunches and afterschool care to underprivileged kids. He put up a website on the internet to get donations to pay for overhead expenses and got volunteers to run the program. It's a great concept."

"What a shame the whole thing is a scam."

"Why does it have to be? It could still work, Dorian. I mean, for real. It would have to have a different name, of course, but the same basic structural concept. We could do this in Fern Lake. You and Brett and me."

Dorian nodded. "It is something to think about."

Chapter Nineteen

acon! And pancakes! Yumm! Kimberlee stifled a yawn as she pushed open the kitchen door. The tantalizing aroma of breakfast hung in the air. She checked her watch. 5:30 A.M. She groaned. Too blasted early for man nor beast, and she was neither.

Imelda stood beside the stove, flipping hotcakes and shoving sizzling bacon around the grill.

Brett poured maple syrup over a steaming stack on his plate as he recounted, again, yesterday's trip to the police station. He stuck his fork into a piece of bacon and sliced it into bite size pieces. "They've put out an all-points bulletin on Wilbur so there's no way he can—"

"What can I fix for you, Miss Kimberlee?" Imelda turned as Kimberlee eased into a kitchen chair.

"Just coffee, Imelda. I'm not much of a breakfast eater." Kimberlee rubbed her eyes

"Oh no, Miss Kimberlee. You must eat big breakfast. You must have food inside to keep you strong. You sit right there. I will make you some hotcakes. Would you like bacon or sausage with your eggs?" She waved a spatula toward the old stove.

Kimberlee groaned. "I never eat a big breakfast, especially this early. I usually just have a piece of toast and coffee while Amanda gets ready for school."

Brett crammed a two-inch high fork full of pancakes into his mouth. "Kimberlee onny agweed to get up so earwy to humow me." He slurped coffee from his cup and swallowed. "I want to show her the sunrise. Harold said it's fabulous this time of year."

"It's not polite to talk with your mouth full." Kimberlee shot him a disapproving glare.

"Miss Kimberlee?" Imelda held up the spatula and waved it from side to side.

"I guess if I must, could you please scramble the eggs and maybe some toast? Thank you, Imelda." She glanced over at Brett cutting into his over-easy fried egg. The yolk flowed across his plate like a pool of yellow lava, surrounding the crisp bacon.

"I guess all this fresh air just makes me hungry." Brett laughed. "Could you rustle up a couple more pancakes, Imelda?" Brett flashed his smile that never failed to charm the ladies.

"Of course, Mr. Brett." Imelda slid two more pancakes onto his plate.

"Could you please pass the marmalade, hon?"

Kimberlee covered her mouth, yawned and handed the jam jar to Brett.

He flipped off the lid. "What are you girls planning to do today?" He smeared jam across his second stack of flapjacks. "Is your grandmother feeling better?"

Kimberlee closed her eyes and turned her head. She'd never understand how men could eat so early in the morning, and enjoy it so much. "It sounds like it. She says she wants to come downstairs and show me and Dorian how to make jam. I guess we'll hang out here at the house with her today."

"Don't make any plans for tomorrow morning. Remember? We have a riding lesson with Harold. Then there's the dance tomorrow night." Brett smeared the last bite of pancake through the egg yolk on his plate and shoved it in his mouth. "Did you think to bring riding boots?" Brett drained the coffee from his cup.

Kimberlee shuddered at the sight of egg yolk dripping off Brett's fork. "I did. I hope I won't fall off the horse and humiliate myself."

Brett laughed. "Not much chance that will happen."

"Right."

"Thanks Imelda," Brett called over his shoulder, setting his plate in the sink. He grabbed Kimberlee and pulled her to her feet. "Just step outside with me for one minute. I have something to show you." He checked his watch and winked at Imelda.

"What is it?" Kimberlee looked around the porch and across the dark yard.

"Just wait."

Brett wrapped his arm around her shoulder. The sky over the prairie turned from purple to rosy red, then pink with streaks of yellow. "Do you remember our first sunrise?" Brett turned her toward him.

"As I recall, it was about a week after we were married and the water main broke about 4:30 in the morning. You had to run outside in your pajamas and turn off the water." She tried to suppress the giggle that threatened to erupt.

"We were mopping the floor until after sun-up," Brett laughed. "And, watching the clock until 8:00 A.M., so we could call the plumber." He looked up at the pastel sky. "Remember? I promised I'd make it up to you one day?" He tipped up her chin and ran his finger over her lips. "Well, here it is. Special ordered just for you, sweetheart. The perfect sunrise, and not a mop in sight."

"We have had some interesting adventures this past year, haven't we?" She dropped her head to his shoulder.

"I wouldn't trade a minute. I didn't even mind mopping that morning because we were together." He leaned down with a gentle kiss.

"You say the sweetest things." Within minutes, the edge of the sun peeked over the horizon, like a giant fireball rising out of a lake of fire. Kimberlee drew in a quick breath. *It's so beautiful.* God's magnificent handiwork surrounded the ranch as the sky lightened and the sun crawled upward into morning.

Brett squeezed her shoulder. "There, now, aren't you glad you got up early? Was it worth it, sleepy-head?"

"It was perfect. Just what I needed to brighten my spirits. Thanks, hon."

He stifled her words with another kiss. "I'm going out to the barn. The stable hands are shoeing horses this morning. I'll see you later."

"Oh, no you don't." She grabbed his arm and spun him around. "You're not getting away that easy. Come back here and tell me how much you love me."

Brett pulled her closer and mimicked her voice. "How much you love me."

"Not good enough, you goose. Say it right or those stable hands will have to shoe horses without you."

"I love you more than the prongs on a pitchfork. More than stickers on a cactus. More than burs on a burro..."

"I get it. Get out of here and go shoe your horse."

Brett gave her a quick peck on the cheek and hopped off the porch.

"Go get em, cowboy." Kimberlee shook her head, waved and returned to the kitchen.

"Did you enjoy the sunrise, Miss Kimberlee?" Imelda stood at the sink, her hands up to her wrists in soapy water.

"Yes, it was wonderful. Now, I'm glad I got up early. Thanks for fixing breakfast, Imelda. Can I help you with the dishes?"

"I'm almost finished, but thank you. Your breakfast is on the table."

Kimberlee took three bites of scrambled eggs and grabbed her toast as she escaped through the swinging doors before Imelda could fill her plate again. She found Dorian curled up in the rocker in the library. "You're up early."

Dorian stroked Thumper, sitting on her lap. "Couldn't sleep. Do you think Grandmother is up to hearing about the Children's Benefit Program this morning? We have to tell her sooner or later. It would be best if she knew before the authorities get involved. And I think we should tell her together."

Nothing like dropping a bomb on Grandma to ruin a gorgeous sunrise. So much for the beautiful memory. Kimberlee sighed. "I guess it has to be done. Let's wait until after she's had breakfast. I'm going upstairs and spend some time with Amanda. Why don't we meet up in

Grandmother's room about 9:00 A.M.?"

"Good idea. I'll work up some courage between now and then. What I really need is a stiff drink. How strong did Imelda make the coffee this morning?"

"You goose." Kimberlee chuckled and hurried up the stairs. She turned at the top stair, "See you later."

The smell of bacon drifted through the swinging door as Dorian disappeared into the kitchen.

At the crack of the appointed hour, Kimberlee and Dorian stood outside Grandmother's door. Dorian tapped gently. "It's us, Grandmother. Kimberlee and me." She rolled her eyes toward Kimberlee.

"Come in, girls."

"Ready?" Dorian pushed open the door.

Grandmother sat in her easy chair by the window; her head back, her eyes closed, her foot resting on a hassock. The sun streamed through the window. She opened her eyes and sat up as the girls came into the room. "How nice of you girls to come and visit. Make yourselves comfortable."

Kimberlee sat in the rocking chair, pleased to see Grandmother in a good mood. "Have you had breakfast?"

"Imelda brought me a tray. I like to eat my breakfast here by the window. I can see most of the ranch from here, you see."

Dorian sat on the bed and drew her legs akimbo, under her. She cleared her throat and took a deep breath. "Grandmother, we've come to talk to you about the Children's Benefit Program. Has Wilbur even taken you to visit one of the sites or have you ever talked to any of the volunteers?"

Grandmother shook her head. "Wilbur always said I shouldn't be bothered with the day-to-day stuff. He said it wasn't very pleasant down there and I'd just be upset seeing all the children in raggedy clothes. He thought it best that I should just finance it and let others do the dirty work. Why do you ask?"

Please, Lord, give us the right words. Kimberlee glanced at Dorian. "What if you found out that Wilbur lied to you? That there wasn't any program, at all. How would you feel about that?" She looked closely for a reaction.

The frown on Grandmother's face suggested that her words didn't set well with her. Her brow wrinkled and then her mouth tightened.

Here it comes.

"How stupid do you think I am? Do you think I would give him thousands of dollars if there wasn't a real organization serving the children?" Her face flushed.

Dorian rose from the bed and stooped beside her grandmother's chair. "I'm sorry, Grandmother. Please don't be upset. Just listen to what we have to say. I know you trusted Wilbur. Why would he tell you not to come and see what the program was doing for the children? Why should you stay away?"

"I told you. He has my best interest at heart and doesn't want to upset me—"

"Why should it upset you to see the children eating good food and having a safe place to play after school? Isn't that what Wilbur told you the money was for?" Dorian laid her hand across Grandmother's arm.

"I don't know. When you put it that way…" Grandmother stared out the window. "A few times I suggested we should visit one of the locations, but they were all out of town, you know. He always had some reason why I shouldn't go. Once they closed the Carrizo Springs facility for a few days because a water pipe broke. Another time…" She looked from one face to the other, her eyes widening. "What do y'all know that I don't know?" The color drained from her cheeks.

"I'll be right back." Kimberlee hurried down the stairs to the kitchen. "Imelda? Would you bring some coffee to Grandmother's room? As quickly as possible, please."

Imelda laid a dishtowel on the counter. "Is everything okay? Missus Lassiter?"

"I'll explain later. I must get back." She turned and rushed back to Grandmother's room.

Dorian leaned over her grandmother.

Grandmother twisted a hankie in her lap, her eyes riveted to Dorian's face.

"...and when Brett and Kimberlee visited the sites, they found empty lots. The police are investigating." Dorian finished up with the details. "You're not the only one he's taken advantage of. Wilbur's website claims to have programs in ten cities, but it's not true. There are no facilities anywhere." She looked up as Kimberlee came into the room and sat back in the rocking chair.

Grandmother shook her head and burst into tears.

Dorian handed her a box of tissue.

"We can show you the computer website, if you like," Kimberlee added. "He's soliciting money on the internet."

Imelda pushed open the bedroom door, carrying the coffee tray. She stopped in the doorway. "Oh, Missus Lassiter. What is the matter? Why are you crying?"

"It's okay, Imelda. Thanks for the coffee. We'll handle this." Kimberlee waved her hand, dismissing the housekeeper.

Imelda set the tray on the nightstand and backed out the door, leaving the door slightly ajar.

Kimberlee handed a cup of coffee to Grandmother. "I know this is a shock. Here, try to drink this. You'll feel better." Probably should have put a slug of whiskey in it. That definitely would have made her feel better.

"No, thank you, Kimberlee. I'd like to lie down. I'm completely exhausted. Will you please help me over to my bed?"

"Of course." Kimberlee set the coffee back on the tray. "It's here if you want it."

Dorian took her arm. Grandmother rose unsteadily and stepped toward the bed.

Like shadows, Noe-Noe and Thumper slipped into the bedroom, jumped onto the bed and flopped down next to her hip.

Dorian slid a pillow under Grandmother's legs and covered her with a crocheted comforter. "There now, how is that? Are you comfortable?" She fluffed the pillows.

Grandmother's hand went down, as if by habit, to stroke Noe-Noe's head. She closed her eyes. "I can't believe Wilbur would do something like this. I'd have trusted him with my life." She clenched her fists. "If I was a man…" She dabbed at her eyes with the tissue. "Oh, what's the use?"

Dorian nodded. "He won't get away with it. Brett has notified the police. I expect they'll bring Wilbur in for questioning soon. The whole truth will come out and he'll likely be charged with internet fraud and embezzlement. If you want, tomorrow, we can take you into town to speak to another attorney."

"You know, I don't want to hear another word about this right now. Can we change the subject?"

"No problem. We understand." Dorian sat quietly for a few moments.

Kimberlee stood and checked the time on the wall clock. "Look. I promised Amanda I'd play Candyland with her. Do you want me to stay? I will if you need me."

"No…no… Y'all run on. I'll be fine. Perhaps Dorian will stay and talk with me for a while." Grandmother gulped down a tear.

"Okay. I'll see you downstairs. Remember? We were going to make jam today. Do you still feel up to that?" Kimberlee smiled.

"Perhaps tomorrow morning would be better, dear. I'll see you later."

Kimberlee leaned down and gave Thumper a pat. "Now, you and Noe-Noe stay here and help Grandmother, do you hear?"

Thumper dozed, listening to the murmur of Dorian and Grandmother's voices. Despite the pleasant breeze drifting through the window, the hot sun on the back of his neck grew uncomfortable. And his tummy felt a little queasy. Maybe the tuna fish sandwich he found this morning on the patio had sat out all night? *Yuck!*

He peeked one eye open. *Aha!* The top of the tall Victorian dresser across the room looked more appealing, out of the direct sunlight. He stood and gave his fur a shake, starting with his head, all the way down his back. He leaped off the bed and pussyfooted across the rug, calculating the distance to the top of the dresser. *Four feet to the 9th power of thrust, multiplied by the velocity quotient of 6 minus πr^2.* His stomach rumbled. *Or is it 7 minus πr^2? Oh I can't think....*

He stooped and gathered his feet together, gave his somewhat vague calculations another quick think and leaped.

Whoops!

He'd underestimated his velocity, leaving him grappling the edge of the doily, trying to gain a grip on something solid to pull himself up. His claws hooked into Grandmother's padded sewing basket, tipping it off the dresser. Twisting to regain equilibrium, he and the basket tumbled to the floor. *Geronimo!*

Thud!

He made a perfect four-point landing in the middle of buttons, thread, knitting needles, lace trimming and a couple of envelopes spilling out of the sewing basket.

"Thumper, what on earth!" Grandmother sat up, her hand to her cheek.

He licked his lower legs and then hopped onto Grandmother's bed where he slumped against her pillow. *Don't worry. I meant to do that.*

Dorian crossed the room. "Never mind. I'll pick it up." She gathered buttons and lace and dumped them back into the sewing box. She picked up an envelope lying among the pile of sewing notions, turned it over and glanced at the faded return address. Her hand shook as she picked up the second envelope. "These are my mother's letters," she whispered. "The ones you told me about. May I read them?"

Letters? Of course. Melody's letters.

"Please, dear. I meant to show them to you. Go ahead and read them aloud. I'd like to hear them again myself." Grandmother laid her head back on the bed pillows and closed her eyes. "It will take my mind off Wilbur."

The envelope crinkled as Dorian pulled out the faded stationery. She began to read from the letter.

> *September 1, 1985*
>
> *Dear Mother:*
>
> *We've settled in the house. It has a nice yard for Dorian. Hubby found a good job as a civilian cook at the military base. I've enrolled Dorian two mornings a week at the preschool Kimberlee used to attend, The Little Tikes and Trikes. Enclosed are recent pictures of her.*

Dorian laid the letter on the bed, pinched the envelope open and turned it upside down. It was empty. She continued to read.

> *I told you about my dreams, about Mark fighting with a guy in a red coat, a black cat and a dock next to the lake. Mark's house is right next to a lodge with a boat dock, just like in my dream. And they have a black and white cat! It can't be a coincidence. So far, I've had no luck tracing Carol. They say she left town with Kimberlee right after Mark died.*
>
> *I did make a friend at the lodge. Jack is about sixteen years old. He's very nice, but terribly shy. He knew Mark and Carol and used to babysit for Kimberlee. He doesn't know I'm Mark's sister.*
>
> *Jack showed me a litter of kittens born at the lodge about three weeks ago. One is the cutest black and white female. She looks like the lodge*

cat–probably the father. I'm going to bring her home for Dorian in a couple of weeks. Jack is more talkative when we play with the kittens. I'm sure he knows something about Mark's murder but I haven't figured out how to get him to talk about it.

I hear Dorian waking up, so better run. Give everyone a kiss for me. We're making plans to come visit next summer. I can't wait to see you and so miss the horses. We must plan a trail ride and a barn dance. Maybe by then, I'll have some answers. The police aren't doing anything. They wouldn't even talk to me when I told them I was looking into Mark's murder.

Love, Melody

Dorian dropped the first letter on the bed and opened the second envelope. Her hand shook as she pulled out the pink stationery.

September 19, 1985

Dear Mother,

Just a quick note to bring you up to date on things here in Fern Lake. Jack and I are now buddies. He showed me how to bait a hook and cast and I caught a fish. Another day, I rented a boat and took Dorian for a ride around the lake. We played with the kittens both days. Our kitten, Spook, is almost ready to come home.

I have to tell you, Mom. Something really scary happened today. I overheard Mr. Herman and a man talking on their boat. I heard them say, 'I'll dispose of the body.'

Boy, was I scared. 'Body? What body? says I.' I know you'll think I'm crazy, but I think they're planning to kill someone and dump him in the lake. I'm going to the police station, again, tomorrow and tell them what I heard. This time, they have to believe me. Something fishy is going on and it's not just fish in the lake. I wanted you to know in case something happens to me. Ha. Ha. Next time you hear from me, I'll have my new kitty-girl, Spook. I'll send pictures of Dorian and our new baby next time.

Love, Melody

Grandmother opened her eyes. "Now, you see why I had to bring Spook back to the ranch? That kitten was Noe-Noe's great-great-grandmother."

Noe-Noe lifted her head when Grandmother spoke her name. *Did you hear what she said? That's how my ancestor came to Texas.* Noe-Noe licked Thumper's ear.

Dorian replaced the letters in the envelopes. "I don't remember reading anything in Mark's police report about my mother talking to the police. Are you sure she went to the station the next morning?"

"I guess that's where she was headed." Grandmother pulled a tissue from the tissue box and dabbed her eyes. "She was downtown near the police station when witnesses saw her dash into the street for some reason. They say a dark truck hit her and took off." Grandmother leaned back on her pillow and closed her eyes again. "I'm sorry, Dorian. Didn't your father tell you any of this?"

Dorian shook her head. "I was only four years old when she died. When I was old enough to understand, he just said she was killed by a hit and run driver. This is the first I've heard about her interest in Mark's murder. Are you suggesting there was a connection between hearing the conversation on the dock and the hit and run?"

"I don't know what to think. Maybe the lodge owner knew she'd overheard them talking." Grandmother shook her head and tucked her tissue back into her housedress.

"After Melody's funeral, I took a copy of her letter to the Fern Lake Police Department. They promised to look into it. Maybe they did, maybe they never bothered. If a body never washed up on shore, they probably thought she just imagined the whole thing. But, I always wondered…"

Dorian held the letters with a trembling hand, rocking and looking out the window.

Grandmother closed her eyes and appeared to be sleeping.

Poor things. They both look so unhappy. Thumper rolled on his side and continued his bath, licking his front foot and drawing it over the opposite ear. Only a hint of breeze came through the window now, gently moving the curtains. He closed his eyes and laid his head on his front paws, thinking of Melody and Dorian and Grandmother.

Memories from his ancestor, Black Cat, flooded his mind. Black Cat apparently was a witness to the terrible day Melody died—no surprise there. Thumper lay on the coverlet, his eyes closed, as the images washed over him…

Black Cat had walked through the quiet alleys behind the Fern Lake Deli. He jumped onto a box next to the owner, smoking outside the deli. "How ya doin', Black Cat?" The man tossed the cigarette, ground it out with the ball of his foot, and stroked the cat's head.

Black Cat arched his back, welcoming the caress. He stretched and kneaded the wooden box.

"You hungry?" The deli owner disappeared into the market and returned with end cuts off rolls of ham and pastrami.

Black Cat purred his gratitude, dispatched the hunks of meat and hopped off the box, headed for the center of town. Next to the flower shop, a wrought iron stand overflowed with red, white and blue flower arrangements. Black Cat stopped in a patch of sunlight. Occasionally, a shopper paused to pat his head or stroke his back.

He basked in the sun puddle, mesmerized by the flag flipping in the breeze across the street in front of the Fern Lake Police Department and City Hall. Next door, a fire truck sat half way out the door of the fire station. A puppy wandered up the sidewalk, sniffing and lifting his leg from time to time.

Black Cat settled into a half-dozing nap, his tummy full of ham and his heart full of the beauty of the morning. Through his veil of sleep, he heard a familiar voice. "Well, good morning, Black Cat. Lovely day, isn't it?" He opened his eyes. *Ah,* Melody. The young woman who came to the lodge and played with Jack and his kittens. He stood and rubbed her ankles.

The shrill clang of the fire bell shattered the quiet morning.

Firemen rushed out of the station and jumped into the fire truck. The engine roared as it zoomed out of the station house.

The puppy cowered near the firehouse door and then darted down the driveway, into the street, where it hunkered in terror.

Melody clapped her hands. "Come here pup, come here!" The pup started toward her, then, terrified, crouched in the middle of the road. A black pickup truck hurtled down the street.

"No!" Melody raced into the street, directly into the path of the oncoming truck. Instead of slowing, the driver gunned the engine and swerved toward her. The bumper struck her, head on. Still clutching the puppy, her body flew across the hood of the truck and crumpled onto the pavement.

Mrs. Herman hunched behind the wheel of the battered pickup. She gunned the engine and careened down the street and away from the woman she'd just run down.

Passers-by screamed, rushed into the street and clustered around Melody. The puppy wiggled free and disappeared around the firehouse.

Thumper's images faded and the bedroom came back into view. So, Ted Herman wasn't responsible for Melody's death. His wife was the hit and run driver.

Over the years, they never identified the truck or driver that caused Melody's death, but, now, Mrs. Herman lay in a convalescent hospital, nearly paralyzed, her mind active, but her body in a virtual prison. Perhaps justice, long delayed had finally caught up with her.

Dorian ran her hand over Thumper's head. It felt ever so much like Melody's caress in his ancestor's memory. His racing heart slowed as she stroked his back.

"Oh, you're still awake." Dorian leaned over and kissed Grandmother's cheek. "I thought you dozed off."

Thumper lifted his head and shifted positions.

Noe-Noe stood and hopped off the bed.

"I wasn't asleep. I was thinking of Melody and wishing I had a second chance to raise a daughter. This time I'd do things different…" Grandmother's face turned bright pink. She put her hand to her mouth and turned her head away.

Thumper pulled his ears down. *So, now she's admitted it. She plans to steal Amanda to satisfy her own selfish whim to raise another daughter.* But, at what price?

Dorian walked to the door and touched the doorknob. She paused, and then wheeled around. "I'll let you rest for a while. Thanks for answering my questions about mother's death. I'm terribly sorry about the Children's Benefit Program." She opened the door and stepped into the hall.

"Yes... I'm sorry too. I'll…I'll see you later."

Dorian's footsteps echoed down the hall.

Grandmother put her hands over her face and rocked forward and back. "Now, what am I going to do about Wilbur?"

What, indeed, was she going to do? She was starting to love Kimberlee and Dorian in spite of herself, but not enough. She hadn't changed her mind one whit about Amanda.

Chapter Twenty

"*D*orian, child, take one of those pans from the cupboard." Margaret pointed toward the apricot tree in the back yard where the morning sun cast a glow on the golden fruit. *I doubt these girls know one thing about making jam...* "Run out and fill it with apricots. I think you can reach enough from the ground without a ladder." She waggled her hand in the direction of the tree by the fountain. *Maybe this will take our minds off Wilbur.*

"Okay." Dorian took the pan and stepped out the kitchen door. "Come on, Sam. Come with me." She and Sam crossed the yard to the apricot tree where she pulled the apricots off the limbs and dropped them into the pan.

Sam hopped around her feet, picking up fruit from the ground.

"Are you comfortable, Grandmother?" Kimberlee brought a sofa pillow from the living room. "Sit down and put your foot up on this chair." She shoved the pillow under her foot. "There, now, isn't that better?"

"Why, that's not necessary, but thanks." *She doesn't have to be so gol-blasted nice all the time.* Margaret turned her warmed cheeks away from Kimberlee.

"What should I do first?" Kimberlee looked around the large kitchen.

"Get a big kettle from under the counter and several large mixing bowls. The sugar and Sure-Jell is in the cupboard over the oven. Imelda already washed and stacked the jars on the counter for us yesterday."

Kimberlee banged around the kitchen, following orders.

"Fix up a large kettle with cold water and ice. After the apricots are placed in the boiling water for a few minutes, we'll drop them into ice water. That loosens the skins so they slip right off. Once the pits are cut out, we'll be ready to start the jam."

The kitchen door squeaked open and Amanda came in clutching Thumper to her chest.

"Fumper says he's hungry, Mama." She staggered across the room, her arms wrapped beneath the compliant cat's front legs. His long body knocked against her knees with each step.

Kimberlee shook her head. "I don't think so, sweetheart. Daddy Brett gave him breakfast early this morning."

"*Uh-huh.* He's hungry. He tode' me so. He wants some bacon." Amanda squinched up her mouth and glared at her mother.

"Amanda. Don't make naughty faces at Mama. Now, you run on and take Thumper outside to play. There's a good girl." Kimberlee gave her head a pat, and a little push toward the back door.

"Amanda, you come on back here." Margaret spread her arms wide. "Come and give Grandma some sugar." She turned to Kimberlee. "If Amanda wants to feed da kitty bacon, that's dust' what her can do, 'cause Grandma says so."

Amanda stood still by the door. Her gaze moved from her mother to Margaret.

Kimberlee stepped between her and Amanda. "Please don't contradict me when I discipline her, Grandmother. It just confuses her and makes it harder for me." She knelt beside Amanda. "Now run along, Amanda. Go find Nanny." She gestured toward the yard.

The muscles in Margaret's face tightened. *Who does she think she is, chastising me in front of the child, right in my own kitchen?*

Amanda sidled across the room and put her hand on the refrigerator handle. She paused, as if waiting for the winner of the tug-a-war to make the final decision.

Margaret smiled. There! It was working already. Amanda was accepting her authority and turning against her mother. She was half-way home.

Kimberlee gave Amanda's shoulder a shove toward the door. "I said, take Thumper outside."

The warmth crept up Margaret's cheeks. She made a half-hearted effort to control her voice, without much success. "Kimberlee, where are your manners? You're still a guest in my house. I said the child may do as she pleases. If Amanda wants to feed the cat *caviar*, she can feed the cat. I won't hear another word on the matter."

The color drained from Kimberlee's cheeks. The kettle slipped from her fingers and clattered to the floor just as Dorian opened the door and stepped in with a pan full of apricots.

"What's the matter? What's wrong?" Dorian scanned both their faces and set the apricots on the table, picked up the kettle and placed it on the counter.

Kimberlee's cheeks flared with color. "Amanda and I are having a difference of opinion as to whether Thumper needs bacon. Grandmother feels that since it's her kitchen, she should make the final decision and I feel that Amanda and Thumper should get outside before one of them gets spanked. Now, if you'll excuse me…" She rushed through the swinging door. Her feet pounded up the stairs. A bedroom door slammed.

Margaret turned toward Dorian, the faint smile of success on her lips. "Just a little disagreement. Nothing to worry about. Now, if you'll wash those apricots and put them on to boil for a few minutes, I'll show you how to get the skins off in a jiffy."

Dorian glanced between Margaret and the door where Kimberlee had disappeared. "Perhaps we can get back to this later. I think I'll go see if she's okay."

"She's just…" The swinging door between the kitchen and the hallway sprang back and forth as Dorian hurried from the kitchen. "Fine." *I swear, I don't know what she's so upset about. What difference does it make if the child feeds the cat or not?*

"Grandma?" Amanda dropped Thumper, her hand still on the refrigerator door. Her eyes were wide.

Margaret turned. "Amanda?" The inside of her head felt like a bottle rocket on the Fourth of July. She lifted her foot off the pillow, stood and shuffled across the kitchen. She yanked open the refrigerator and grabbed the bacon. "Here! Feed the damn cat." The plate of bacon clattered onto the counter.

Amanda set the plate of bacon on the floor in front of Thumper.

Margaret limped out of the kitchen into the library. The fax machine on the desk hummed, and then began to spit out a printed report. Her heart thumped. Was it the information from the detective agency? Information that would prove Kimberlee an unfit mother and lay the groundwork to get custody of darling Amanda? She ripped the paper from the fax machine.

The library door squeaked open.

"Grandma?" Amanda stood in the doorway, holding Thumper upside down in both arms.

Margaret's head whipped around. She shoved the paper behind her back. "What is it, now?"

Amanda shifted the cat to her shoulder like a baby and patted his back. "I guess Fumper's not hungry. He doesn't want bacon." She dropped him to the floor and wandered out the slider door onto the patio.

"Oh! Okay."

Margaret whisked the paper from behind her back. The words danced across the page as she tried to focus on the tiny print. She opened the desk and pulled out her reading glasses.

Ableman Detective Agency—48 Hour Report.

We have already done a thorough investigation on your granddaughter, Kimberlee Larson Clark. We don't find no grounds to support a claim of unfit mother or for legal grounds to petition the court for the removing of her same minor child, Amanda Jean Larson. Please tell me how you wish us to proceed and move forward.

Tears spilled down Margaret's cheeks. All hopes of taking Amanda from Kimberlee were dashed, and with it, her chance to regain her youth and raise another child...at least legally. Was there another way?

Kimberlee rubbed her forehead. A tingle of a pain threatened to sprout into a full-blown migraine. She blocked the Children's Society from her mind and tried not to consider the questions about Harold. She tried to concentrate on what he was saying as he threw the saddle over her horse's back and tightened the cinch.

"I've picked a saddle with a nice seat for you, Kimberlee, since you're a beginner. I think you'll be more comfortable with this." Harold patted the deep seat on the saddle.

"Thank you, I guess." Kimberlee ran her hand over the tooled leather. "I wouldn't know one saddle from another. They all look the same to me."

She tried to push this morning's *scene* from her mind, but Grandmother's words roared into her head. 'You forget, you're still a guest in my house.' As if she could forget for one minute the last few days since they'd arrived and became *guests* in Grandmother's house. *Ha!* Guests implied vacation. Vacation implied fun, not like having a continuous pitchfork in the rump from the devil's spawn. As she stroked the horse's nose, the image of Grandmother's face popped into her head. The resemblance was uncanny. A smile twitched her lips. *Shame on me.*

Harold laid the saddle blanket across his mount. He glanced over toward Brett, working at saddling the third horse. "You doing okay over there, Mr. Brett?"

Brett nodded and fumbled with the cinches hanging below the horse's belly. He leaned down and buckled the strap. "How's that?" He beamed at his instructor.

"I wouldn't recommend you get on that horse just yet, son. You haven't pulled the cinch tight enough." Harold unbuckled the strap, gave the Appaloosa a nudge with his knee, and tightened it another notch. "They bloat their stomachs so the straps aren't so tight, you see. If you don't cinch it tight enough, the saddle will slip around and you'll go flying."

Brett's cheeks turned crimson.

Harold laughed. "Never mind. You couldn't have known. You'll do better next time. Okay, little lady, put your foot in the stirrup here and I'll give you a leg up." He took Kimberlee's hand.

She looked down into Harold's eyes as she lifted her new Justin boot into the stirrup. He grinned and put his hand on her thigh, boosting her into the saddle. He was enjoying this way too much. "Oh, I'm up so high." She gripped the saddle horn. "I hope I live long enough to tell about it."

"You'll be okay," Harold said. "Now take the reins in one hand and grip the horse a little with your knees, not too tight or he'll take off running. That's it. Let me adjust the stirrups." He moved the straps, adjusted the buckle and guided her foot back into the stirrup. "That's better. Don't worry. We'll take it easy at first. You won't fall off."

Harold checked Brett's saddle and straps again and then swung onto his mount. The three animals walked out of the paddock toward the gate.

Forty-five minutes, 4000 cactus, 2200 various colored shrubs later, and with her tee shirt clinging to her bosom, Kimberlee turned in her saddle. A light breeze cooled the perspiration on her forehead. How many miles had they come? She shifted her weight and the saddle creaked beneath her bottom. She couldn't even see the ranch house any more. And sooner or later, they'd have to travel the whole distance back to the land of the living. *Is this what you call having fun?*

Harold blathered on, waxing poetic about keeping their backs straight, their heels down and their shoulders back, *blah, blah blah*, until Kimberlee tuned him out.

The heat waves rose up from the ground making the distant hills dance and shimmer. "Oh, look over there, a mama jack rabbit and her baby." The mother rabbit hopped a few feet ahead. "Isn't she cute?

Look at her ears. They're bigger than the rest of her combined." The baby rabbit hopped into a clump of shrubs behind his mother.

Harold turned and looked back. "Keep your eyes open. You're apt to see more than jack rabbits. We might see a coyote or the mountain lion that lives over yonder." He nodded toward the canyon. "We won't be going that way, just in case. We don't want nobody to get *et* up by a mountain lion, now do we?" He chuckled.

Kimberlee looked back toward the canyon, heart picking up a beat, her thoughts on the coyote she heard the other night and Harold's aforementioned mountain lion.

Harold guffawed. "Let's kick them up and give them a little exercise." He clucked to his horse and shook the reins.

Brett and Kimberlee's horses followed close behind, breaking into a trot. Her arms flailed. Her bottom rose and slapped on the *comfortable seat* as her horse clopped behind Harold. "Stop, Harold. Make them stop. *Oww.*"

Harold pulled up on his reins.

Kimberlee's mount slowed to a gentle walk.

Harold turned in the saddle. "Won't make much difference, Miss Kimberlee. Your butt's gonna ache tomorrow whether we walk or trot."

He pointed back toward the bush where they'd seen the rabbits. "Look back there. It's a Harris Hawk, huntin' his dinner."

They twisted in their saddles just as the hawk struck, his talons driving into the baby rabbit's neck. The hawk stood over his victim, glaring at the riders for a moment, as though daring them to challenge his rightful kill. Then he spread his gold and brown wings and lifted off the ground, clutching his prey. The baby rabbit hung from his sharp talons, its long ears flopping with each stroke of the hawk's wings.

Kimberlee's gaze followed the gold and brown hawk as he soared over the prairie, then swooped down and disappeared into the distant canyon. Tears prickled her eyes.

"He's probably taking food to his young." Harold jerked his chin toward the rocky abutment jutting up from the prairie floor. "It's the male what feeds the family while the female tends the young."

Kimberlee blinked. She wasn't going to cry and embarrass herself. She wiped the back of her hand across the arch of her cheekbones.

Harold glanced at her and nudged his horse. "Better keep moving, folks." The riders plodded along in silence. "You've got to understand, miss. It's nature's way. The hawk has to feed its young and some things is just meant to die in the process. It's not a bad thing. Out here, you get used to livin' and dyin'. It's part of the overall scheme of things."

She nodded. Another tear careened down her cheek. She dropped her head to hide her face. Brett handed her his handkerchief. She dabbed at her eyes, leaving black smudges of mascara on the white handkerchief.

He reached over and rubbed her shoulder. "It's okay, sweetheart. I understand."

Her cheeks warmed. She tucked the soiled hankie into the waist of her pants. "I really think I'd like to go back now, Harold."

He nodded and turned the horses toward the ranch. "Sure. You don't have to learn to ride all in one day."

"We should spend some time with Amanda this afternoon," Brett said. "And you'll want to rest a while before the barbecue and the barn dance tonight. That'll be fun, now, won't it?" He gave Kimberlee a big smile.

She nodded and tried to smile. "It was just…the little rabbit…" She sighed. Her mouth clamped into a firm line. That's how Grandmother made her feel this morning. *Just like that little rabbit…* She'd avoided the old crab-apple at lunch and they hadn't spoken since.

Dorian graciously agreed to skip the riding lesson and stay behind to help Grandmother when she insisted they go through with the barn dance and barbecue in spite of the news of Wilbur's betrayal.

Kimberlee wiped her face again with the soiled hankie, squared her shoulders and faced the path back toward the ranch house. What did Harold say? 'Some things is meant to die in the process…'

A tombstone appeared up ahead, off to the right, cold and grey concrete in the shape of a cross casting a thin shadow across the sand. The horses plodded closer. *Whose name was carved on the front?* Her eyes squinted, trying to bring the words into view. Odd they hadn't noticed it on the way out.

Heat waves quivered in front of the gravestone, blurring the name. She leaned forward, trying to bring the words into focus. As suddenly as the image had appeared, it was gone, leaving only sand where it had stood moments ago. A chill swept down her spine, as though someone had stepped on her grave. Had she imagined it or was it an omen? Were Harold's words a warning? Like the baby rabbit, they were all victims trapped by circumstances beyond their control. And some things is meant to die…

Chapter Twenty-One

nly a few more hours and it would all be over. Wilbur's hand shook as he gripped the steering wheel of his restored 1945 Jeep. Adrenaline rushed through his body at the sight of the package in the passenger seat—the simple explosive device Garcia had built for him in Crystal City. No way was he going to let Harold foul up his plans. It would only take a few minutes to attach the dynamite to Imelda's stove burner. Tomorrow morning, when she turned on the stove, in the little house she and Harold shared, they'd both be toast.

He glanced at his watch. 8:00 P.M. All the guests and the family should be at the barn dance by now. They'd be too busy partying to get in his way. First, he'd install the bomb in Imelda's kitchen and then… deal with the old lady. With the music in the barn, no one would be the wiser.

Everyone in town had heard the story he told about his plans. "What a shame I'll have to skip Mrs. Lassiter's shindig. I'll be out of town. I've got business in Crystal City Thursday and I'm planning to stay overnight."

Wilber laughed. This afternoon, his arrival at the Crystal City motel was memorable. The fat chick at the registration desk had squirmed like a puppy when he complimented her eyes. *Pa-leez!* He'd taken his overnight case up to his room and then sneaked out the back door. Tomorrow morning, he'd make another fuss over the clerk when he checked out. If he was questioned about Harold and Imelda's *horrible accident,* the motel clerk would give him an alibi. Perfect. He'd planned it right down to the last gnat's eyebrow.

Overhead, the darkening sunset painted a canopy of purple and red across the horizon, a typical Texas summer evening. His heart thumped. Perspiration dotted his forehead as he approached the ranch across the prairie from the rear. His Jeep circled behind the ranch house. "You can do it, Wilbur." His words sounded hollow in the car.

Wilbur parked his Jeep about a quarter mile from the barn and checked his watch again. 8:25 P.M. He stuffed a pair of black gloves and a nylon stocking into his dark jacket pocket.

He crept forward, moving from one clump of bushes to the next until he came in sight of the barn. Music wafted across the prairie. The party was in full swing, as guests spilled out of the barn, around the stables and into the yard.

Wilbur stretched out full length beneath a manzanita bush. He put his binoculars up and peered at the guests cavorting and romping around like idiots. Juan had some girl backed up against the wall in the shadows. He pulled her blouse away from her throat, kissed her neck, working his way down toward…

Wilbur screwed the binoculars tighter. What the heck? Oh, yeah! His heartbeat picked up its pace when Juan yanked her blouse out of her skirt and fumbled with the buttons, then with one hand busy at her breast, he reached for the hem of her skirt.

Wilbur held his breath. Would he…

Juan pulled the girl further into the shadows. *Huh!* Guess she was okay with it.

Wilbur turned his field glasses toward Star's paddock where a stable boy stood guard against admiring visitors getting too close to the mare and doing something stupid.

He flipped the glasses back to the barn. There stood Harold by the door, laughing and drinking a beer as if he didn't have a care in the world. Little did he know his chance of drawing Social Security was about as good as a Popsicle left in the sun on the sidewalk.

Wilbur swatted another fly. Did the blasted thing think his motionless body was yet another cadaver dumped in the desert for its dining pleasure? His mind segued to Bunker and his threats. If there had ever been any doubts that he'd made the right decision, they disappeared as he remembered the remains of ole Danny's bloated body when they brought him back to town.

He shifted his position, his back stiffening from lying in the sand.

The aroma of spicy barbecued chicken drifted toward the bushes. His stomach growled.

He swallowed and licked his lips. How long had it been since lunch? He should have eaten something before coming out here. Waves of nausea flowed through his belly. From hunger or fear? *No choice. It's them or me.*

Dorian came into view once, her hands flying as she flirted with some cowboy outside the barn door. The cowboy put his arm around her waist and pulled her back onto the dance floor.

From time to time, Brett and Kimberlee passed into his field of vision, laughing.

The kid and several neighborhood brats ran in and out of the barn with the dog at their heels.

As he had figured, Imelda and Margaret must have stayed in the main house. He hadn't thought Margaret could walk to the barn on that bum ankle. Good news for him. He could take care of the old sow while everyone was partying hearty, carrying on like a Roman orgy.

Overhead, stars finally dotted the silky velvet sky. Okay. Time to go. He sneaked across the yard toward Harold's house and around to the dark kitchen. He peeked through the glass and shoved up the kitchen window.

Squeak!

He dropped back into the bushes, crouching, listening, and trying to calm the staccato beat of his heart. Had someone heard?

Nothing.

He hefted his small duffel bag over the sill and dropped to the linoleum floor, paused again to listen, then crept across the kitchen, smiling at his illogical fear. Those fools couldn't hear anything over that blaring crap they called music. It was loud enough to crack the ice in the punch bowl.

A square of moonlight, streaming through the window cast a glow onto the kitchen range. Wilbur lifted off the burners and set them on the counter. Next, he raised the stove lid. *Skreeeek!* He froze, his heart thudding. Moisture beaded his forehead and trickled down his cheek.

Several seconds passed. *You jerk! Get on with it.*

He fingered all the exposed wiring connected to each gas burner, and then pulled the bundle from his duffel—three sticks of dynamite, tightly bound with packing tape affixed to a battery. Placing the bundle precisely in the center of the burners, he attached the wire protruding from the battery to the switch. He wiped his gloved hand across his forehead and swiped it down his pant leg.

It was so simple. Tomorrow morning, when Imelda turned on her burner…*poof*! No more Imelda. No more Harold. No more problems. Perhaps the house would go up in flames and they'd blame the fire on a gas leak. Wilbur smiled. Who would think his problems were so easily solved?

He grit his teeth, lowered the top of the squeaking panel and replaced the burners. A slight movement in the corner sent his heart thudding against his damp shirt. *What was that?*

He pulled Brett's flashlight from his back pocket. His shaking hand cast a jiggling stream of light across the linoleum as he searched. *Who's there?* The light passed over the bottom of the cupboards and the refrigerator. Just past the broom closet, twin glowing orbs burned holes in the darkness, like coals of fire. The luminous globes shifted to the side, as though searching for some unsuspecting victim to drag back to Hell.

Wilbur swallowed a lump in his throat. *Oh, God!* He made the sign of the cross and jerked the light toward the specter.

The marmalade cat hunkered in the corner. She blinked and the glowing orbs slid from full circles to quarter moons.

He stomped his foot. "That blasted cat again! *Scat!*"

Noe-Noe hissed and dashed through the cat door. The plastic flap slapped back and forth, sounding like firecrackers in the dark house.

Wilbur put his shaking hand to his pounding heart and took a deep breath. Committing murder was darn nerve-wracking! He glanced around the kitchen. No trace of his handiwork. He crawled out the kitchen window, slid the window down and crept into the darkness. What a fool he was to let his imagination run away with him like that.

He circled the yard, scrambling behind the shrubs and garden structures as he approached the main house. Two down, one to go.

Wilbur pulled open the screen door on the main house. He held his breath when the hinges squeaked. *Does a guy have to bring his own oil can to a murder?* A smirk pulled at his lips. There, see? If he was able to think up a joke at a time like this, everything was going to work out just fine. Thankfully, the dog Margaret sentenced to the porch was now cavorting around the barn with the guests.

He sneaked through the kitchen, stopping every few steps to listen. Nothing but the sound of drums pounding in the barn. His nerves were under control now, the fright of seeing the cat dismissed. He wasn't really scared. The cat just startled him.

He moved soundlessly up the back stairs. Adrenaline thrummed through his body, invigorating, electrifying, and addictive. Maybe he should advertise in a mercenary magazine. *Killer for Hire. Price Negotiable.* He grinned. Another joke. This wasn't so hard after all.

The hallway was in semi-darkness. A small scented candle burned inside a glass hurricane lamp on the hall table. Wilbur removed the stocking from his pocket and pulled it over his head as he crept down the hall. A light glowed beneath Margaret's bedroom door. She was still awake! But, was she alone? Or was Imelda in there with her? She wasn't in the kitchen.

His fingers tightened around Brett's black metal flashlight. His thoughts raced to the scene tomorrow when Mrs. Lassiter would be found dead with Brett's fingerprints all over the murder weapon. Oh, he'd protest his innocence, alright, saying he'd been at the dance. But proof beyond a reasonable doubt would be lying on the dead woman's floor. They'd say he must have left the barn during the dance. He could have returned, unnoticed, when the deed was done.

Brett might protest, 'Why would I do such a thing?' To guarantee his wife got a share of the million-dollar ranch, and not risk losing it all to Dorian. Maybe they'd ask Wilbur to defend the poor sap. He'd even do it *pro bono*, as a favor to the family. What a shame Brett would be convicted in spite of Wilbur's best effort to win the case. Not!

Wilbur's sticky fingers inside his gloves gripped Margaret's doorknob. Wait! Voices inside the bedroom? Imelda was still in there. He'd have to wait until she left.

Back he went, across the hall into the bathroom, like he had the night he stole Brett's flashlight. He left the door ajar. *Déjà vu*, all over again! This was getting tiresome. The stupid bathroom had become much too familiar.

He peered through the crack in the door, his heart throbbing in his ears. *Get out of there, Imelda! Tomorrow morning is your date with destiny.*

Wilbur sat in the bathroom for twenty minutes before Imelda finally opened Margaret's door. She came out carrying a dinner tray; the rotten little marmalade cat winding around her feet, mewling its disgusting gurgle.

"Alright, little one. Come with me. I'll get you a treat." Imelda hummed as she started down the hall.

The cat paused and looked back over her shoulder toward the bathroom.

Wilbur froze, willing his heart to stop pounding. Did she know he was in here? Would the cat from hell come back and give him away? Wilbur closed his eyes and wished fleas as big as horse flies on all four-legged creatures plaguing him this week.

Imelda's footsteps faded at the foot of the stairs. He gasped for air and blinked to clear the flashing lights from his eyes. How long had he held his breath? *Don't faint now, you fool.*

Margaret's light finally went out. Now, he'd have to wait until she fell asleep. He sat on the toilet seat in the darkness, his buttocks growing numb, going over every detail. He'd smash her head in with Brett's flashlight, run down the back stairs to his Jeep and rush back to the motel.

Brett would be arrested. Surely, that rat, Bunker, should be willing to wait for his money until the reading of the Will and the estate was handed over to the Children's Benefit Program. Perfect! Like clockwork. What could go wrong?

Every few minutes, he checked his watch. She should be asleep by now. He sneaked across the hall, slowly turned the doorknob and pushed open Margaret's door.

Margaret's bed rested in a puddle of moonlight. The lump under the covers must be his unsuspecting victim.

Kimberlee dabbed a tissue across her brow and collapsed onto a bench, breathing hard after a line dance with Brett. Thank God, the band had finally taken a break. She couldn't dance another minute if her life depended on it.

Across the barn, Dorian chatted with neighbor ladies while they filled their plates at the food table.

"Having a good time?" Brett sat between Kimberlee and one of the Eagle Pass detectives whose eyes roamed over Grandmother's guests.

"Best stake-out I've been on for months." The agent popped an olive in his mouth and slicked a cowlick off his forehead. "Wish they were all as much fun. Name's Michaels, by the way." He shook Brett's hand.

"Doesn't look like Wilbur intends to show up tonight." Brett turned and smiled at Kimberlee, sitting on his opposite side. "Can I get you anything to drink, babe?"

She shook her head. "I'm fine." Her gaze passed over the guests until she spotted Amanda, sitting on a bale of hay with Sam stretched out at her feet. Nanny Sally stood nearby, talking to one of the ranchers. Sometimes, Nanny Sally was a pain in the *patooties*, but she did a good job of watching Amanda. Was she going to miss her when they got back to Fern Lake?

"We don't take kindly to folks around here embezzling old ladies and internet solicitation. Who'd of thought a pillar of society like Wilbur Breckenridge would stoop so low." Agent Michaels shook his head and took a long swig from his diet Coke, his eyes still moving around the barn.

Kimberlee eyed his soda. Guess he didn't drink while he's on duty. "It's certainly a shock to Grandmother and the family. The sooner this thing with Wilbur is settled, the sooner we can go home." Kimberlee blew a strand of hair off her forehead. A couple in Western gear danced past as the music started up again.

Thumper snuggled close to Grandmother's side, floating between wakefulness and sleep, comfortable and warm as the music from the barn drifted through the window. Noe-Noe went downstairs with Imelda. He'd stayed to guard Grandmother.

The doorknob creaked. Thumper's eyes popped open, fully awake now! His ears pricked forward. Had Imelda come back? His muscles tensed. His paws hit the floor without a sound. He levitated to the top of the dresser where he had the advantage of height. This time, the calculations were instantaneous and correct. He crouched, his gaze riveted on the doorknob as it slowly turned. Not that he cared much for Grandmother. Her plans for Amanda were despicable, but she *was* family and he had agreed to stay with her.

Fear smell emanated from the figure just outside the door. It wasn't Imelda! The hair on Thumper's back stood on end. He waited.

The door inched open. Wilbur poked his head around the corner. He looked up into Thumper's eyes. "Not *you*, again! Damn, cat! You won't stop me this time." Wilbur shoved the door wide open and rushed across the room. He swung the flashlight, striking the side of Grandmother's temple. Blood gushed from her skull. She lay as still as death.

Thumper shrieked and leaped from the dresser onto the bed and onto Wilbur's back, digging all twenty-four claws into his shoulders. He was too late to save Grandmother, but Wilbur wouldn't get off without the mark of the beast this time.

Wilbur screamed and jerked from side to side, trying to dislodge Thumper's claws. Brett's flashlight fell onto the rug and rolled toward the door.

Thumper sank his fangs deep into the back of Wilbur's neck. His claws sunk deeper into his shoulders.

Wilbur cursed as he reached back, grabbed Thumper around the throat and yanked him loose, tearing a gaping wound in his neck. He cursed and flung Thumper across the room.

Thumper's head whacked the dresser with a *thunk!* Everything went from gray to black.

Chapter Twenty-Two

 *oww!*

Thumper's yowl, like a demon escaping from the fires of hell, shattered the tranquil evening, reverberated across the yard and echoed through the barn, chilling the blood of all who heard.

Kimberlee's head jerked toward the barn door. Her heart skipped a beat. *Thumper! Grandmother?* Not again! Hadn't she learned her lesson last time with the pills?

Conversation ceased as the guests looked anxiously around the barn. Faces paled, feeling something terrible must have occurred, but not knowing what, they scattered like ants, running every which way toward children and spouses.

Agent Michaels jumped up. "Norris! Murphy! Come with me. Everybody! Keep calm and stay in the barn."

"I don't think so." Kimberlee ran toward the bales of hay where Amanda sat with Nanny. "Amanda. Stay with Nanny. We'll be right back."

Brett and Kimberlee raced toward the house. He pulled open the screen door, dashed through the kitchen and toward the back stairs.

Imelda's screams from the second floor echoed down the stairs. "Help. Help. He's killed Missus Lassiter!"

Kimberlee rushed toward the staircase. A crushing pressure pounded across the top of her head. An icy hand clutched her heart. She grasped her forehead and took a quick breath. Not now! She didn't have time for a migraine.

She grabbed the banister and pushed through the pain, placing one foot ahead of the other, slowly ascended the stairs and hurried down the hallway toward Grandmother's bedroom. She stopped in the doorway, each throb of migraine pain matching her pounding heart.

Agent Michaels stood just inside Grandmother's door. "Murphy! Search the house. Norris. Go out and check around the house. Report back in ten minutes. Brett, run to my car and bring back the First Aid kit."

Imelda knelt beside Grandmother's bed, her hand over her eyes. She clutched the crucifix at her throat. "Oh, my God! Missus Lassiter."

Kimberlee gazed in horror around the semi-dark room. The bedcovers lay askew. Blood drenched Grandmother's pillow. Specks of blood clung to the lampshade on the nightstand and spattered across the headboard. *Grandmother! Dead?*

Dorian pushed Kimberlee aside, flicked on the light switch and rushed toward the bed. "Someone. Call 911. We need an ambulance." She yanked a pillowcase off a pillow and wound it around Grandmother's head, staunching the flow of blood. Dorian placed her fingers on Grandmother's jugular vein. "She's still breathing, but just barely."

Kimberlee collapsed into the rocking chair, her arms clasped across her chest. The last time they spoke was in anger. How could this happen? Was it Wilbur! Wait! How could it be? He wasn't at the party tonight, so it couldn't have been him. Maybe a burglar, using the cover of the music to break into the house? That didn't make sense. Why would a burglar come upstairs into her bedroom? Any money would likely have been downstairs in the library. This was a personal attack. Why was she alone? Hadn't Imelda agreed to stay with her?

Questions. Questions. No answers. Why? Why? She clasped her hands and began to pray.

Brett returned with the First Aid kit. He handed it to Dorian.

Agent Michaels strode across the room to where Imelda knelt by the bed, wringing her hands. "Ma'am? Can you tell us what happened?" He pulled out a notebook and a pen.

Imelda shook her head and wiped her eyes with the corner of her apron. "I took Missus Lassiter's tray to the kitchen and I heard the cat…" She turned and searched the room, then pointed a shaking finger toward the dresser. "There! By the dresser!"

All eyes turned toward Thumper. He lay motionless beside the bloody flashlight.

Kimberlee clutched the arm of the chair, unable to move as Brett rushed over and knelt down. He ran his hand over Thumper's head and down his back and then moved his fingers to Thumper's throat. "He's alive. There's blood on his face and feet." Brett tilted Thumper's head, pried his mouth open and leaned closer. "Something here… It looks like a piece of skin."

Kimberlee rose unsteadily and stumbled across the room. She knelt beside Thumper. "Oh, dear God, don't let him die."

Michaels bent down. He pulled on rubber gloves, picked the skin from Thumper's teeth with tweezers and placed it in an evidence bag. "Looks like the cat took a bite out of the guy." He used a cotton ball to swab the blood on Thumper's feet and dropped it into another plastic bag. "This should be enough to identify the attacker. From the blood and the tissue, looks like the guy's going to have some teeth marks and scratches and a whole lot of explaining to do."

The agent replaced the evidence bags in his kit. He leaned down and examined the bloody flashlight. "Here's the weapon," he said, gesturing to Brett. "You can see blood and hair. I'll bag it for evidence."

Brett gasped. "That looks like my flashlight. How did it get…?"

Kimberlee's heart seized. Brett! That wasn't possible. He was in the barn with everyone.

The agent grabbed Brett's arm. "Let me see your hands and arms."

Brett's face turned chalky-white. He laid Thumper down on the floor, stood and held out his arms. "You're not serious. You can't possibly think I had something to do with this."

The icy tone in his voice chilled Kimberlee's heart. She rushed to Brett. "Honey. He doesn't know you. None of us think…"

Agent Michaels turned Brett's hands from front to back and pushed up his sleeves.

Brett's arms had no sign of scratches.

Michaels checked both sides of Brett's head and neck. "Sorry, sir. No hard feelings. You did admit the flashlight was yours."

Brett nodded and shoved his shirtsleeves down over his arms. "I understand." He stooped and gathered Thumper in his arms. "Can I take him now, or will you need to examine him further?"

"We've got enough to process DNA from these." He nodded toward the evidence bags. "Go ahead and take your cat."

Kimberlee stood and stroked Thumper's head. "Is he going to be okay?" Oh, why had they ever brought him here? *Please, God, let him be alright.*

Brett shrugged and shook his head. "Let's take him downstairs and clean him up. If he doesn't come around in a few minutes, we'll find a vet."

"You go ahead." Kimberlee turned toward the bed. "I'll stay here with Grandmother. I'll be down in a few minutes."

Brett nodded and left with Thumper cradled in his arms.

Kimberlee went over to Grandmother's bed, knelt and took her hand.

Humph!

Kimberlee looked up. Who was there?

Harold stomped into the bedroom, his face pale, his mouth drawn into a straight line. He strode to Imelda's side, pulled his handkerchief from his pocket and handed it to her. "Here, honey. They told me what happened downstairs." The furrows deepened in his brow.

Imelda dabbed her eyes and wadded the hankie into a ball. "Oh, Harold." She turned toward Agent Michaels. "I must tell you..." She looked from his face to Harold's. "I know who's responsible for this."

Kimberlee's mouth dropped open.

Harold's face turned a lighter shade of gray. "Imelda," he stammered, "Do you...do you know what you're saying?"

She tipped up her face, smiled and reached for his hand. "Yes, Harold. We can't hide the truth anymore."

Harold ducked his head and gripped her hand. "Shouldn't we talk about this? You know what it means. We could—"

"For God's sake, woman, speak up." Michaels stepped closer to Imelda. "If you have information about the attacker, tell us. Why didn't you say something sooner? Who's responsible?"

Dorian pushed Agent Michaels away. "You're frightening her. Perhaps we should take her downstairs..." She gestured toward the bed where Grandmother lay, her head swathed in the bloody pillowcase. "...away from this. There's nothing we can do here. The ambulance will be here any minute. We'll just be in the way." She took Imelda's hand, pulled her to her feet and propelled her toward the hall.

Harold followed.

Agent Michaels nodded and turned to his men, just walking through the bedroom door. "Norris? Murphy? Any luck?"

Officer Norris shook his head. "I've checked all around the house and the barn. But, there're so many people. The guy could have mingled with the crowd. What do you want me to do?"

"Come with me down to the library. Murphy, stay here with Mrs. Lassiter." He stepped toward the door.

Kimberlee followed Agent Michaels down the stairs and into the library where Dorian had seated Imelda on the sofa. "I'll make some coffee. Kimberlee, will you stay?" Dorian met Kimberlee's eyes, nodded toward Imelda and left the library.

Harold paced the floor. He stopped beside the couch, his face a mask of whatever turmoil was in his heart. Was he sad that his employer had been attacked, or feeling guilty for attacking her? Whatever Imelda had to say could change the course of his life forever and he didn't look too pleased with the possibilities. Harold shoved his hands in his pockets.

Kimberlee sat beside Imelda and took her hand.

Agent Michaels stood nearby, with a pen poised over his notebook.

"Now, take your time, Imelda," Michaels said. "Who attacked Mrs. Lassiter? Start at the beginning."

Harold stepped in front of the sofa, between her and Michaels. "She doesn't know what she's talking about. Leave her out of it." He reached for the officer's arm. "I'll tell you what you need to know. She didn't have anything to do with it." The color in his face took on a shade like Amanda's dried out Play Dough. His hand fell away from the agent's arm and dropped to his side.

Kimberlee drew in her breath. "Did you know this would happen, Harold? Could you have prevented it?"

Harold ran his hands over his eyes. "I should have said something, but I didn't think…"

Agent Michaels glanced between Imelda and Harold. "I think we better hear what Imelda has to say before we go any further. We may have our attacker already.

"Imelda, you have the right to remain silent. Anything you say…" He proceeded to read Imelda her rights.

"Imelda?" Kimberlee pressed her thumbs to her throbbing temple. "Tell us what you know about this." Would the hand grenades never stop coming in this purgatory?

Imelda took a deep breath and gulped back tears. Her gaze dropped to her lap. Then, the words burst out like a dam flooding the valley. "Harold didn't want anything to do with it. He told me… He promised he wouldn't go through with it. He promised to give up the business with The Children's Program."

Agent Michaels exchanged startled glances with Kimberlee. "Go on, Imelda. Was Harold mixed up with Wilbur's Children's Program?"

"Imelda, for God's sake, shut up. Let me handle this. Leave her alone. I'm the one you should be talking to." Harold shook Imelda's shoulder.

She burst into tears.

Agent Norris pulled handcuffs from his belt and placed his hand on Harold's arm. "We've got a lot of questions for you, too. Harold

Marlowe, you have the right to remain silent...”

Dorian stood in the doorway with a tray, coffeepot and cups. “Harold! Before you say another word, you should speak to an attorney.” She set the tray on the table, though no one reached for a cup. With everyone's nerves on edge, coffee was the last thing on their minds.

“He's not under arrest yet, but I've read both of them their rights.” Agent Norris's gaze traveled up and down Harold's face. “Now, are you and Imelda willing to go downtown and answer questions, or should we take you in handcuffs?”

Harold glanced at Imelda, the look in his eyes like an antelope run to ground, waiting for the final snap of the predator's jaws. “There's no need for that. We'll come with you and answer all your questions.” He reached down and helped Imelda up from the couch. “Come, dear.”

Kimberlee stood and hugged Imelda. “I...I don't know what to say.”

Agent Norris took Harold's arm and marched out the door. Agent Michaels walked beside Imelda, his hand on her arm.

The shriek of the ambulance grew louder until it screeched to a stop by the front lawn. The silence after the wailing siren was almost palpable.

“Dorian. Will you run to the barn and tell Nanny to keep Amanda away from the house. I don't want her to see them taking Grandmother out like this.”

“I'll make sure she keeps her out there until the ambulance is gone.”

“I need to find Brett and check on Thumper.”

“Go...go...tend to Thumper. I'll check on Amanda and then follow the ambulance into town. I'll call you as soon as I have any word.”

Kimberlee hurried down the hall and passed the paramedics carrying a gurney, rushing up the stairs.

She pushed through the swinging door into the kitchen. Thumper lay hunkered under a towel on Brett's lap. “Oh, my poor baby.” She knelt beside Brett's chair. "Why did I ever bring you to this terrible place? Why didn't I listen to Jack and leave you home with him?"

Thumper lifted his head. Kimberlee. He tried to concentrate on her voice, but everything looked out of focus and she sounded far away, dulled by the ringing in his ears.

He swallowed. A string of drool dripped from his mouth onto the towel in Brett's lap.

Noe-Noe paced the kitchen, howling and switching her tail, her gaze locked on Thumper. *What was she saying?* It was so hard to understand.

"*It's my fault,*" Noe-Noe yowled. "*Grandmother is my person. I should have protected her. I shouldn't have gone downstairs with Imelda. I'm such a pig, always begging for snacks. Pig, pig, pig! Now Grandmother's dead, Thumper's going to die and it's my fault! I'll be an orphan and an old maid all in the same night.*"

Thumper focused on her twitching ears and whiskers. Why was she so distraught? If he could just control his quivering head, things would make sense. "*Shh-nah-ju-foot. Ish-nor-flut.*" That hadn't come out right. He shook his head, trying to clear his fuzzy thoughts. "*Owh. Hurtz. I shed ish nah yer… Oww.*"

Noe-Noe still had three heads, none clearly in focus. He tried again to comfort her. "*Ish not yer fault. It coulda happen ta anyone. You shed so yersef.*"

Noe-Noe ran to Brett's side and put her paw on his knee. "*Is he alive?*"

"I think Thumper's going to be okay." Brett patted Noe-Noe's foot. "Listen. He's trying to tell us something."

Thumper stared into Kimberlee's three blurred faces and three Bretts, now coming together and settling down into two each, then each had one clear face. He twisted in the towel and began to lick his shoulder. He was so embarrassed. He couldn't even carry on a coherent conversation with *mi amour*.

"Look, he's grooming," Kimberlee said. "That's always a good sign."

Brett rubbed the top of Thumper's head. "I can still feel the lump, but I think the swelling is going down a little. I don't think we need to vet him."

"How could we have prevented this? We both thought Grandmother might be in danger when Wilbur learned about her plan to change her will." Kimberlee reached over and stroked Thumper's back. Thumper turned and licked the top of her hand.

"Short of posting a guard outside her bedroom, I don't think there's much we could have done. I thought she'd be okay with all of us staying in the house. We gave the police a head's up about Wilbur. And Imelda agreed to stay with her while we were at the party." Brett glanced out the kitchen window toward the yard where guests were headed toward their cars. Apparently, the news of Grandmother's attack had spoiled the holiday spirit and the party was over. "What else could we have done?"

"You think it was Wilbur? You don't think Harold did it? You heard Imelda."

Thumper lifted his head and stared into Brett's face. *It was Wilbur. I took a chunk out of his neck. You'll see when you catch him.*

"Well, yeah, I think it was Wilbur." Brett wrapped the towel tighter around Thumper's shoulders. "The police will know for sure with the DNA test. Thumper bit him. But, that's going to take a few days. It's not like on TV when they do it during a half-hour program."

Thumper glanced at Noe-Noe. *Told ya. Brett is brighter than the average guy.* Kimberlee twisted her hankie. "I wish Grandmother never sent the letter. I don't want her stupid horse ranch. I wish we never came to this horrible place." She dabbed her eyes.

"I know. We'll leave as soon as we can. It's probably going to take several days to sort things out. At this point, we don't even know if your grandmother's going to make it. I know it's tough, hon…" Brett stroked Kimberlee's hair and kissed her forehead. "We'll just have to take it a day at a time."

Thumper eased off Brett's lap, landing with a thud beside Noe-Noe. "*Oww…uh… I mean…come on, Noe-Noe, let's go outside. I need a bit of fresh air.* Thumper weaved a little as they jumped through the little cat door and waddled out to the back porch.

"Was it really Wilbur?" Noe-Noe rubbed Thumper's shoulder.

"He had a stocking on his head. After I bit him, he pulled it off. It was Wilbur, alright."

"I can't believe the old turkey-bait would do it. Tell me everything."

"He hit Grandmother before I could get to him. I scratched and bit him good. Then he pitched me across the room. That's all I remember."

Noe-Noe bumped against his head. She lowered her eyes. "You're my hero."

"*Oww…* I mean… Oh, it was nothing. I couldn't stop him, could I?"

The dust in the driveway rose as the police car followed the ambulance beyond the stone fences to the county road. The whine of the sirens split the night and faded into the distance as the vehicles raced toward town.

Chapter Twenty-Three

agged breaths, his chest heaving and heart pounding, Wilbur stumbled through the darkness toward his Jeep. He felt as though his heart would explode through his chest. The scratches on his ears stung and the back of his neck throbbed like fire where Thumper's claws and teeth had left their mark. He reached up, touched his neck and pulled his fingers away, sticky with blood. Curse the beast that alerted the family before he could finish the job.

His plans—all in shambles. His blood was all over the crime scene, thanks to the wretched cat. It wouldn't take the authorities long to connect the dots. His carefully planned alibi in Crystal Springs wouldn't hold water once the blood was tested for DNA.

No one was supposed to find Mrs. Lassiter's body until tomorrow. Imelda and Harold were supposed to be dead and unable to spill anything about the Children's Program. Eventually, when they read Margaret's will, the Children's Program would inherit the ranch and he was the Program. At least his plan for Harold and Imelda was still in place. Their date with destiny still awaited them tomorrow morning. Unfortunately, it might be too late. Now that the cat was literally out of the bag, Harold would sing like a little bird. A plague on all cats, especially the big black and white one.

Wilbur clenched his fists and grit his teeth. He hoped the damn thing broke its neck when it hit the dresser. He smiled at the thought and stumbled on through the darkness.

Just ahead, a shadow melted into his 1945 Jeep. A warm glow flowed through his chest at the sight. Its familiar outline eased some of his despair, like coming home to a warm fire and an easy chair.

His cheeks bent in a smile, but disappeared when another stab of pain surged through the back of his neck.

Now, what to do? Should he go back to the motel and try to tough it out? No, the blood in the bedroom would prove he was the attacker when they did a DNA test. How long would that take? He probably had a day. Maybe two. Not long enough for the bite to heal. Maybe he should grab his passport and head for the border. If Harold talked, which was likely, the cops might come around asking questions as early as tomorrow. The hope of Mrs. Lassiter's bequest to the Children's Benefit Program was down the drain. He should have chucked the whole thing before he got in so deep with the loan shark. He could have cashed what was left of his mutual funds and headed for the Cayman Islands. Harold was right, after all. Why hadn't he listened? Now look at the mess he was in. He had no choice. He had to leave the country.

He flung himself through the open door into the driver's seat, grabbed the steering wheel, turned the key and pressed the starter with his foot. There was a click as the solenoid tried to engage the flywheel, but didn't have enough power to turn over the motor. He pressed it again. Expletives burst from his lips. There was another click and then silence. The battery was completely dead. Vintage cars were beautiful, but, oh, so unpredictable.

Wilbur slammed the heel of his hand into the steering wheel. Now what? He was half a mile from the ranch house and fifteen miles from Crystal City and the only shred of alibi that might buy him a few hours to plan his get-away. He ground his fists into his eyes and fought back the sting. *Must have got some dust in my eyes walking across the sand...*

Wait. The Mexico border was only four miles away.

Even if he could get the Jeep started, how would that work? The authorities were likely at the border watching for him. Oh, look there. Here comes the only 1945 restored Jeep in the state of Texas. Do you think its Wilbur Breckenridge, the guy with no alibi, a chomp out of the back of his neck and blood all over his clothes? Do you think?

Forget the Jeep. It wouldn't start, anyway.

How screwed could a guy get? He might just as well confess and get it over with.

Wilbur stared across the dark desert. *What am I going to do?* He pulled out his cell phone. "Now, all I need is a signal." He held his breath and breathed a sigh of relief when two bars lit up. He punched several keys and crossed his fingers as it rang. Thanks to his unique legal maneuvering, he'd kept Rodriquez out of jail several months ago. The scumbag never paid the bill. Pay-back time.

"Hello?"

"Hello, Rodriquez. Wilbur. Look, I've just got a minute. You know that marker you owe me for getting you off that rape charge?"

"Yeah? So, what of it?" Rodriquez sounded leery.

"I need some things from my office and I can't get back into Eagle Pass."

"What I gotta do to square the score?"

"Bust into my office down town. There's a strongbox inside a locked cabinet behind my desk. Break it open and bring me my passport and all the cash inside. Then, torch the place on your way out and—"

"Hold on, Wilbur. That's arson. I could do plenty of time if I'm caught. I don't owe you that much. Something like that is gonna cost you. "

"Okay. Okay. I'll make it worth your while. Say… $1500? And don't get any ideas about crossing me and stealing the strongbox. Don't forget, I know things that can put you away—"

"Okay, but $2000 is more like it, considering the risk I'm taking. Just the strong box? And torch the place. Where and when do you want to meet?"

"Take some of the money and rent a boat and meet me…say… about 7:00 A.M. tomorrow morning. You know the spot. On the Rio Grande, near the rocks at the end of the canyon on the Lassiter ranch. You can drop me off in Piedras Negras. If you see any of my jackets or clothes in the office, bring those too."

"Okay, tomorrow morning. 7:00 A.M. And you agreed on $2000

bucks. By the way, Wilbur, when this is done, we're square. Don't ever call me again."

"I'm counting on you. Don't let me down." Wilbur clicked off the phone, scrunched down in the seat and tightened his light jacket around his shoulders. He pulled a bottle of water from a Piggley Wiggley grocery bag and drank from it. A lottery ticket fell from the bag to the floor. He glanced at it. *With my luck, I probably hit the jackpot.* He put his hand to the back of his neck. "Damn cat."

Chapter Twenty-Four

ncomfortable and cold, Wilbur shivered and drew his legs into the fetal position. The temperature had dropped overnight to an uncomfortable forty-five degrees.

He lifted his head to the chirps and hums of birds and other critters. It sounded like a religious serenade worshiping the coming of dawn. He shifted his legs and whacked his knee against the gear shift knob. His eyes popped open and an oath cascaded from his lips. He rubbed his eyes and pulled his knees tighter to his body. *What time is it?*

Pinpricks of stars still held court across the early morning sky.

Wilbur glanced at the luminous dial on his Rolex. 4:50 A.M. Nearly dawn. He covered his mouth, yawned and blinked to clear his vision as he stared through the front windshield. The ragged edges of the boulder loomed beside his Jeep, just visible in the early morning light. *What the...* Why was he sitting in the middle of the desert? Last night's events crashed through his brain. He drew a breath. The cold air snapped against his teeth. Nausea grabbed his belly. *My God, I killed her. I really did it.* Now, what was he going to do?

He closed his eyes against the memory of Mrs. Lassiter's blood-soaked head. A twinge of pain pulsed through the back of his neck. He reached up and pulled away his fingers, speckled with dried blood. With a grimace, he wiped his hand on his pants. Now, all he needed was Cat Bite Fever.

His eyes squinted as he peered out the open door. Cactus and rocks began to separate themselves from the darkness, becoming darker lumps in the surrounding terrain. Better get moving. Only three hours until he was to meet Rodriquez. If he showed up at all... What Rodriquez would do when he opened the moneybox was anybody's guess.

It was a mighty big temptation to a dishonest man, giving him access to the strongbox. Rodriquez might take the money, torch the place and take off. He had to take the chance. He had no choice. With the evidence in the old lady's bedroom, it was a cinch he'd be identified as the killer before the bites on his neck could heal.

Wilbur's heart leaped. Maybe the Jeep would start this morning! He turned the key, hit the starter and crossed his fingers. *Click. Click.*

Nothing.

Wilbur cursed and drained the water from the bottle. He stepped out of the Jeep and pulled his rifle from its scabbard by the front fender. He slammed the bolt back and then forward, chambering a round and set the safety. At the sound of the sharp metallic clank, all the desert critters went silent. The rifle was loaded and functional. With the binoculars around his neck, the box of shells in his jacket pocket and his flashlight tucked in his waistband, he turned back for one last look at his baby.

Wilbur caressed the fender and gave it a pat. "Good-bye, old friend. Guess this is where we part company." He set his mouth in a firm line and trudged across the prairie toward the canyon.

Several hours later, the sharp outline of the canyon walls loomed ahead. At last, the road leading down into the canyon came into view. Wilbur paused to wipe the sweat from his face and checked his watch. 6:28 A.M. Hiking through sand across the desert had taken longer than he thought.

Wilbur pulled up his binoculars and scanned the terrain toward the Rio Grande. There. Just at the water's edge, he was able to make out the outline of a boat. Rodriquez! He was early. Probably counting the money in the strongbox and worrying that the police might show up any minute. He should have told him 8:00 A.M.

No time to walk around by the road that led down into the canyon. He'd have to climb down the rock face directly into the canyon and then run the rest of the way if he was to make it by 7:00 A.M. Rodriquez wasn't likely to wait much past the appointed hour. Maybe he could reach him on the cell phone this morning. He checked his phone. No reception.

Wilbur perused the edge of the canyon. Where was the easiest place to traverse the wall? About 200 yards to the west, it was possible. Climbing anywhere along the rock face was dangerous, but if he had any hope of connecting with Rodriquez and making his get-away, he'd have to risk it.

Chapter Twenty-Five

mages of her home, Fern Lake and her bookstore melted, driven from her dream by the drone of a tractor somewhere in the distance. Kimberlee sighed and opened her eyes. Morning? Already? Myriads of stars still twinkled in the predawn sky.

She reached for Brett. Her hand fell on his cold pillow. She rubbed her eyes, trying to read the clock on the dresser. 5:30 A.M. Where was Brett? A little trill of worry coursed through her chest. She forced herself to take a deep breath. He's either in the shower down the hall or already out checking on the stable hands. The men must be concerned, knowing the police had taken Harold in for questioning last night. *Of course, that's where he is*. Brett would want to respond to the men's concerns.

She climbed from the bed, dressed quickly and hurried downstairs and into the kitchen. "Dorian! You're up early. Something smells good."

"Thought I'd make waffles. I didn't know when you and Brett would be up. I've sent a tray up with Nanny for her and Amanda. The three of us need to make some decisions about Grandmother. I didn't think you'd want Amanda involved in that discussion."

Kimberlee poured a cup of coffee, sat at the table and wrapped both hands around the warm cup.

Dorian slapped a hot waffle onto a plate in front of her.

"Thanks. Have you seen Brett?" Kimberlee spread butter across the waffle and poured syrup over the top.

"He went out to the barn. He said he'd just be a few minutes."

Kimberlee's knife and fork clanked against the china. She looked up as Brett opened the screen and stepped inside. "What did the men have to say about Harold and last night's events?"

Brett shook his head. "They knew the police took Harold and Imelda into custody. They aren't home yet. Guess that means they were held all night." Brett wiped his feet on the mat. He rubbed his hands against the morning chill. "Apparently Harold's supporters shut down the gossip around the potbelly stove. One of the more vocal hands was sporting a black eye. He claimed he ran into a door, but I have a feeling he was bad-mouthing Harold and someone set him straight." Brett pulled out a chair and sat at the table.

Kimberlee finished the last bite and carried her plate to the sink. "Do you want something to eat?"

Dorian poured more batter into the waffle iron and closed the lid. "I'll have this ready in a minute, Brett. Do you want eggs?" She reached for the refrigerator door.

"No thanks. Waffle's fine."

"So, what else did you find out?" Kimberlee brought Brett a cup of coffee and leaned against the kitchen counter.

"It seems Grandmother always treated the men well, providing barbecues and dances several times a year. She even hired a Mariachi band and let them invite their wives and girlfriends to a dance on the Fourth of July. And, they each got a fat turkey at Christmas.

"Everyone agreed Harold was firm but fair. He'd even turned a blind eye when *relatives* came over the border to *visit.* He'd help them find work at neighboring farms."

Kimberlee chuckled. "I don't suppose having the Rio Grande River touch the edge of Grandmother's property in the canyon was just a coincidence." She poured another cup of coffee, opened the refrigerator and peered inside.

Dorian slid a hot waffle onto Brett's plate. "Dr. Turner called a while ago. He said Grandmother is conscious and he expects a full recovery. They've transferred her out of Intensive Care to the Surgery Ward. She can have visitors later today. She'll probably need physical therapy."

Kimberlee closed the refrigerator. "We're out of cream. Someone's going to have to do a grocery run." She glanced around the kitchen.

Dorian pulled a tablet, a pencil and the phone book from the drawer. "We've got a lot to do. Let's make a list. What's first?" She tossed the pencil on the table and sat.

Kimberlee paced the floor, rubbing her forehead. "Should we call Wilbur for some legal advice?" The pressure in her head was like a helium balloon, about to burst. Would this nightmare never end? How she wished to be back in her bookstore with fourteen boxes of best sellers to open and a line of people pounding on the door, screaming, 'Open, open, open!'

Brett pushed his coffee cup to the side of the table. "Kimberlee, honey. You've got to be kidding. Who do you think attacked Grandmother?"

Kimberlee's cheeks chilled. "I…I…know we thought it might be Wilbur…but I guess I just didn't want to believe it." She sighed, sat at the table and folded her hands. "Imelda was alone in the house with—"

"Surely you don't think it was Imelda." Dorian leaned across the table.

"No. But, Imelda did say Harold was involved…somehow."

Brett shrugged. "Wilbur had motive and he wasn't at the dance, so that gave him opportunity. He must have heard about the attack by now. It's all over the news. If he was innocent, don't you think he would have come by this morning or called? No one's heard from him."

"Maybe he doesn't know yet… We should consider every possibility." Kimberlee reached across the table and pulled Dorian's pencil and paper toward her.

"We'll know soon enough. There's an APB on him about the Children's Society. And we have blood and skin from the attacker. They'll have the DNA results soon, if they rush it." Dorian ran her hands through her ponytail and readjusted the rubber band.

Kimberlee drew circles on the sheet of paper. Her head swirled, like the circles on the page. Despite an overwhelming desire to run for the airport, they were stuck here until Grandmother had a support system in place.

"Dorian, will you call the police headquarters and find out Harold's status?" Brett stood and paced the kitchen. "If they're going to hold him, we'll need a new stable master. Someone has to be in charge." The lines in his forehead deepened. "The sooner things are settled, the sooner we can get the heck out of Texas. What's next?"

Kimberlee wrote. *Stable master.*

"Someone's going to have to be an administrator, since Grandmother's not able to handle her affairs for a while." Dorian shrugged. "The men have to be paid along with everyday ranch expenses. Someone needs to have access to her bank account."

"But, who? I don't want to stay in Texas to take care of this stuff." Tears stung Kimberlee's eyes. "I want to go home!"

Brett patted her hand. "We need an attorney to help sort out this mess." He drummed his fingers on the table. "I'll check Harold's office and see if there's any money to pay the men. I'll have the men choose a foreman, so at least there's someone in charge to make ranch decisions."

Hire new attorney.

"You girls go through Grandmother's purse and search the library." Brett stood and glanced at his watch. "It's nearly 7:00 A.M. Look for anything that might be an insurance policy, maybe an address book to notify any friends and family we're not aware of. Let's meet back here about 8:30 A.M. and we'll compare notes."

The three scattered like pigeons from a telephone wire. Kimberlee—to search through Grandmother's library. Brett—to the barn to rifle Harold's desk. Dorian stepped onto the patio and called the police department to check on Harold and Imelda's legal status.

The desk in the library was littered with envelopes, stacks of papers and a clutter of paperclips, pencils and a key ring. Kimberlee looked up when Dorian came through the door with Sam at her heels. "What did you find out?" She swiveled the desk chair around to face Dorian. "Are they holding Harold?"

Dorian collapsed onto the sofa and drew her legs under her. Sam flopped down beside the sofa. "Harold confessed to being a partner in Wilbur's Children's Society scam. They arrested him on internet fraud charges. They're questioning him as a person of interest for Grandmother's attack. He claims he wasn't involved. In fact, Imelda claims that Harold was trying to stop Wilbur from going through with it. Of course, if that's the case, he should have notified the police. Wilbur had him convinced he'd changed his mind. Things aren't looking too good for Harold right now.

"They shut down the Children's Benefit headquarters in Eagle Pass and questioned the bookkeeper. Apparently, Maria thought everything was above board. She's not the sharpest tool in the pump house."

"Brett and I got the same impression."

"Wait. I saved the best for last. Wilbur's office mysteriously burned to the ground during the night, so a lot of the documents are gone, but they probably have enough just from the website and Grandmother's records. The fire looks like arson, of course. No surprise. They've extended the APB statewide. Wilbur's wanted for internet fraud, arson, as well as a person of interest regarding attempted murder. He'll be going away for a *looooong* time when they catch up with him."

"So, they got the DNA results back? They're sure it was Wilbur?"

"Not yet. So far, until the DNA comes back, he's just a person of interest. Don't worry, honey, they'll catch him. Thumper's evidence will see to that."

Kimberlee jumped as the phone rang on the desk. She grabbed the receiver. "Hello? Imelda? Are you alright? We've been so worried about you." She nodded to Dorian, mouthed the word, *Imelda*, and then punched the speaker button.

"I'm okay. They charged me as an accessory on the internet charge, but my sister posted bail. Oh, Miss Kimberlee. I am so ashamed. It was wrong to take Missus Lassiter's money, but please believe me. We would never hurt Missus Lassiter. Harold tried to stop Wilbur. He thought everything was going to be alright. We didn't know…"

"I believe you, Imelda. I'm so sorry. What are you going to do now?"

"They're moving Harold to Dallas for the arraignment. My sister lives near there. She has asked me to stay with her, so I can be near Harold. My arraignment will probably be next month." Imelda honked into the phone, blowing her nose. "Is Missus Lassiter going to get well?"

"The doctor says he thinks she will be okay, but it will take time. You take care of yourself, okay? And don't worry." Kimberlee picked up a pen and drew boxes on a paper.

"I must go now," Imelda sobbed. "My bus is leaving."

"Imelda, wait. Did Grandmother keep any money in the house? The men need to be paid tomorrow."

"Please deposit $1.80 for another three minutes," the operator interrupted.

"Oh, yes. In Missus Lassiter's desk, there is a secret compartment where she keeps—"

The phone went dead.

"Hello? Imelda?" Kimberlee hung up the phone. She sighed and turned to Dorian. "Well, you heard... She got cut off." She stared out the window at the paddock where Star leaned over the fence, dozing in the sun. What a lucky horse. Nothing to worry about but eating and sleeping and winning blue ribbons... It was a sad day when you wished you were a horse instead of...

Dorian nodded and lay down on the sofa, pulling a pillow under her head. Dark circles under her eyes professed a sleepless night and the strain they'd all been under for the last several days. She put her hand over her puffy eyes.

Sam laid his head across her legs. Dorian reached down and stroked his ears.

Kimberlee leaned toward the sofa. "Are you okay? You look really tired. You didn't get home from the hospital till all hours last night."

"I didn't sleep very well after I got home. This has all been such a nightmare."

Kimberlee swiveled back toward the desk "We need to search this desk." She pulled on the bottom, left drawer. "It's locked. We'll have to force it."

Dorian stood and pulled a knife from her pocket. "Knew this would come in handy one day. Lead on, Sherlock. I'm right behind you." She wielded the pocketknife toward the desk. "I hate doing this, but I guess we don't have any choice." Dorian moved a stack of papers from the side of the desk to better reach the left bottom drawer. "Grandmother wasn't the neatest person, was she?"

Kimberlee glanced nervously around the library, feeling like a thief. As if the library police were going to burst in any minute.

Dorian wiggled the pocketknife in the lock. *Click.* "That does it." She pulled it open. "Here it is. Now, where would you hide a secret compartment? Got it." The panel in the back of a cubicle slid back revealing a stack of bills inside. "*Jeeze*, look at this." Dorian began counting bills, stacking them up in piles of $100 each. She looked up, meeting Kimberlee's eyes. "There's over $8,000 here!"

With the sun just tinting the horizon, Sitka, the mountain lion, awoke. Her stomach rumbled. She had eaten the last bit of deer she brought down several days ago. With the twilight hour at hand, best to get about this morning's business. She scrambled from her den onto the rock and tilted an ear to the east where tumbling rocks rumbled. Some creature was fairly close by. Her mother's instinct surged. She paced in front of her den, her ears laid back. More rocks rumbled.

She growled and took a few steps. One of the cubs yelped. She turned back, torn between protecting her cubs and confronting the disturbing sounds.

The wind shifted and the distinct smell of *man* drifted by. Her mood flashed from confusion to fury. The man was too near her babies. Saliva dripped from her mouth as her brain went into *stalk-kill* mode.

The man's curses drifted to Sitka's ears. The final insult. With a rush of indignation, she loped across the short distance toward the canyon.

At the rim of the canyon wall, she crouched and peered over the edge. The man-creature clung to the rocks just below. Dirt and shale clattered beneath his feet as he slid down between the rocks. The rifle on his back clanked against the stones.

He grunted and turned to face the wall, dug his fingers into the dirt, and reached his foot down for another toehold.

The smell of sweat coursed upward, stinging Sitka's nose. Her shoulder muscles rippled as she prepared to pounce. Anxiety for her babies, her grumbling stomach, and the stink of man—all that was wrong in Sitka's world, there within her grasp.

The man looked up, terror in his eyes. Sweat poured down his forehead, his face a muddy grey. Ragged breaths escaped his chest. He leaned into the rocks, slung the rifle off his back, and thrust the weapon to his shoulder.

A growl rumbled in Sitka's throat. Saliva spattered the rock beside the man's head.

An explosion shattered the stillness. A stab of pain ripped through Sitka's shoulder. She lunged toward the invader.

He jerked backward. The rifle flew outward and down. He yelled, regained his balance for a moment and then his body pitched out, his arms flailing as he crashed down the canyon wall amidst an avalanche of broken rocks. His shrieks cut through the cold dawn.

Sitka leaped back. A trickle of blood oozed from her wound. The rumble of plummeting rocks ceased and there was silence.

A vulture squawked overhead, then circled and dropped down into the canyon, landing some feet from the man's body. The bird spread its wings, took a cautious step closer and paused. Another hop brought it closer still to the man's body, wedged between two rocks.

The man's hand moved, reaching toward his rifle, just beyond his fingertips. A string of oaths escaped his mouth. His hand fell back on his chest.

A final hop brought the vulture to the man's chest. The man moved his head and the bird took flight, only to land some feet from the body... waiting.

Sitka gave her stinging shoulder a quick lick, turned and limped back to her den. She moved with stealth, the man-creature forgotten, watchful should she encounter an opportunity to flush an unsuspecting creature from hiding. The cubs were ready to eat meat.

Chapter Twenty-Six

orian fanned the stack of bills like a deck of cards. "Why would Grandmother keep so much cash in the house? She should have put it in the bank. At least we have enough money to pay the men tomorrow."

Kimberlee removed an address book from the middle desk drawer. "Hey, check this out." She handed it to Dorian.

Dorian flipped through the pages. She stopped at the L's. "Lassiter. Jeremiah Lassiter?" She glanced at Kimberlee and shrugged. "Maybe he's someone who could help out while she's recuperating."

Kimberlee's face split in a smile. *Please, God. Let it be true. We need to get back to Fern Lake.* She picked up the phone. "I'll give him a call. What's the number?"

"209-555-1004. His name is Jeremiah." She laid the book on the desk.

Kimberlee dialed. The phone rang, once, twice, three times. "Hello?"

"Hello. May I speak to Jeremiah Lassiter?" Kimberlee's heart began to pitter-patter.

"This is Jeremiah. Who's calling?"

"My name is Kimberlee Clarke. Margaret Lassiter is my grandmother. I'm calling from her ranch in Texas. I found your name in her address book. Are you a relative?"

"She's my aunt…sort of. Her husband's brother, George Lassiter, was my father. So, she's my aunt by marriage. Has something happened to Aunt Margaret?"

"Well, it's a long story. Someone tried to kill her. She's—"

A gasp on the phone. "What?"

"She's in the Eagle Pass Hospital with a serious head injury. The doctor says she's going to be okay, eventually. We don't really know much more than that."

"Who did you say you were, again?"

"I'm her granddaughter, Kimberlee. Are there any other relatives we should notify?" Kimberlee turned to glance at Dorian. "I mean, anybody close to her that might be able to help out...*um*...when she gets out of the hospital?"

"Can't you folks take care—"

"Oh, no. We're just visiting from California. We hoped someone could come and help run the ranch. The stable master was arrested—" She touched the dots of perspiration on her brow. *Come on, fellow. Try to follow me here...*

"The stable master tried to kill her? My God!"

"No... He was arrested on another charge... Oh, I'd rather not go into all that right now." Kimberlee frowned "I just wanted to notify her family members. Grandmother will be in a rehab facility for about a month, but after that, she's going to need someone—"

"Maybe I can make some calls and get back to you," Jeremiah said. A child shrieked in the background. "*Shh.* I'm on the phone. Can't you keep that kid quiet? Sorry. Got a six-year-old."

"It's quite alright. I have a daughter just about that age too. Let me give you my phone number. 707-555-1258. Call anytime...cousin. There's another cousin here with me. Dorian. Actually, she's more closely related to you than I am. Your uncle Chuck was her grandfather. We're both from Fern Lake. That's in Northern California."

"Oh yeah? I'm in Hollywood, you know...in the Industry. Commercials—fluoride toothpaste ads, deodorant, that sort of thing. You've probably seen my commercials. On the Magnum PI reruns? Tom Selleck? Right after the evening news."

"Really? How interesting. Have you been able to get work with the economy and all?"

"Frankly, it's not going so good right now. I work in a bar some nights and on weekends. Makes ends meet while I wait to be discovered." Jeremiah laughed. "Gee, it's a small world, isn't it? If you dig deep enough, I guess we're all related some way.

"Look, I'll let the family know what's happened. There's not many of us left. My dad and mom have passed and my sister's in Florida, but I'll call her. We weren't very close to Aunt Margaret. I think the last time I saw her was about…three years ago. I'm sure sorry to hear about it, but I don't know how—"

"Okay, thanks Jeremiah. It was nice talking to you. If we ever get to Southern California, we'll look you up." *Don't hold your breath.* Kimberlee stood and paced the library.

"Sure thing," Jeremiah replied. "Maybe I'll make it up north one of these days. Let's keep in touch. Okay? Bye."

Kimberlee hung up the phone.

"What did he say?" Dorian looked hopeful.

"Oh, I don't know. He's some sort of shirt-tail relative through the Lassiter side of the family. I guess he'd be your second cousin or something. He's a wannabe movie star." Kimberlee wrinkled her nose. "Are there any other names that look promising?"

Dorian flipped the pages in the address book. "It's hard to say. No way to know if they're relations or neighbors or business associates. I don't see any other Lassiter's." She shook her head. "Maybe Dr. Turner has some suggestions. I suppose, she can always hire someone to come and stay with her. She's got enough money." Dorian grinned and gestured toward the stack of bills.

"Well, I'm not sitting here long enough to find out." Kimberlee crossed her arms and walked to the window. "I think if Brett can hire someone to keep the ranch running until she gets home, that's about the best we can do. She'll have to take it from there. We've got a life, too." She turned back toward Dorian.

"Mrs. Watson called today. She only agreed to keep the bookstore open until this weekend. Her daughter is coming from Ohio to visit on

Monday, and she's not willing to keep the store open any longer. We need to go home. I have a business to run." Kimberlee returned to the desk and pulled out the top drawer. "We should keep looking. Might be something more…maybe a disability insurance policy?"

She pulled all the papers from the drawers, divided the pile and handed half to Dorian.

Dorian knelt on the floor beside the desk, sifting through the stack. "Look at these." She fanned out several brochures across the coffee table. "A dance studio, a children's riding school in Eagle Pass, summer camps in the mountains, local 4-H clubs and a private girls' high school in Dallas. What do you suppose she was doing with these things?"

Dorian opened the dance studio brochure and glanced through it. "Could this be where my mom attended?" She flipped the brochure from front to back. "The brochures don't look that old."

"She probably kept them as keepsakes. People are like that."

"Probably." Dorian pulled them together, tapped them on the coffee table and squared the edges. "I'm sentimental, too. I'm going to take them." She set the brochures to the side of the coffee table.

Kimberlee thumbed through her pile of papers and shoved some back into the drawer. "No insurance policies. Just a bunch of bills that need to be paid." She stacked the bills in a separate pile and leaned back in the desk chair.

"At least we can pay the men. That's a good thing." Dorian reached for the bills on the desk and ran a rubber band around the middle.

Kimberlee glanced up as Thumper waddled through the library door and danced stiff-legged across the rug toward the desk. "Hi, Thumper. Where's your little friend? He must be feeling better. Thank goodness, he's alright. He sure gave me a scare." Kimberlee chuckled.

Thumper arched his back, stretched his legs out in front and pulled his ears down. He jumped onto the desk and lay down, his fur puffed out and his big white snowshoe feet pulled together. His tail flipped across the papers lying on the desktop.

"Get down, Thumper. We're done here." Kimberlee gave him a

gentle shove and pulled on the roll top, trying to close the lid.

Thumper stood and pawed at the papers on the desk, scattering them and knocking some onto the floor. "No, Thumper, get down." Kimberlee picked him up by his middle, but not before he pawed a paper from one of the little cubicles and snatched it in his teeth. He dropped it when he hit the floor and raced over to the sofa where he turned in a circle and flopped against a sofa pillow.

Dorian leaned down and picked it up. "You're always making a mess, you screwball. What's this? Oh…" She scanned the paper. The color drained from her face.

"What's wrong?" Kimberlee frowned. What could possibly get such a reaction? *She looks like she's seen a ghost.*

Dorian put the paper behind her back. She glanced at Kimberlee. "I don't think you want to see this."

"Why not? What is it?"

"*Um...*" Dorian stood and walked to the window. She pulled back the curtain. "Where's Brett?"

"He's out in the barn. Why? What's he got to do with it?" Kimberlee reached for the paper. "Let me see. What is it?"

Dorian twisted away from her. "Honey, call Brett. Let's wait until he comes before I show it to you."

Kimberlee squinted. Her cheeks warmed. Her heart quickened. Something was wrong! "Why? Why won't you tell me? I'm a big girl. Why do you think I need Brett to hold my hand?" She stamped her foot. *Just like a baby, throwing a temper tantrum. Guess I just proved her point.*

"Okay, have it your way. Look at it, then." Dorian's face flushed as she handed the paper to Kimberlee. "Don't say I didn't warn you. It's from a detective agency in Santa Barbara."

Kimberlee snatched the paper from Dorian's hand.

Ableman Detective Agency June 14, 48 Hour Report —

Subject—Kimberlee Lassiter Larson-Clarke

> *Investigation of subject's divorce from Doug Larson stated incompatibility. We didn't find no information to prove the subject as an unfit mother. There aren't no legal grounds to challenge custody of the child, Amanda Jean Larson, or to take her from her mother's care. Please notify this office what you want us to do next.*
>
> *Charges 12 hours @ $100 per hour $1200*
>
> *Please remit and send payment at your soonest early convenience. Ableman Detective Agency*

Kimberlee stared at the paper. The letters blurred. Her fingers tingled. Her cheeks felt numb. The room darkened. Perhaps the sun had gone behind a cloud? No. She knew the signs.

"Here, sit down. I was afraid of this. You're not going to faint, are you?" Dorian felt Kimberlee's forehead. "I'll get you some water." She started toward the kitchen.

The front door opened and Brett came in. "Hi, guys, what's—?" He glanced at Kimberlee's face. "What's the matter? You're pale as a sheet." He rushed to her and half-carried her to the sofa.

"I'm fine. I…I…just felt a little dizzy for a minute." Kimberlee shoved the fax toward Brett. "Take a look. Now, we know why Grandmother brought us to Texas. It wasn't about an inheritance. It was just a lie to get us here. She's trying to take Amanda away from us!"

The color drained from Brett's face. "I can't believe that…" He glanced at the paper. His cheeks turned from white to dark.

"Oh!" Dorian gasped. "I just remembered something she said. We were talking about my mom, Melody, and your dad, Mark. She said she wished she had a chance to *do it all over again...* She said she'd *do it different this time.* Then her face got all funny looking, like she was embarrassed or something.

"She was talking about raising another child. She *was* after Amanda." Dorian turned toward Brett. "All this talk about leaving the ranch to one of us… It was all bunk. She probably never intended to change her will. Everything was going to the Children's Program all along."

Dorian glanced at the papers stacked on the coffee table. "The brochures for the schools and the dance lessons. They weren't my mother's. They were for Amanda." She glanced up the stairs toward the nursery where Amanda played. "And, the cash in the desk? I'll bet she intended to pay the detective agency in cash, so there wouldn't be a money trail. My God!"

Kimberlee's gaze moved from Brett to Dorian. Her chest felt like someone had shot a cannon ball through the middle, leaving an eight-inch hole. How could Grandmother have thought…?

Which was worse? Learning her grandmother was trying to steal her child or having a private detective looking for ammunition that would allow her to do so? It was all pretty much the same thing.

The sun came out from behind a cloud, casting a square of sunshine through the window onto the library floor. Amanda's little voice drifted down from the nursery upstairs. "You are my sunshine…my sunny sunshine. I'm so happy your eyes are gray. …if you had a deer, you wouldn't take it…*um*…away."

Just hearing her voice warmed Kimberlee's heart. *My child!* No one was going to take Amanda from her. "Do you think Wilbur knew about Grandmother's plan to get Amanda?"

"I doubt it." Brett began to laugh.

Kimberlee glanced between Brett and Dorian. "I don't see anything funny about this, Brett. What is there to laugh about?" She shot a glare toward him. Grandmother hired Nanny to take care of Amanda. Was she in on the hoax, too? Maybe she should send Nanny packing.

"I know. I know. Listen. Wilbur tried to kill your grandmother before she could change the will from the Children's Program to one of you girls. But, Grandmother wasn't going to change the will at all. She was trying to get Amanda. There's no way he could have known what she was up to or he'd never have attacked her."

Dorian shifted from one foot to the other. "I hate to bring this up right now, but I left word at the hospital that we'd be by this morning to visit. She's expecting us."

"You and Brett can go. I personally don't think I could face her. I'm afraid I'd be tempted to pull her plug." Kimberlee put her hands over her face and dropped her head. She didn't really mean that. How could she have thought such a thing? But, there's no way she was going to leave Amanda alone with that…that…woman upstairs.

"Brett, you and Kimberlee stay here. I'll go by myself." Dorian turned toward the stairs. She paused when the phone rang.

Brett picked up the phone. "Hello? Lassiter residence." He walked to the window. "Yes, this is Brett Clarke. Yes… I see…" He stared out the window and then turned toward Kimberlee. "Okay…thanks for calling." He clicked the button. "That was the police department."

Kimberlee held her breath. Would the DNA prove Wilbur was innocent, or was that just wistful thinking? How she had hoped they were wrong and a stranger had attacked…

"He said they found Wilbur's Jeep parked about a half-mile from the ranch house, but there's no sign of Wilbur. And…the DNA report is back."

"What did they find," Kimberlee cried. "Was it Wilbur?" She held her breath.

"They compared the DNA from a water bottle in his Jeep against the blood and tissue they took from Thumper. It's a match."

Kimberlee's breath rushed out. "Well, I guess we're not surprised. You suspected him from the start." She sighed. "So, what he did was all because of us." Chill bumps raced up her arm. She leaned her head back on the sofa and closed her eyes.

"Why, Kimberlee. How can you say such a thing?" Dorian reached for her hand. "It's not our fault. Our coming brought it to a head, but he was using his fake children's program to steal Grandmother's money. He was desperate to keep her from changing the will, whether she'd promised it to us or to the next presidential candidate. Grandmother set it all in motion with her lies and deception."

"You're right, of course. She told him she was changing the will." Kimberlee got up from the sofa. "Dorian. Go and do your duty. Your grandmother is waiting. As far as I'm concerned, I don't have one.

"Besides, I need to talk to Nanny and find out what she knows about this situation. For her sake, I hope she's as much in the dark as we were."

Chapter Twenty-Seven

"Wake up, honey." Brett shook Kimberlee's shoulder. "We all could use a little R & R this morning. I've arranged for Juan to take us for a sunrise trail ride."

Kimberlee rolled over and put her hands over her ears. Her head hurt and her eyes ached from lack of sleep. She had lain awake for hours, going over and over learning about Grandmother's betrayal yesterday.

Long after midnight, Kimberlee finally slept, her dreams full of images of Amanda screaming, holding out her arms while Grandmother pulled her back.

"Leave me alone. I'm so tired." Kimberlee pulled her pillow over her head. "It's not even light outside. I just want to lie here and rest." She pulled the covers up to her neck.

"It's not good to stay in bed, all gloomy and depressed. Get up and take a shower. You'll feel better, you'll see. I'll wake Dorian. We'll have Nanny bring Amanda down and I'll make Mickey Mouse pancakes. We need to keep our minds busy and have some fun for a few hours." Brett yanked the covers off her body.

Kimberlee shrieked and drew her legs up in a fetal position. "Alright! I'll get up. Don't expect me to have fun, though, and that's final."

"You've made up your mind, *huh*?" Brett laughed. He turned toward the door. "Breakfast will be ready in thirty minutes. If you're not up, I'm coming back here and…you'll be sorry."

Kimberlee stumbled into the kitchen, her damp hair curling around her shoulders. She kissed Amanda and smiled at Dorian and Nanny.

Once you're out of bed, it's half the battle.

Brett scooped up a Mickey Mouse pancake and set it in front of Amanda. "There you go, sweetie. How's that?"

Amanda squealed at the sight of Mickey with big ears and raisin eyes and a mouth. She grabbed her fork.

"Can you eat that big pancake all by yourself, Amanda?" Brett set the spatula on the counter.

Amanda grinned and nodded.

Nanny poured syrup over Mickey's face. "Do you want me to cut it up for you?" She kept her gaze on Amanda, adjusting her napkin and pulling her glass closer to her plate, avoiding Kimberlee's eyes. Ever the dutiful nanny. Yeah, right.

"No. I do it by myself." Amanda pulled away and attacked Mickey's ear.

Where does she get such an independent personality? Kimberlee poured coffee and stared at Nanny Sally. The woman looked so guilty this morning. Last night's conversation still sat on her chest like a ten pound dumbbell. Either Nanny knew nothing of Grandmother's plans for Amanda or she was the best liar in Texas. After fifteen minutes of denials and tears, she had convinced Kimberlee of her innocence. *This morning, I'm not quite so sure.*

"Brett wants to go on a trail ride this morning, but I don't know. I hate to leave Amanda here…" Kimberlee rolled her eyes toward Nanny and then looked away.

"Why don't you and Brett go?" Dorian picked up Amanda's napkin off the floor. "I can stay here with Amanda. I don't mind. I have a few calls to make. I need to talk to my boss and let him know I'm staying longer than I planned. And, I could really use a long nap. After my visit with Grandmother yesterday, I'm exhausted. She cried the whole time I was there and kept asking for you."

Kimberlee tossed her head. "Would you do that? Thanks ever so much. I'd feel better if…well, just thanks, Dorian. Brett would be so disappointed if I don't go with him."

Kimberlee met Brett in the barn where Juan waited with three saddled horses. She tried to remember what Harold taught her several days before. Was it only a few days since she and Brett rode with Harold across the desert? It seemed like a lifetime ago. "Did you put on the special saddle Harold gave me?"

The mention of Harold's name dampened her mood. Her concerns regarding Harold's true identity had been on the back burner ever since Grandmother's attack. But then, how many problems could you concentrate on at the same time? She frowned and shook her head. She just wouldn't think about it now. Brett promised they'd have fun today. "Never mind, this one is fine." She thrust her boot into the stirrup and hoisted her leg up and over the horse's back.

Juan nodded and pulled the last strap on his horse's saddle. "You're doing fine, Miss Kimberlee."

"Say, Juan. Would you loan me a set of chaps? I always wanted to wear a pair." Brett's face lit up with that little boy expression she had learned to love. He was just a big kid at heart.

Juan nodded toward a hook on the wall. "There's a pair over there you can use. Now, you folks remember to stay close. I don't want you to get lost out there."

Brett hurried to don the chaps. He mounted and patted his pocket. "Don't worry about me. I've got my cell phone right here, ready for any emergency."

"Might's well leave that here." Juan shook his head. "It won't be no good out on the prairie. Unreliable signal."

"I'm ready. Let's go!" Kimberlee clucked at her mount and turned her mare's nose toward the prairie.

They passed through the gate behind Juan, heading across the open range. The outline of cactus gouged dark fingers into the red and amber sky. Soon the ranch house and barns grew small in the distance as the sun crept over the horizon, warming the air and changing the dark shadows to recognizable images.

Kimberlee's spirits brightened as the pressures of the last few days slipped from her shoulders. Brett was right. This was exactly what she needed. She cast an air kiss toward him and breathed deep, filling her lungs with crisp morning air. The worries of the week melted away and she was at peace, as though she had stepped from earth onto another planet. Out here, she didn't have to think about attempted murder, Harold's questionable identity, or Grandmother's nonsense.

Juan's saddle squeaked as he turned, pointing to a mound of loose dirt off to the left of the trail. "Keep your horse well away from there. That's fire ants."

Brett and Kimberlee pulled their horses to the right side of the trail and passed the mound on the far side.

The sun rose higher, evaporating the dew on the shrubs. Shimmering colors rose from the prairie floor, giving the illusion that the distant hills were alive, gently weaving and rippling from side to side. At 10:00 A.M., Juan called a halt.

Kimberlee pulled off her jacket. They passed a canteen of water around and stretched their legs. Within fifteen minutes, they were back on the trail, gently sloping upward into higher elevations.

Juan gave his horse a kick. He trotted up the trail, training his binoculars on the path ahead. "If we're lucky, we might run into Quantum and his herd. They're usually somewhere around here this time of day."

The trees and underbrush grew thicker as they edged toward the summit. Eventually, they came to the top of the rise and gazed down into the valley. On the right, jagged fingers of rock reached skyward. A gorge ran the length of the hills toward the Rio Grande. A stand of oaks grew off to the left. A little river ran through a grassy meadow down the center. Beside the river, a group of horses grazed in the meadow.

"There. Off to the right. Can you see them? They're clustered up there by that stand of trees." Juan stood in his stirrups and pointed.

Quantum, the black stallion, trotted beside his mares, guarding against the possibility another stallion might woo them away.

"Can we go down and get a closer look? I'd love for Brett to see them up close, like I saw them last Sunday." Kimberlee nodded toward the herd.

Juan scanned the darkening sky. "We don't have much time. I don't know how long that storm is going to hold off. We might be riding back in the rain."

"I don't mind. I'd like to get closer." Brett leaned forward and shaded his eyes to better view the horses.

Heavy clouds formed overhead as Kimberlee's mare plodded behind Juan with Brett bringing up the rear. They rode single file through the underbrush into the valley. Kimberlee caught her breath as she reached the edge of the grassy meadow and the herd came into view. A streak of lightning crackled across the sky. Thunder rumbled in the distance.

Quantum reared, whinnied and took off at a gallop. His black mane whipped in the wind as he led his mares away.

"Let's catch up with them." Brett gave his mount a kick and sprinted past Kimberlee and Juan. Kimberlee's horse lunged after him.

Kimberlee grabbed the pommel with one hand and gripped the body of the horse with her knees. The wind beat at her face. Her heart thumped in time with the thundering hooves.

Brett's horse raced beside her, creating a cloud of dust and wind and noise. Adrenaline mingled with terror as she rode, reveling in the exhilaration of the moment, yet knowing how dangerous and foolish it was.

Her body throbbed with each stride of the beast's surging muscles, driving through her legs. Her throat burned with each breath. She was neck and neck with Brett. His horse's mane whipped against her hands with each stride, stinging like fire. Never had she felt so close to death and yet…so alive.

She turned and stared into his horse's giant brown eye, the dark and the light of it looking like land and water on a distant planet floating through the universe. Her heart soared as she became one with the wind and the grass and the dirt and the noise, overcome with abounding joy.

As she raced beside Brett, the tragedies of the week disappeared like a magician's rabbit. She swallowed a sob, as the ecstasy of the moment washed over her and she wished it would never end.

Quantum's herd pulled away and seemed to disappear in a cloud of dust.

Kimberlee's mare skidded to a halt beside Brett.

Juan pounded up behind them and pulled his horse to a halt. "What's the big idea? What were you trying to prove?" His face was as dark as the clouds overhead. "You both could have been killed!" Lightning streaked and thunder rumbled.

"*Wow*! Wasn't that great? I've never had such a thrill." Brett pulled off his hat and beat it against his leather chaps.

Kimberlee could only nod, still panting from the exertion. Her body tingled. She had no words to express what she felt and reveled in the joy of it.

"We need to get moving. These summer storms can be vicious. We don't want to be caught out here on the prairie if we can help it. Let's make tracks, guys." Juan turned his horse back and the riders moved off at a trot toward the ranch.

Great drops of rain pelted down. Kimberlee sniffed and tasted the scent of it as little puffs of dust bounced in the dry earth. The smell of damp earth would forever remind her of this wonderful afternoon.

The lump in her throat rose up. The exhilaration, sharing Quantum's joy and following his herd, filled her heart to overflowing. She couldn't gulp down her sobs. Rain mingled with the tears streaming down her face.

Juan held his hand up. "Are you alright, Miss Kimberlee? Do you want to get down and rest a minute?"

Brett slid off his horse and handed the reins to Juan. "What is it, honey?" He pulled her from the saddle and wrapped her in his arms.

"It was all so wonderful. The wind, the lightning... I...I've never felt anything like that before. I needed to be a part of it, to become one with all this. I needed to remember that God is in control and we are powerless to change what happens around us. I don't know how to explain it." Tears trickled down her face.

Brett nodded. He pulled his handkerchief from his pocket and dabbed her cheeks. "I understand. I—"

Kimberlee pulled her head back and stared into his eyes. "No. You don't. I don't understand it myself. We were riding and the thunder and lightning… It was like, all at once I understood." Raindrops left damp circles on the sleeves of her jacket.

"Tell me, honey. Understood what?"

"All that's happened here on the ranch. Grandmother and Wilbur— what Wilbur did and what Grandmother tried to do. I didn't think I could go on. I was losing control, losing…me."

Kimberlee looked out across the meadow where the rain poured onto the dry earth, and then back at Brett. "Now I understand. It's not important, none of it. What's important is you and me and Amanda—our family." She waved her hand. "Just look at this...this is important. Quantum and his herd—they're important and the lightning and the thunder. But, Wilbur and his greed and Grandmother's shenanigans, they're not important at all.

"As soon as she's settled, we'll leave. We'll go back to our own lives and that will be the end to all the unhappiness of this week." She smiled. "I'm ready now. Let's go."

Brett squeezed her arm and helped her mount her horse. "We're ready, Juan. Lead on."

A streak of lightning slashed across the sky and thunder crashed in the distance as the storm moved further across the plains. As suddenly as it started, the rain stopped and the sun came out.

The bushes sparkled with clustered rain droplets, catching the sun and glistening like diamonds. The hills jutted up from the prairie floor like mounds of cookie dough. A brilliant rainbow of red, yellow, green and blue circled the top of the canyon. And, there again was the contrariness of the prairie, intense and challenging one minute and God's beautiful garden the next.

Juan pointed up at the colorful archway. "Mother Nature's pallet. We should push on now. We'll ride along the canyon and then cut straight across toward the ranch house. It's the quickest way back."

They rode in silence, single file toward the jagged canyon rim. Occasionally, small rodents and lizards scurried across the trail. As they approached the gaping chasm, a circle of vultures hovered near the boulders along the south wall. The horses plodded ahead. The raptors circled, riding the air currents and dropped down into the canyon, and then rose up, catching the wind and circling, only to drop back down.

Juan pulled his horse to a stop. "Looks like something big died over there." He gestured toward the birds. "Maybe a deer?"

A chill started in Kimberlee's toes and worked its way up her body, leaving chill bumps on her arms and throat. Brett's words echoed. *They found Wilbur's Jeep parked about a half mile from the ranch house.* "It's Wilbur." Kimberlee closed her eyes and dropped her head.

"What?" Brett stared at her. "Why do you say that?"

"I just know. You said they found his Jeep but they didn't find him. It makes sense. If he were on foot, he'd head this way, through the canyon to the Rio Grande River and into Mexico. Where else could he go?"

"Let's check it out." Juan prodded his horse into a trot.

Kimberlee clucked at her mare to follow.

She hung back as Juan and Brett rode to the edge and looked over the ledge. "It's a body, alright. Looks like it could be Wilbur…or what's left of him." Brett turned and held up his hand. "You don't need to come any closer, honey."

She had stopped about ten yards from the canyon rim. Then, she nudged her mare closer. "It's okay. I can handle it."

About half way down, a rifle lay catawampus across a boulder. What remained of Wilbur's crumpled body lay further down the canyon. The vultures and scavengers had fed on the corpse. A bit of dark jacket flapped against a rock. Flying insects buzzed over the remains.

Brett pulled out his cell phone and flipped it open. "No signal.

We'll have to go back to the ranch and call the police from there."

Kimberlee shuddered. She turned her mare away from the canyon wall, locked away the image of Wilbur's battered body and threw away the key. *I refuse to let this take away one minute of my mountain top experience with Quantum.*

Chapter Twenty-Eight

Unable to stop time, no matter how much he wished he could, the family was scheduled to leave Texas in forty-eight hours. Thumper sat staring at the kitty cat clock on the wall. Its eyes clicked back and forth in its empty head, like the hollow place in his heart. Its tail swung from side to side as each second ticked by, bringing the moment of departure closer. The lump in his throat felt like he'd swallowed Wilbur's Jeep. The hands on the clock crept imperceptibly, but time moved too fast. When he and the family left the ranch, he'd never see Noe-Noe again.

He bumped Noe-Noe's shoulder. "Come with me. I'm going to take you to brunch."

She flicked her ear. "We're doing this again?" She followed him through the cat door.

"Trust me. We'll get it right this time." Thumper led her into the back yard where the fountain burbled and the little birds hopped in its spray.

He scrunched beside her as they inched closer to the fountain. His ears laid back, eyes glittering at the sight of the little birds on the brunch menu. "Listen. We'll double down. I'll go to the port side and draw their fire." One eye squinted. "You bear starboard and catch them unawares when they make a break for it. We'll share the booty 50/50. Can you remember now, which way is starboard?" He cocked his head, his eyes half closed.

Noe-Noe lowered her ears and pulled back her whiskers.

Thumper turned his head away. "I'm just sayin'." He shut his mouth before he put his hind paw in it.

"Now!"

Thumper flew across the grass, grabbing left and right at the elusive capons. Out streaked his paw. He seized a little tan bird with red feathers and flung it to the grass. Given a choice, tan birds with red feathers had always been his favorite.

Noe-Noe hadn't moved. She sat crouched in the grass, her gold eyes locked on the intended snack struggling beneath Thumper's huge white foot.

"Here you are, my dear, *capon al fresco*. You may have the pleasure of dispatching our feathered friend and inculging in the first bite." Thumper shoved the struggling bird toward Noe-Noe, being careful to keep pressure on its head, lest brunch should *take a powder*.

Noe-Noe flicked her whiskers and turned her head aside. "You go ahead. I really don't have much of an appet:te in the mornings when I'm expecting." She stood and waddled away.

"Well, that's a fine thing. I've already had breakfast. I only suggested brunch to please you. I might as well let it go." Thumper lifted his foot and the sparrow flew up into the tree where his bird mates twittered. "Wait a minute." His head went up, his ears moved forward. "What did you say? Expecting? Expecting what?" The word echoed in his brain. *Expecting!*

Water splashed louder in the fountain. The leaves overhead came alive with chirping birds, apparently delir:ous with relief at their pal's narrow escape. The whole world took on a sharper dimension. *Expecting!* The word struck into the core of his being. "I'm going to be a father? That's wonderful. I mean...that's terrible. I'm leaving in two days. I'll never get to see my children. They'll never know their father."

Noe-Noe ambled toward the house, her hips swaying. At the porch, she turned. "Of course they will. They'll know everything about you and our ancestors. They'll have all our memories, just like all the Fern Lake Cats." She flicked her tail and disappeared through the cat door.

Thumper gulped. *My beautiful Noe-Noe, with stripes the color of mustard and eyes the color of marigolds.* She was having his babies. How would he ever live without her?

"What am I supposed to say to her?" Kimberlee reached for the car door handle. The twenty-minute drive to the hospital to visit Grandmother had ended much too soon for comfort. Her heart thumped as Brett pulled the car into a parking space. There were a million places she'd rather be right now, including the gynecologist for an annual PAP test.

"Maybe you won't have to say anything." Brett opened his door and stepped out. "Just say you hope she'll soon be well and say good-bye. We'll be leaving in a couple of days. You'd want to say good-bye before we left, wouldn't you?"

"Would I? Knowing what we know about why she brought us here?" Kimberlee slammed the door.

"Even so. After what she's been through with Wilber and Harold," Brett nodded. "I think you would want to say good bye. That's the decent thing to do, regardless of what she did. You know I'm right." He walked around the car and took her hands. He pulled her toward him.

She looked down at her feet. She could stand anything but the accusation in his eyes and knowing he was right.

"Kimberlee. Look at me. You know I'm right, don't you."

She lifted her head, stared into his eyes and choked out an answer. "I guess so." The words sounded hollow and not at all what she felt in the hardened core of her heart. *I'd sooner eat chocolate covered potato bugs, but, I'll do it for you.*

"Then, let's get it over with." Brett grasped Kimberlee's hand and struck out across the parking lot toward the hospital like he was headed for a fire sale at the hardware store.

Inside the hospital, Kimberlee caught the faint scent of antiseptic soap and flowers. Passing the Java City kiosk, the enticing aroma of coffee and cinnamon buns tickled her nose. She paused. "Do we have time for a—?"

"No." Brett pulled her down the hall, stopped at the Information Desk and asked directions to the Surgery Center. The girl behind the counter directed them to the second floor, post-surgery ward.

Within a few minutes, they stood in front of Room 202. "Ready?" Brett grabbed Kimberlee's arm in a vice-like grip. Was it for encouragement, or did he think she might bolt? Maybe he was right. Running was right up there at the top of the list. *Things I'd Rather Do Today Instead of Confront Grandmother*.

She swallowed a lump in her throat and forced her mouth into a smile. "Let's do it."

Brett shoved open the door. The shades were drawn against the afternoon sun, placing the hospital bed in shadow. The *beep, beep, beep* from a monitor measured Grandmother's heartbeat. Green dials glowed in the semi-darkness.

Bandages swathed Grandmother's head, framing her pale face. The wrinkles in her cheeks and forehead looked even deeper than Kimberlee remembered. *She looks so fragile lying there.*

"Grandmother, are you awake? I've brought Kimberlee." Brett shook Grandmother's shoulder.

She opened her eyes, pulled her arms out from under the covers and reached for Kimberlee.

Surgical tape held a needle affixed to the back of her hand. Blue veins stood up like jagged little rivers running from her wrist toward fingertips callused from years of hard work.

"Kimberlee, I was afraid you wouldn't come. I wouldn't blame you if you didn't want to see me. I've done a terrible thing. I'm so sorry." Grandmother's dark eyes roamed Kimberlee's face, holding a plea for understanding—for forgiveness.

Kimberlee took her hand. She tried to hold on to the anger she had harbored since Thumper sent the detective's paper to the floor. She tried to harden her heart against Grandmother's plea, because there was nothing that could excuse her despicable plan.

Kimberlee's anger slipped away as she looked down at the broken woman in the bed. Grandmother wasn't rational. She was old and sick and likely demented. Kimberlee's heart swelled with pity. She dropped to her knees by the bed and put her head on Grandmother's hand.

Grandmother coughed. "You don't know what I've done." She choked back a sob. "I wanted to be young again. I thought…if I could raise another child…but I was wrong. So wrong… I deserve to die." Sobs wracked her body. "I should have died when…" She pulled her hand away from Kimberlee and touched the bandages on her head.

"No. No…Grandmother. Wilbur was wrong." Kimberlee turned toward Brett. *A little help here? I don't know what to say.*

He shook his head and shrugged. "Here, now." Brett pulled several tissues from the side table. "That's enough of that kind of talk." He handed one to Kimberlee, the others to Grandmother.

"Now, let's put it behind us. It's over. Let's move on." Brett glanced around the room. "My, look at all the lovely flowers. You must have a lot of friends, Grandmother. Who are these from?" He touched a bouquet of roses sitting on the nightstand next to her bed.

Leave it to Brett to say just the right thing at the right time.

Grandmother sniffed and blew her nose. "I think those are from my great-nephew, Jeremiah." She pressed the button to raise her bed higher. "Wasn't that nice of him? There was a nice get-well card too. How do you suppose he knew about—?"

"Dorian and I found your address book. We talked to him…*um*… I think it was Friday."

Kimberlee glanced toward Brett, now standing by the window, staring down at the parking lot. No one spoke. The *tick-tick* of the wall clock grew louder. Kimberlee shifted from one foot to the other. *Somebody, say something. This is awkward.* None of the events of the week were good topics of conversation. *How's that private detective thing coming along? Finalized your plans to steal my child? Taken another over-dose lately? Hired another attorney to embezzle the rest of your money, yet?* I don't think so.

Brett turned toward the bed. "Grandmother, let's get serious for a moment. How much have they told you? Do you know what happened to you?" He pulled the visitor's chair over and gestured for Kimberlee to sit.

Kimberlee breathed a sigh of relief. Better he was the one to bring it up.

Grandmother sighed. "The police stopped by a couple of times. And, Dorian talked to me yesterday. I know Wilbur attacked me. Harold's in jail for embezzling my money. And, I was trying to…" Her mouth quivered. Tears gathered in her eyes. "There's more?" She ran her hand over her face.

Brett glanced briefly at Kimberlee and then at Grandmother. Was he checking to see how she was taking all this or getting up the courage to discuss an uncomfortable subject?

He gave Kimberlee an encouraging smile and then turned back to Grandmother. "They found Wilbur's body. He apparently fell, trying to climb down the canyon wall near the Mexico border. He's dead." He cleared his throat, letting that information sink in, and then continued. "So, about the ranch. With Harold in custody, I've assigned the job of stable master to Juan, with your approval, of course."

Grandmother nodded. "Good choice. He's a hard worker."

Kimberlee pulled Jeremiah's flower arrangement closer and smelled the roses. "We thought Juan and his family could move into Harold's house. We'll clean out Harold's personal belongings tomorrow. As soon as Juan's family is settled, we'll be leaving." She sneaked a look at Grandmother to see how she was taking the news.

"Dr. Turner says you'll be transferred to the Rehabilitation Wing in a few days. He thinks you can go home after a few weeks of physical therapy. Do you have any thoughts about who might help out when you get home?"

Grandmother shook her head. "I suppose there are practical nurses. I don't specifically know anyone. Maybe Nanny would stay and help.

I'll speak to her about it."

"Well, good. That's settled." Brett glanced at his watch. "You must be tired. We should be going."

Grandmother laid her head back and grimaced when the back of her head touched the pillow. "I am tired. And my head hurts. Perhaps you could ask the nurse to come in, on your way out?" She closed her eyes.

Kimberlee stood and backed toward the door. "Good-bye, Grandmother. I hope—"

Grandmother lifted her hand in a dismissive manner. She didn't open her eyes.

Kimberlee followed Brett into the hall and pulled Grandmother's door shut behind her.

"I suppose that meant good-bye or good riddance."

The door had no sooner clicked shut, than Margaret sat straight up and fluffed the pillow behind her head. So, they were leaving and taking Amanda with them—the last hope she had of raising a little girl. She sighed. *Too bad things didn't work out with Amanda. If they think I'll give up my plans that easily, they don't know Margaret Lassiter.*

She drummed her fingers on the bed sheet for a moment and then pulled the phone into her lap.

She'd always wanted another little boy. Little boys meant baseball games, holes in the knees of their pants, and frogs in their pockets. Little girls were sweet, but little boys could grow up to make you proud, raise lambs and rabbits for the 4H clubs, build hotrods and become high school football stars. Not like Mark who ran away and joined the service when he was seventeen… *Yes, that's the ticket. Why didn't I think of this before? Whatever made me think I wanted a girl?*

She dialed 411.

"Information. How may I help you?"

"Can you please give me the number of Jeremiah Lassiter in Hollywood?"

The operator gave her the number. She dialed. The phone rang once, twice…

"Hello?"

"Jeremiah, dear! This is your great-aunt Margaret. I called to thank you for the lovely flowers. How sweet of you to think of me." She coughed, with just enough anguish to evoke sympathy.

"Aunt Margaret? My goodness. Are you alright? We heard what happened."

"Oh, I'm fine." A pitiful whine crept into her voice. "The doctor says I'll be out of here before you know it. Jeremiah, dear, the reason I called… Since this happened, it's made me realize I should make some plans and settle my financial affairs before it's too late. We never know, do we?

"I'm seriously considering leaving my entire estate to you. I'd like you to come and visit so we could discuss it." *That should do it.*

Jeremiah gasped. "Aunt Margaret, I never thought—"

"Perhaps you could come for a while when I'm discharged from the hospital in a few weeks? We'll have barbecues, hayrides, maybe a barn dance with the neighbors. It would be a good idea if could stay for a month or so and help me manage some issues here on the ranch. We could work out the details of the inheritance while you're here."

"Aunt Margaret. I'm overwhelmed. "I—"

"Of course, you must bring darling little Dickie. How is our precious little boy? What is he? Six-years-old now? My! How times flies. I can't wait to get my hands on him…"

Chapter Twenty-Nine

Various excuses, including needing to help Brett clean out Harold's house, resulted in Kimberlee staying at the ranch Monday morning while Dorian drove into town to shop for groceries and visit the hospital one last time.

Kimberlee pulled on a sweater and tied a scarf around her head.

"You ready?" Brett pushed open the kitchen door, carrying an armload of cardboard boxes. Kimberlee picked up several more boxes stacked by the front door. They hauled them across the yard to Harold's house. Brett used Grandmother's master key to unlock the front door.

Kimberlee followed Brett into the living room and dropped the boxes to the floor. "*Brrr…* It's cold in here. It's warmer outside. Let's leave the front door open. It might warm up quicker." She pulled her sweater tighter around her neck.

Thumper and Noe-Noe traipsed through the front door. He circled the room, sniffing each stick of furniture.

Noe-Noe ambled down the hall toward the kitchen. She raced back into the living room, her fur puffed up and her mouth twisted in a grimace.

"Brett. Look at her." Kimberlee laughed at Noe-Noe's expression. "She looks like she smelled a skunk."

"How do you want to do this?" Brett moved a box toward the bookcase. "If you want to work in Imelda's room, I'll start boxing up their books."

"I guess I'll just pack their personal things like clothes, knick-knacks, that sort of thing. If Juan wants to move furniture in or out, he can do that later."

Kimberlee's heels clicked across the hardwood floors down the hall to the bedroom. The house felt empty and barren, like an eggshell, cracked and spilled out, as if it sensed that Harold and Imelda would not return.

The bed in Imelda's room was neatly made, her toiletries carefully arranged on the bureau. *I feel like a thief, pawing through her personal things.*

Imelda had been genuinely upset the night of Grandmother's overdose. Or so it seemed. Was it just a façade to manipulate an unsuspecting old woman? A true friend wouldn't betray her friend. Had it only been a week ago? How time flies when you aren't having fun.

Kimberlee opened Imelda's dresser drawer and emptied her clothing on the bed.

"Hey, honey." Brett called from the living room. "Would you put on the tea kettle? I could use a hot drink. There must be tea somewhere in the kitchen."

"In a minute." Kimberlee picked up a pink sweater, refolded it and laid it on the bed beside Imelda's nighties. She gave it a pat. *I remember this sweater. Imelda had it on the day we arrived. I remember thinking the color was so becoming against her dark skin.*

She sat on the end of the bed gazing at Imelda and Harold's wedding picture on the bureau. They looked so happy. She shook her head, stood and started down the hall to make the tea.

Noe-Noe faced Kimberlee in the kitchen doorway, blocking her entry. She hissed, her back arched, every hair standing on end, her tail the size of a bottle brush. Her ears lay against her head. She snarled and raised her paw, claws extended, as if to say, "No one is getting past me."

What on earth? "What's the matter, Noe-Noe?" Kimberlee reached out to stroke her.

Noe-Noe's claws streaked across Kimberlee's hand, leaving deep scratches.

"Oww!" Kimberlee jerked her hand back. "Dang it, Noe-Noe!

Shame on you!" Drops of blood oozed from the scratches. She sucked the back of her hand where the scratches stung like fire.

Darn cat! What's her problem? Kimberlee stepped into the bathroom and ran cold water over her hand, washing away the blood. She opened the medicine cabinet and found a bottle of hydrogen peroxide. She poured it over the scratches, dried her hand and applied an adhesive bandage.

Reflected in the mirror behind her, stockings hung over the shower door. She turned. Imelda's bathrobe dangled from a hook on the wall. An electric curling iron lay on the counter, still plugged into the light socket. Shampoo and hair conditioner sat on the counter next to an electric toothbrush. When Imelda left home, she had every intention of returning that night. How fate had intervened, a result of her own greed and betrayal.

What a waste. Why wasn't she happy? She had everything—a husband who loved her, a good job, and a nice home. Now, it's all gone. She'd been arrested and waiting indictment, out of work and homeless.

Kimberlee returned to the bedroom and pulled out another drawer full of Imelda's slacks and tee shirts and set them alongside Imelda's pink sweater. *Imelda. What have you done?*

Thumper crouched on top of the mantle beside an old metal box. His front feet hung over the edge as he stared down at Brett, packing photographs, magazines and books. On days like this, not having opposable thumbs was a good thing. Let Brett do the work.

Brett flipped open a book and stared at the pages. He glanced up at Thumper. "Maybe I shouldn't pack all these books. Juan and his wife might want to read them." He shrugged. "I guess it doesn't make much difference to you, one way or the other, does it?" He shoved the book back onto the shelf and pulled out another. "This looks interesting. I haven't read this one, either."

He laid the book on the floor near the front door and smiled up at Thumper. "Harold won't mind if I borrow it. He's not going to need it any time soon." Did Brett really expect him to have an opinion about Harold's books?

"Hey, honey? How's that tea coming? Is it ready yet?"

Kimberlee's muffled reply came from the bedroom. "Oh, shoot! I forgot all about it. Give me a minute."

Thumper stood and stretched. As he lay back down, his back foot shoved the metal box closer to the mantel's edge.

Brett pulled another book from the bookcase and packed it in the cardboard box.

Noe-Noe scampered down the hall, meowed and touched his sleeve.

"Hey, little kitty. Did you come to help?" Brett scratched her head.

Noe-Noe faced the bookshelves, reached up her paw, clawed the back of a book and pulled. It flipped out of the shelf. She jumped back when it thudded to the floor. An old, faded photograph, bent and curled on the edges, tumbled out.

What the... Brett picked up the photograph and turned it from side to side. "What's this? How did this get in here? Did Kimberlee give it to Harold?"

Thumper leaped off the mantle and landed on the rug. He looked up into Brett's face. *And just what does it mean?*

Brett touched the photograph. "It's Kimberlee's picture of her Dad and Ted with the deer." He ran his finger over his mouth. "Wait. It can't be her picture." He glanced down at Thumper. "There aren't any teeth marks in it. It's a *copy* of Kimberlee's picture." Brett put the book back on the shelf and scratched his head. "Where could Harold have gotten this picture?" He stared at the photo.

Thumper rubbed against his leg. *You're almost there, Brett. Keep thinking.*

Brett pulled out his cell phone, went out onto the porch and punched in a number. He glanced around the yard and then back over his shoulder. "Hey, Jack. It's me, Brett."

Thumper sat in the doorway. *If Brett's on the right track, no way he'd want Kimberlee to overhear him now.*

Brett lowered his voice. "Listen, I've only got a minute. We're cleaning out Harold's house. I just found an old photograph. It's Ted and Mark with the deer, like the one Kimberlee carries. What do you think?" He murmured. "What? You found records? Okay, give me the good news first."

Thumper twitched his whiskers. *At last, we're finally getting somewhere.*

Brett rubbed his forehead. "That's right. Harold Marlowe. You found both? A birth and a death certificate? How old was he when he died? Yeah, that's usually how it's done. Then, that's the proof we need. Ted used a dead baby's birth certificate to create a false identity. So the tall tale he gave Kimberlee about meeting Ted in the Caymans was a bunch of crapola! *He is Ted Herman!* Guess it doesn't make much difference now. He's in jail.

"Listen, I'll let the girls know. We'll let the authorities know about the fake identity. They can do what they want with the information. Thanks for your help, Jack. We're getting things settled here as quickly as we can. We'll be home in a couple days."

Thumper followed Brett back into the house where he knelt by the boxes of books. He put the faded photograph in his pocket. He stroked Thumper's head. "Now, how am I supposed to tell Kimberlee?"

Thumper put his nose in the air. *I believe it was the famous author, H.H. Munro who said, 'A little inaccuracy saves tons of explanation.'*

Thumper ambled over to Noe-Noe and rubbed her side. *"How did you know Ted's picture was in that book?"*

Noe-Noe huffed. *"Did you forget that I was outside the library the other night when you dumped her purse on the rug? I knew Harold had a photo over here like the one you guys were looking at."* She sat up and scratched behind her left ear. *"I told you then, I knew things. You aren't the only cat with the memories."*

"You knew the photo was in the book?"

"Some years ago, Imelda gave Harold a wallet and a book about the Kickapoo Indians for Christmas. He transferred all his pictures into his new wallet, except that one. He put that one in the book. I doubt he ever intended to read it and he thought no one would ever find it there. He wasn't very interested in the Kickapoo tribe."

"Do ya think?" Thumper sniffed. He crawled into an empty cardboard box. *"Hey. Peek-a-boo. Come play with me."*

Noe-Noe lifted her head. *"Wait a minute. Did I just hear Kimberlee go back into that blasted kitchen, again? Good grief!"* Noe-Noe dashed down the hall."

Kimberlee opened the kitchen cupboards. She set two cups and saucers on the counter. After rifling through several more cupboards, she found a can of tea with the lid stuck tight. At first it wouldn't budge, and then it flipped off, spewing loose tea across the counter and onto the floor.

"Oh, fudge!" She wiped the tea leaves from the counter with a dampened sponge and grabbed a broom. Brett was going to think she was growing the tea plants in here.

She filled the teakettle at the sink and placed it on the stove. As she reached for the stove knob, Noe-Noe mewed, leaped onto the counter, and pawed at her hand.

Kimberlee turned. "Oh, so first you beat me up and now you think I should give you a treat? What a caterwaul you're making." She smiled at the sound of the word. *Caterwaul!*

Noe-Noe jumped off the counter and rubbed against her leg, still crying.

"You must have a very short memory." Kimberlee opened more cupboards, searching for the cat treats. "You sound like you're starving to death. I really don't think so."

Noe-Noe paced the kitchen, yowling piteously.

"Alright! I'm looking. I'm looking. Give me a minute." Kimberlee slammed door after door. She found the cat food under the sink and shook some into a bowl.

Noe-Noe ran out of the kitchen, still meowing. She turned at the doorway, looked back and then raced into the living room.

"Well, fine. I guess you didn't want it that bad, after all." Kimberlee put the cat food back into the cupboard and glanced at the stove. *How's that teakettle coming along?*

"Oh, for heaven's sake! I forgot to turn it on."

She reached again toward the stove.

Brett called from the living room. "Kimberlee, come in here. Quick! I have something important to tell you."

"Be right there. I'm putting the kettle on now." She flipped the stove knob, turned and hurried through the door. As she stepped through the kitchen door into the hallway leading to the living room, an explosion rocked the kitchen.

Her hands flailed as the concussion threw Kimberlee flat to the floor. Her head spun. A wave of nausea swept through her stomach. She swallowed down an overwhelming desire to vomit. Her ears rang like church bells. Something whooshed past her head and hit the floor with a metallic clunk.

Fire roared and crackled—the acrid scent of melting plastic. She struggled to sit up and turned toward the kitchen. Flames had already fully engulfed the walls. A trickle of fire zigzagged across the kitchen floor, following a path of oil and shattered glass from the oil lamp that fell from the top of the refrigerator.

Brett! Must find Brett. Kimberlee got to her knees. Flames trailed across the carpet, snaking toward the living room. She stood and put her hand to her head, then lurched toward the bookshelf. *Brett?* He lay motionless on the rug. A metal box lay beside his head. A gash in his forehead trickled blood. *The box must have hit his head.*

A window shattered in the kitchen and glass clattered to the floor.

She knelt and touched Brett's clammy face. "Brett, wake up. We've got to get out of here." She pulled his arm.

He didn't move.

She staggered to her feet, grabbed Brett's arms and tried to lift him. Too heavy—she only moved him a few inches. She loosed her grip. His arms fell back across his chest.

Heat from the approaching flames warmed her face. Hadn't she complained about it being cold in the room? *Be careful what you wish for.* "Oh, Brett! Wake up. We don't have much time. We have to leave!" She shook his shoulder. Her face prickled with chill fingers despite the fire inching closer. "Oh, God, help me. What shall I do?"

Smoke billowed down the hall, filling the living room with a haze. It was impossible to see halfway across the room, except for the light streaming through the open front door. *Must get Brett out.*

Flames roared closer. She coughed and screamed again. Where were the men? Dorian? They must have heard the explosion. Why didn't they come? Her chest ached with each breath.

She leaned down and grasped her hands beneath Brett's shoulders and yanked—two more inches. *I can't do this.*

The searing flames rose up like a fiery beast. A flare reached out and touched her hand. She jerked back. Terror gripped her heart. *If I don't get out, we'll both die.*

She loosened her hold on Brett and looked toward the door. Safety—only a few steps away. I need to live for Amanda! She bit her fist, her body wrenched with sobs. Each breath a struggle. Safety—just beyond the open door. *I must save him. I am strong enough. Strong like Quantum.* Strong enough to fight for the one she loved.

The flames licked at the carpet just beyond Brett's feet. She grabbed under his arms again and pulled. An inch. Another inch. *Strong, like Quantum.* Closer to the door now, but still not close enough. Where were the stable boys? Near blinded from the smoke and tears, she pulled and his weight lightened—surged. A wet nose and furry shoulder touched her arm. A familiar whine. *Sam?*

"Sam! Thank God." Sam grabbed the back of Brett's shirt again and tugged.

"Good boy, Sam, pull! *Strong.* Pull. Pull. Pull!"

Kimberlee held her breath and strained. *I can do this! Pull.* They were at the front door. *God bless the dog.* Then, somehow, together they were twenty feet from the house and safety. She collapsed on the grass and drew Brett's head into her lap.

The stable hands rushed up carrying a fire extinguisher and made several attempts to approach the house. One of the boys aimed the garden hose toward the flames shooting through the windows. The feeble spray barely reached the edge of the porch.

Kimberlee yanked the scarf from her neck and wrapped it around Brett's forehead, tightening it around the wound. He tossed his head, moaned, and then opened his eyes. Kimberlee's heart leapt. "Brett?" She leaned down and kissed his forehead, tears stinging her eyes. "You're going to be alright." *Thank you, God. Thank you, Sam.*

"Are you guys okay?" Dorian knelt at her elbow, her hand resting on Sam's head. She glanced up at Juan. "I heard the explosion. Did someone call the fire department?"

Juan nodded, plying the water from the garden hose toward the side of the porch not yet burning. "It's no use. It's too far gone."

"What happened?" Dorian touched Kimberlee's shoulder.

Kimberlee shook her head. "I don't know. It must have been a gas line. It started when I turned on the kitchen stove. Brett called me, so I just flipped the knob and hurried down the hall. If I had stayed in the kitchen even for a few moments, I would have been killed." She shivered as a wall crumbled.

Kimberlee scooted back, pulling Brett toward her. Even at that distance, the heat from the fire felt uncomfortable. Flames shot through several holes in the roof sending bits and pieces of charred ash skittering through the air like fireflies. Glass shattered somewhere in the back of the house.

Prickles raced up Kimberlee's arms. Tears trickled down her

cheeks. Her head hurt. She reached over and patted Sam's back. "We could have both died if it hadn't been for Sam." Goose bumps galloped up the back of her neck. She touched the stinging scratch on the back of her hand.

Kimberlee jerked her head back toward the burning house. She slid Brett's head off her lap, and scanned the yard. "Where's Thumper and Noe-Noe? Both cats were in the house when the explosion… Oh, Dorian, where are the cats?"

Chapter Thirty

"Here, Noe-Noe. Where are you, Thumper?" Kimberlee struggled to her feet. "Thumper!" Her gaze searched the yard and out to the barn. She ran back toward the burning house. "Thumper, Thumper! Noe-Noe!"

One of the stable hands grabbed her and spun her around. "You can't go back in there, Miss." He pulled her further from the fire.

Kimberlee tried to jerk her arm away. "They must be here somewhere. I've got to find them. Thumper! Noe-Noe!" The crackling and snapping of the blaze blotted out her voice. Another wall crashed inside the house. Flames spurted through the broken front windows like Fourth of July fire fountains.

"Honey. Come back, please." Brett's voice sounded so weak. He struggled to sit up, holding his head, and then tried to stand.

Dorian pulled him back down. "You stay where you are."

"Kimberlee. It's no use. There's nothing you can do." He reached out and grabbed her hand.

Kimberlee sank down beside him, her face streaked with tears. *Why? Why?*

Brett held her in his arms and rocked her. *"Shh. Shh."*

She put her head on his shoulder. "That's what Noe-Noe was trying to tell me." Kimberlee touched the bandage on her hand. "She tried to stop me from going into the kitchen. She scratched me and I scolded her. Then she tried to warn me in the kitchen, too. I didn't pay attention. How did she know?"

"Maybe she could smell the gas. Cats have a better sense of smell than we do." Dorian patted her arm.

"I should never have brought Thumper here. What more? Oh, Brett, take me home. I want to go home." She buried her face in his shirt and sobbed.

"We'll go, honey. Only another day or so." His voice raw and catching in his throat. He ran his hand over her head.

"What am I going to tell Amanda?" She burst into another fit of sobbing.

Big, fat, soft Thumper, who came into her life last year, the catalyst that brought her and Brett together when they searched for clues to the Fern Lake mysteries.

How was it possible that the loss of a pet could create a hole in her heart big enough to drive a truck through? Thumper was a comfort to her and Amanda when she fled from Brett, lost and disillusioned in his love. Thumper was the glue that held them together; her and Amanda, Brett and Dorian, held in the spell he wove just by being *Thumper*. Would Amanda understand that as surely as there is a Heaven, Thumper would greet them at the gate when it was time to meet their Maker?

A siren whined in the distance, growing louder as the fire engine neared the driveway lined with stone fences. Kimberlee dried her eyes and watched the firemen leap from the truck, unroll their hoses and attack the fire. Once the men had brought the fire under control, the fire chief approached with a clipboard. "What happened? I need to fill out a report."

"I guess the stove exploded."

The medic removed Kimberlee's scarf and bandaged Brett's forehead. "I was in the living room and something fell on my head. The next thing I know, I was outside on the ground. My wife pulled me out of the house. She's my hero." Brett took Kimberlee's hand and kissed her knuckles. "I didn't know I was married to Wonder Woman."

She looked into his soot-blackened face. Perspiration had run down his cheeks, carving rivers though the blackness, like canyons cut into a dark mountainside. Her mouth twisted in a weak smile. "Not so wonderful. I couldn't have done it without Sam, and we didn't save…"

Tears blurred out the surroundings. "Our kitties."

The fire chief looked up from his clipboard. "I'm sorry?"

Brett shook his head. "Our cat, Thumper and Grandmother's cat, Noe-Noe...." He glanced at Kimberlee and then looked away.

Dorian put her arms around Kimberlee's shoulders. "I know how much he meant to you. He was pretty special to me, too. I'm so sorry. If it had been Sam..." Her eyes filled with tears.

"I know," Kimberlee whispered.

"I think that's all I need from you folks right now. We'll finish up here and get back to you if we need more information. I'll send a report for Mrs. Lassiter's insurance once the fire investigator examines the scene." The Chief snapped his clipboard shut.

A second fire truck wailed up the driveway. Kimberlee looked back at the charred and smoldering remains of the house. The last vestige of Harold and Imelda had just gone up in smoke—erasing any evidence they had ever been a part of the ranch. "We're in the way here. Let's go back to the house and let these men do their job. At least they've kept the fire from spreading over to the barns." She dried her eyes and turned toward the ranch house.

She grit her teeth against the rock in the pit of her stomach and fought tears that threatened to spill down her cheeks again. *How am I going to face Amanda?*

Dorian and Kimberlee walked on each side of Brett, supporting him with their arms.

"If you guys want to get some rest, I'll go up and sit with Amanda."

"Thanks, Dorian. I think we could both use a nap and a shower. We'll see you later."

Kimberlee made a quick stop in the nursery to hug Amanda. Now, she lay on her bed, feeling as though her head would explode. Her heart wanted to cry out, but her tear ducts were as dry as the prairie that surrounded the burning rubble of Imelda's former home.

Brett took a shower, dressed and sat staring out the window, as though he was in shock from the ordeal. No small wonder. Coming that close to death was a sobering experience. He pulled his chair closer to the bed. "Kimberlee, honey, I found something over at the house just before the explosion. I've been trying to figure out how to tell you about it." He touched his pocket where something crinkled.

Kimberlee sat up, her hand on her forehead. "Now what? Isn't it enough that we've nearly been blown to bits and our cat is dead? There's more?" She laughed, a wild and uncontrolled laugh, the kind of laugh that without much more cause, could dissolve into hysteria. "How much more do you think I can stand?" She threw herself back on the bed and pulled the pillow over her face.

She raged into the pillow. "Is it anything that will make one bit of difference one way or the other today?" She yanked the pillow off her face; her eyes swollen from weeping and her throat sore from breathing smoke.

"*Umm*…well, when you put it that way, I guess it can wait." Brett looked away.

"Then considering all we've been through today, I'd just as soon not hear about it right now." She rose from the bed and grabbed a change of clothes. "I'm going to take a shower and take a nap. Don't even think about waking me unless the house is on fire. No pun intended."

Chapter Thirty-One

With a wag of his tail, Sam greeted Kimberlee as she pushed open the swinging door into the kitchen the next morning. "Good morning. I guess I overslept. Something smells…" Kimberlee stopped just inside the door and stared.

Dorian slid spices back into the cupboard and milk into the refrigerator. She turned. "I made breakfast. Do you want some eggs?" She wet a sponge and ran it across the counter and top of the stove.

Kimberlee stopped short. Even holding a carton of eggs in one hand and a frying pan in the other, and all they'd gone through the day before, Dorian still looked like she just stepped off a New York fashion runway. Again! Mascara perfect. Lipstick like a crimson bow. Eye shadow matching her pale blue sleeveless top, while Kimberlee's puffy eyes screamed of a night of tossing and turning and too many tears. Even her shirt, pulled from the suitcase, resembled one of the ponies rode hard and put away wet.

Kimberlee pushed her hair behind her ears and wet her lips. *How does Dorian do it?* Not fair. After going through hell's half-acre this past week, lucky she even had shoes on the right feet. "Just coffee for now. I'll eat something later."

She opened the back door and stepped out on the porch. The acrid smell of burnt wood still tainted the air. Ragged timbers crisscrossed the ashes of Imelda's house. Twisted pieces of metal suggested what might have once been a kitchen stove or a water heater. The fireplace was now a stack of crumpled bricks against the back wall, jutting up among the blackened ruins.

Where there once was a structure that had been a home, now only ashes remained, symbolic of the status of Harold's current life.

She sighed and came back into the kitchen. "Did Brett and Amanda already eat?"

Dorian nodded. "He ran into town to pick up our airline tickets and get some groceries." She handed Kimberlee a cup of coffee.

"Good. I can't wait to leave, though things won't be the same without…" Kimberlee pinched her lips.

"I'm back." The screen door slammed behind Brett, laden down with grocery bags. "There's another bag in the car, if you want to get it." He nodded toward Grandmother's van parked in the driveway. "I picked up a bucket of fried chicken for dinner tonight." Brett set the groceries on the table.

"I'll get it." Dorian disappeared down the steps. "I hope you remembered milk."

Brett kissed Kimberlee's forehead. "How is my little hero this morning?"

"I've felt better. A little headache. It's my heart that's broken. Thumper…" How do you get past a near death experience? How do you forget that your pet died in the process?

She swallowed hard to stop the tears that threatened to tumble down her cheeks. *I've got to get a handle on this. I've cried so much this week, I must have lost ten pounds.* "I'll be a sight better when we're on a plane headed back to California. Did you have any trouble changing our airline reservations?"

Brett shook his head. "We leave tomorrow at noon on Air America. I'll get things settled with Juan this afternoon. We'll go over the books in Harold's office. Juan can handle things until Grandmother gets home. Since he won't be able to live in the house…" He jerked his thumb toward the ruins of Harold's house. "I offered him more pay. Hopefully, Grandmother's okay with that."

Amanda's voice drifted down the stairs from the children's room. "You are my sunshine…my sunny sunshine. *Mmm…mmm…*when my eyes turn gray. I'd be so happy… If you had a deer, you wouldn't take my deer...away."

Kimberlee smiled. *One of these days, I should teach her the right words, but I love the way she sings it.*

Precious Amanda.

Those pesky tears rose to the surface again, just remembering the scene late last night in the nursery. Her fears that Amanda would be devastated when they told her about Thumper were unfounded. She had been more concerned for her mommy's tears than about losing Thumper.

"Don't cry, Mommy," Amanda said. "Daddy Brett says they're in Heaven. They'll be happy there, won't they?" Indeed, they all agreed.

"Heaven is a good place for Fumper and Noe-Noe. Fumper *woves* her. Now, they can be together."

Amanda's childlike faith had touched her heart.

Kimberlee strode to the counter to refill her coffee. Just get me through one more day. Once they were home and took up the threads of their disrupted lives, she could put all this behind her. That is, their routine without Thumper. His absence would leave a mighty big hole in their lives.

Amanda tugged on Kimberlee's skirt. "But, Mommy, why can't I bring my pony home with me? He won't take up much room."

"Air America won't let us take ponies on the airplane. He needs to stay here on Grandmother's ranch." Kimberlee looked helplessly at Brett. He shrugged and smiled.

Amanda's lower lip turned down and her chest heaved. A storm of weeping threatened on the horizon.

"Brett. Will you take Amanda out to see the horses? I have to finish packing." Kimberlee glanced at her watch and shoved Amanda toward Brett.

"Come with me, Amanda. Let's go and say good-bye to Star."

Amanda swiped her arm across her cheeks and opened the front door. Brett followed her onto the porch.

The house was in turmoil as Kimberlee and Dorian ran back and forth, taking clothes out of the dryer, packing suitcases, cramming little souvenirs into the corners of bags.

Kimberlee took clippings from Grandmother's rose bushes and stuffed them into the toes of her extra shoes. Would she dare smuggle them back into California? Was *smuggle* really the right word?

At last it was time to leave.

Brett loaded the last piece of luggage in the van. He locked the front door as Kimberlee lifted Amanda into her car seat. "That's the last. Just need to put in Sam's crate."

Dorian shoved Sam's carrier into the car. He jumped in and she turned the key on the padlock.

Juan turned toward Kimberlee. "Are you ready, Miss?"

Kimberlee nodded. Were they finally leaving? How many times had she wished for this moment? But, how could they leave without Thumper. "As much as I want to go home, I'm going to miss the prairie and the horses." An unexplained ache throbbed in her heart. "I almost wish…oh, I don't know what I wish. Yes. Let's go."

Kimberlee turned for one last look at the ranch house. Could she forget her grandmother's betrayal, the unanswered questions about Harold's true identity, Wilbur's death, and Thumper's loss in the burning house? Memories, particularly bad ones, tend to cling, like foxtails on your pants leg, no matter where you were.

The dust rose up behind the van as it bumped down the driveway. Juan signaled a left turn at the edge of the country road.

A great need swelled up in Kimberlee's chest. *What is it?* She grasped Juan's shoulder. "Wait. Wait a minute."

Juan slammed his foot on the brakes. He turned to look over his shoulder. "What's wrong?"

Everyone turned toward Kimberlee. Seconds passed in the silent car.

"Go back. Juan, take me back." Her eyelid twitched. She felt each heartbeat throb in her forehead.

Brett reached for Kimberlee's arm. "What is it? Did you forget something? I checked everywhere. I don't think—" He eyed his wristwatch.

"I don't know." Kimberlee put her hands to her cheeks. *What is it?* "I just have the oddest feeling. Like, something's wrong. We can't leave yet. We need to go back and check again."

"Honey, we don't have much time. We have to check into the airport at least two hours before flight time."

Juan turned the car and headed back up the long driveway toward the house.

As the car pulled back into the yard next to Grandmother's house, Kimberlee saw the outline of two small figures on the front porch, as though they were waiting for someone to come home and fix their dinner.

Brett leaned forward in his seat. "It can't be… I don't believe it."

Kimberlee's heart leaped. "Is it possible? It is! It's Thumper!"

"Mama! Thumper and Noe-Noe comed back from Heaven!" Amanda pounded the edge of her car seat.

Kimberlee flung open the door and jumped from the car almost before Juan could bring it to a stop. "You're alive." She knelt and kissed Thumper's head and stroked the little marmalade cat by his side. "Where have you been all this time?" *Oh, thank you, thank you!* She wiped tears from her cheeks. *Look at me. I'm crying again. Happy tears this time.* She turned as Brett and Juan climbed out of the van.

"Give me a minute. I'll get his carrier." Juan dashed toward the barn where he had stashed it the day of the fire. Had he removed it lest the sight would cause her more pain?

Brett stroked Thumper's head. "Well, I'll be. They must have gone out on the prairie when the fire started. Then, with the fire trucks and all the confusion, they were afraid to come back." He smiled and stood gazing past the stone fences, out across the plains where Quantum lived with his herd, and to the mountains beyond.

Kimberlee saw the wistful look in his eyes as he gazed around the barnyard.

Brett waved to the stable boy exercising Warrior in the paddock next to the barn. Had Brett developed a fancy to become a gentleman rancher? Did he have a secret desire to remain on the ranch? Could that be the *something important* he'd tried to tell her the day of the fire? Something important he'd learned at Harold's house, he'd said. Something they needed to talk about another day. Not today. Right now, it was all about Thumper.

Dorian unbuckled Amanda's seatbelt and lifted her down from the van. "Run quick and kiss your kitties. We have to hurry."

Amanda squatted on the porch and threw her arms around Thumper. She hugged him to her chest. "Didn't you like it in Heaven, Thumper? Do you want to come home with us now?" She gave Noe-Noe's head a pat.

Kimberlee tilted up Noe-Noe's face and looked into her gold eyes. "They haven't eaten for two days. They must be starved."

Brett knelt beside her. "Come on, Kimberlee. Think about it. They're cats. There's probably a pile of mouse bones picked clean in the barn." He leaned down and kissed her cheek.

Amanda lifted Noe-Noe and clutched her to her chest. "Can we take Noe-Noe with us, Mama?" Amanda whined. "Thumper *woves* her. Please." She cradled the cat in her arms.

Kimberlee stroked first Noe-Noe's gold head and then Thumper's black silken ear. *Do we dare?*

Thumper rubbed against Kimberlee's leg, leaving his fur on her dark pants, marking her again, as his personal property. *Come on Kimberlee. We planned it all so carefully. We need to bring Noe-Noe home with us.*

"Please, Mama. Can we bring her?" Amanda begged, hands folded as if in prayer.

"Well, I don't know. What would Grandmother have to say about it?" After all the grief Grandmother had put her through this week, did she really care?

Dorian laughed. "You can call Grandmother in a couple of days. Under the circumstances, I really don't think she could deny you anything you asked."

Juan hurried back across the yard with Thumper's carrier. He opened the wire door and gestured toward Thumper. "We better go. It's getting late."

"What do you think, Brett? What should we do?" Kimberlee looked down at the cats.

Thumper ponied up into Kimberlee's hand. *I promise I'll eat all my liver and kidneys like a good kitty. Please?*

"It's your call, honey. You know how your grandmother is. If you think we should, make up your mind. We *have* to leave!" Brett lifted Amanda back into the van and buckled her seatbelt.

Kimberlee picked up the marmalade cat, held her up and looked into her gold eyes.

Noe-Noe blinked and opened her mouth in a heart-rending silent meow.

That's the way. You go, girl! Thumper meowed.

"Juan, grab Thumper. Put them both in his carrier. We'll make arrangements with the airlines when we get there. If there's a problem, you can ship Noe-Noe on a later flight." Kimberlee glanced into the front seat at Brett. "I know. This isn't the first cat I've cat-napped, but I promise this will be the last."

Brett grinned and shook his head.

"I can see it now," Dorian chuckled. "Your face plastered on the wall at the Fern Lake Police Department. *Wanted. Kimberlee Clarke, Repeat Offender. Callous capricious Cat-Napper!*"

Juan stuffed Thumper into the carrier and Kimberlee shoved

Noe-Noe in behind him. The two cats curled together.

Noe-Noe turned to Thumper, her whiskers pulled back. *I wasn't sure she'd go for it. I thought she'd hold it against me because I scratched her hand. I was trying to keep her from turning on the stove.*

She probably doesn't even remember that you scratched her. She's happy because we're not dead. I knew she'd give in if we hid out long enough. Thumper put his paw on Noe-Noe's head. *But, we almost got left behind because you wouldn't leave that mouse hole. What if they hadn't come back?*

It was the mouse's fault. He kept taunting me! It could have happened to anybody—

Just sayin'...

Thumper peered through the wires of his carrier and out the side window. Puffy white clouds dotted a brilliant blue sky. The mountains wobbled, seeming to come alive in the morning haze. He lifted his head. A cloud of dust in the distance could only be Quantum, leading his herd across the prairie. The van drove past fields of waving grass.

Star galloped beside the stone fences, pacing the vehicle to the edge of the country road where it turned left toward town, and home.

About Elaine Faber

Elaine Faber is a member of Sisters in Crime, Inspire Christian Writers, and Cat Writers Association. She lives in Northern California with her husband and four housecats. She volunteers at the American Cancer Society Discovery Shop and works with the Elk Grove Library on the Friends of the Library Board.

Elaine started writing poetry and short stories as a child. She has completed four novels. Many of her short stories are published in magazines, on-line weekly magazines and short story collections (anthologies). She favors writing in the cozy mystery and humorous mystery genre. Black Cat and the Lethal Lawyer is the second of three Black Cat Mysteries, featuring Thumper, the cat with his ancestor's memories.

(Books)

Black Cat's Legacy

Black Cat and the Lethal Lawyer

Look for Elaine's novels on Amazon and barnesandnoble.com.
Book reviews are always welcome.

(Coming Soon)

Spring 2015–*Black Cat and the Accidental Angel*–Thumper loses his memory until Angel steps in and helps him save a family. He learns that there are more important things than knowing your name.

Fall 2015—A humorous mystery set during WWII. Mrs. Odboddy, an elderly lady, fights the war from the home front, but can't help but see conspiracies and Nazi spies around every corner.

Elaine welcomes your comments. Write to her at:
Elaine.Faber@mindcandymysteries.com

Website: http://www.mindcandymysteries.com

Also by Elaine Faber

Black Cat's Legacy

Thumper, the resident Fern Lake black cat, knows where the bodies are buried and it's up to Kimberlee to decode the clues.

Kimberlee's arrival at the Fern Lake lodge triggers the Black Cat's Legacy. With the aid of his ancestors' memories, it's Thumper's duty to guide Kimberlee to clues that can help solve her father's cold case murder. She joins forces with a local homicide detective and an author, also researching the murder for his next thriller novel. As the investigation ensues, Kimberlee learns more than she wants to know about her father. The murder suspects multiply, some dead and some still very much alive, but someone at the lodge will stop at nothing to hide the Fern Lake mysteries.

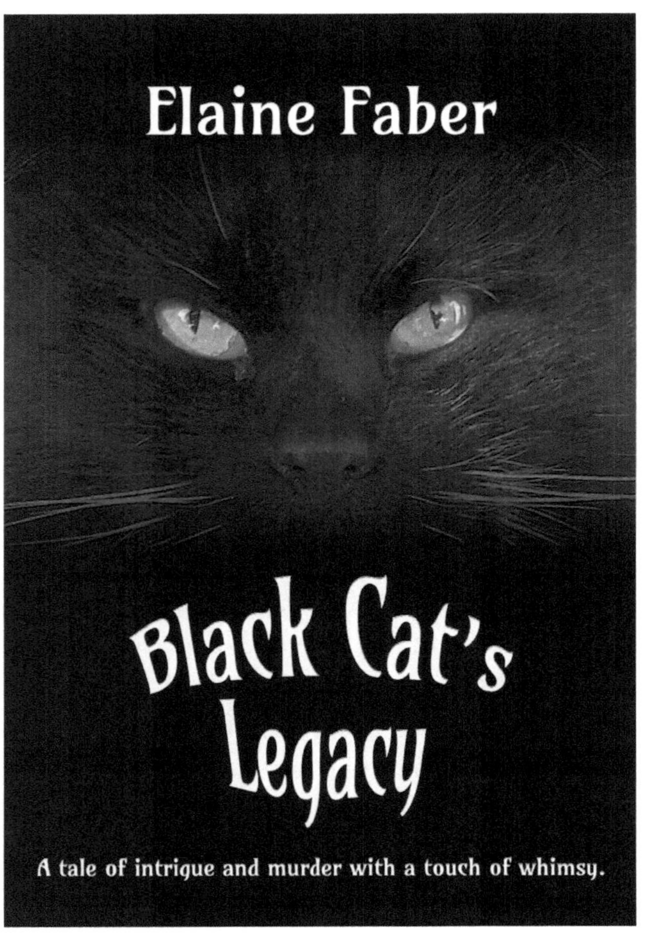

Cover photo *Boot's Eyes*: © Elaine Faber

Coming Spring 2015

Black Cat and the Accidental Angel

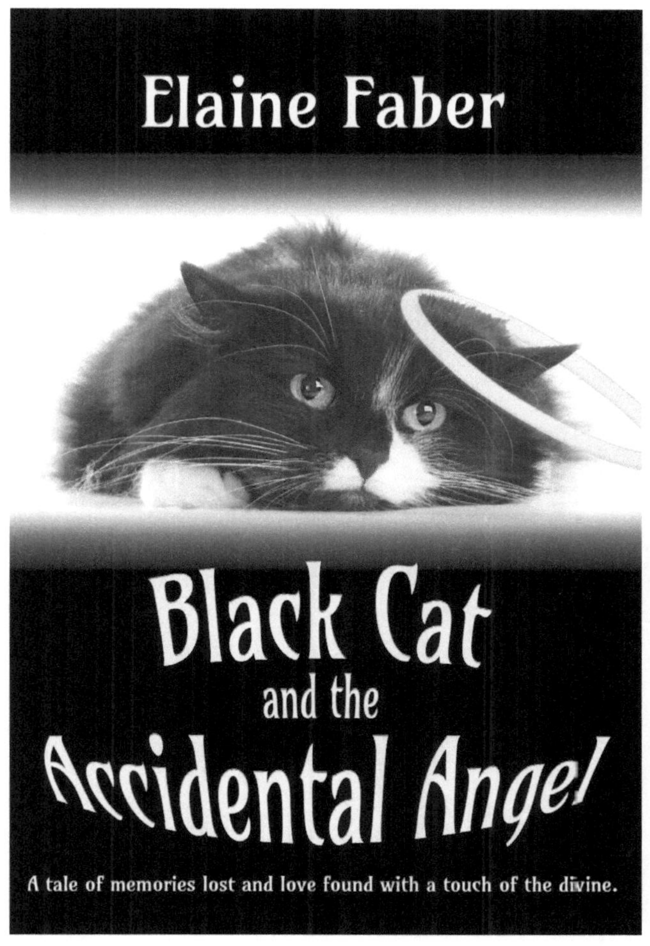

When the family SUV flips and Kimberlee is rushed to the hospital, Black Cat (Thumper) and his soul-mate are left behind. Black Cat loses all memory of his former life and the identity of the lovely feline companion by his side. "Call me Angel. I'm here to take care of you." Her words set them on a long journey toward home, and life brings them face to face with episodes of joy and sorrow.

The two cats are taken in by John and his young daughter, Cindy, facing foreclosure of the family vineyard and emu farm. In addition, someone is playing increasingly dangerous pranks that threaten Cindy's safety. Angel makes it her mission to help their new family. John's prayers are answered in unexpected ways, but not until Angel puts her life on the line to protect the child, and Black Cat finds there are more important things in life than knowing your real name.